A ROSE IN
LITTE FIVE POINTS

VMH PUBLISHING

ATLANTA I NEW YORK

AN EMPOWERING NOVEL

A ROSE IN
LITTE FIVE POINTS

Journey with Meredith through
the vibrant streets of Little Five Points, Atlanta - a
place filled with vivid characters and rapid social changes.

DEIDRE ANN DELAUGHTER

Quantity sales. Special discounts are available on quantity purchases by corporations, associations, and others. For details, visit the publisher www.vmhpublising.net

Paperback ISBN: 978-1-0879-7262-6

EBook ISBN: 979-8-8689-4440-6

This is a work of fiction. The characters depicted in this work are purely fictional. Any resemblance to actual persons is coincidental. Any errors regarding events or locations are entirely the responsibility of the author, and the publisher cannot be held responsible for errors or omissions, or for any consequences arising from the use of information contained herein.

Printed on acid-free paper.

Publisher Disclaimer: The publisher of this story hereby declares that it is not responsible for the content, views, opinions, or any other material expressed within the story. The publisher is not responsible for websites, or social media pages (or their content) related to this publication, that are not owned by the publisher.

Published in United States of America 10 9 8 7 6 5 4 3 2 1

VMH™Publishing

A ROSE IN LITTLE FIVE POINTS is dedicated to these women who have enriched my life beyond measure:

To SZ, who continues to get back up again and again and again. You have more strength and caring to offer than you give yourself credit for. I am grateful for our friendship and our ability to commiserate over health challenges. To MB, MH, and MW, the other Wild Wimmin, your abiding friendship through many of life's seasons—and some of them have been doozies!—has sustained me. And to LMK, EKKS, and CJKJ, my three beloved daughters, I am in constant and eternal awe of what wonderful human beings you are. Truly, I am blessed to be your mom.

A Rose in Little Five Points

Prologue: 1993

As I sit in my daughter's tiny walk-up apartment in San Francisco, watching her lovingly prepare a cup of tea for me, scenes play from the movie reel of our life together. We have hurt each other in many ways, and I'm grateful we finally got to this place in our relationship. I admire how poised, lovely, and smart she is, and I recall that I, as a young woman the age she is now, was self-aware, but only to a point. I think about how my self-doubt and self-loathing nearly destroyed us both. I now understand that her lashing out at me mirrored the adversarial relationship I had with myself but was too oblivious to see. The change in me has been so gradual that I am only now able to look back on my younger self with any degree of tenderness and objectivity. And I only now understand all too well that heartache is often the starting point for change, but only if we do not try to push it away before it can become our great teacher. Oh, how the tectonic plates of the mother-daughter relationship seem to constantly shift! I hope we are, from now on, standing under the same protective doorway during each subsequent rumble.

Chapter One: 1975

THE EASTERN AIRLINES pilot announces we'll be landing shortly and that the weather in Atlanta this fine Ides of March afternoon is a mild 72 degrees. Before the airplane even touches down, I unbuckle my seatbelt. I gently rouse Cameron, who had fallen asleep in my lap, moist curls pasted to her forehead. Pointing out the window seat, I say to my one-year-old daughter, "Look, Honey. There's our new home."

In the midst of our packing and rushing about the past few weeks, I attempted to explain what was behind all of this disruption to her normal routine. Puzzled, sleep still clouding her eyes, she scrunches up her face, and her bottom lip quivers. I know she'll begin wailing piteously if I don't divert her attention. "Let's ask Mr. Whiskers what he thinks, okay?" I pull her favorite stuffed animal, a rabbit with love-worn floppy ears and now-stubbly whiskers, out of the canvas carry-on tote bag.

Once Cameron is holding Mr. Whiskers up to the airplane window, engaging with him in baby babble, I nudge Kenneth awake, mere minutes before the landing gear announces our final descent into the Atlanta airport. "We're home," I whisper. Kenneth grunts. He's been just as fitful on the international flight as our daughter. Ordinarily, his irritability would rub off on me and trigger the three-headed FearGuiltShame self-recrimination monster that is, I think, my factory setting, but I'm too keyed up and deliriously happy to let Sir Grumpy steal my joy. Home!

Kenneth groans, then tries valiantly to smile, but I can tell that he is still not pleased to be leaving Africa and returning to the US. I had hoped seeing the familiar Atlanta landscape from the air—Stone Mountain, Lakewood Fairgrounds, downtown high-rises like the blue-domed Regency Hyatt House, and the Interstate highways snaking through our hometown—would dissolve the rest of his doubt, but I can tell that it has not. I accept partial blame. I essentially blackmailed him into relocating our little family after Cameron had her fourth ear infection in as many months. "I'm done here, Kenneth. I cannot live here anymore. I'm moving back to Atlanta and taking the baby with me. You're welcome to join us." I left him very little choice and very little doubt about his options if he wanted to be with me or watch our daughter grow up.

When we moved to Africa three years earlier—to be exact, Cameroon—we were younger, naive, newly married, and excited to be accepted into the Peace Corps and serve an area of the world that desperately needed us and what we had to offer. Even when our daughter, a pleasant surprise and an interruption to our plans to save the world, was born two years later, we continued to embrace our calling—Kenneth as a civil engineer, helping villages develop better infrastructure, and me as an English teacher to the children of the diplomatic corps. But I'd had enough. Enough of Kenneth taking side trips to other African nations, leaving me home alone for weeks at a time to care for our baby. Enough of trying to schedule English lessons around nap times and unreliable babysitters and spending time with other people's children when I wanted to be with my own. Enough of the anguished screams of Cameron with ear infections, which always seemed to come on in the middle of the night. I wanted my daughter to know both sets of grandparents in the city where we grew up. I wanted to sleep in air conditioning without mosquito netting, and I wanted to take a hot bath without having to fetch and then heat the water myself. I wanted electricity that was available any time I flipped a switch and not at the whim of the government. I wanted to once again get my food from a grocery store, to stand in the meat section, nearly paralyzed with the dilemma of over-choice rather than paralyzed by the task of wringing a pet chicken's neck and then plucking and gutting it. I never got used to that, and now I wouldn't have to. Home!

- - - - -

We're renting, with the option to purchase, the cutest little house on Hurt Avenue in Little Five Points. In the years we've been gone, this area has undergone a transformation. Actually, that might be a bit of an exaggeration. There are still lots of derelict properties that barely hint at their former glory days. But there are many homes flying the butterfly flag of neighborhood renewal, and said urban renewal allows Kenneth to land a job less than a week after our return. Now he works for the City of Atlanta in the Planning Department, and instead of khakis and steel-toed work boots and the occasional pith helmet, he wears suits and ties and crisply ironed button-down Oxford cloth dress shirts, crisply ironed by Yours Truly.

Also, maybe I read too many Harlequin romances in my teen years, but I really expected us to celebrate these recent accomplishments by opening some champagne and christening our new bedroom with the kind of passion we shared on our honeymoon. I know Kenneth is tired after work. I, too, am tired from chasing after Cameron all day. But I miss those pillow-talk nights with my husband. Do I need to resort to covering myself in Saran Wrap to get his romantic attention, or would that gross him out? I could end up looking like an overstuffed sausage since I gained so much weight with Cameron. How long can I call this baby fat?

- - - - -

The war in Vietnam is over. Maybe now the people who opposed the US's involvement and the people who promoted it can begin being nice to one another again. I do not know what side I would have been on if I had a son or spouse who was eligible for the draft. Kenneth was not called up due to his being so nearsighted and his exceptionally high draft card number. What I do believe, though, is that if mothers of young children from all over the world could get together to talk while their children played, we would not have as many wars.

- - - - -

I have just returned from grocery shopping at A&P. I'd nearly forgotten what a luxury mere grocery shopping can be! All that delicious food and all that delicious air-conditioning under one roof on a 90-degree summer day is nearly indescribable when I compare it to how we got most of our provisions in Africa. And we had it easy compared to many others, for the diplomats' families were often quite generous. But our choices were limited. The sheer variety of options we have stateside is almost mind-numbing, whereas there was little decision-making in Cameroon. Pity the soul over there who doesn't like cassava, yams, rice, potatoes, and corn. It took me awhile to adjust to the lack of green vegetables, but adjust I did. My affinity for starches and their affinity for my bottom, hips, thighs, and belly are all too evident. Over there, I fit in as just one of many Rubenesque women, especially in those loose-fitting cotton dresses. Here, though, shorts and t-shirts are no good at disguising my matronly figure. If I'm to be honest, this is the main reason I have not tried to look up old classmates. I'm embarrassed by how I look. So I'm trying to retrain my palate because, truly, I could eat tapioca pudding three times a day.

One way I hope to get more green vegetables into our diet is to buy local produce and work for it. To that end, I have joined Sevananda, a local co-op. They're new to the neighborhood, within walking distance, and their concept is quite appealing. It seems so modern American and yet so rural African. It's also a great place to indulge my habit of people-watching. I hadn't realized so many Atlantans had embraced the hippie culture. Anyway, I hope to wean myself and my family off of so many starchy foods, introduce new foods and textures to Cameron, and drop a few pounds by walking to get my produce.

- - - - -

I can no longer ignore the fact that we're being watched. Whenever I'm in the front yard with Cameron or returning from Sevananda, I can see the neighbor across the street peering out at us from a narrow opening behind the sheers in her front window. Doesn't she know they're called sheers for a reason? Mostly I pay her no attention, but when I do look directly at her window, she yanks the sheers closed and then pulls the drapes closed, too. It's a little unnerving, but mostly it's annoying. I believe she's harmless and perhaps has appointed herself the unofficial neighborhood hall monitor, watching everyone, but I do not like the idea of being spied on. Surely, we're not that curious. One of these days, I'm going to march right up to her front door and ring the doorbell, introduce myself and Cameron, and ask her if her television set is broken or something. I cannot think of any other reason she'd be so interested in us.

- - - - -

Some mornings, while Kenneth is at work, I take Cameron either to my in-laws' house or to my parents' home on the rare days they are not working. The adults drink coffee while we chat and glory in Cameron's cute toddler antics. Kenneth's parents have dubbed themselves Mema and PopPop Fields, and my parents are Mama Jo and Papa Don. After we leave, Cameron and I go home for naptime. After she wakes from her nap and has a snack, I put Cameron in our little red wagon and walk over to Sevananda to buy fresh produce for dinner. It turns out I love being a full-time mother and domestic goddess. I feel born for it, as if teaching English were merely a waystation before reaching my true destination. Whether or not Kenneth feels the same about his change in career is anyone's guess. He's less moody, but he also shares less about what it is he does for the City of Atlanta. I must be patient. His re-acclimation to the US is apparently more difficult than mine, although I cannot imagine why.

- - - - -

I am watching Cameron and Kenneth play with her Fisher-Price Little People Farm. They are sprawled out on the floor in the living room, and he is just as absorbed in the make-

15

believe as she is. I'm seeing more and more ways in which Cameron is like her father. Cameron puts the cow in the barn, closing the barn door, brow furrowed in concentration. She repeatedly takes the cow out, puts her in the pasture, which is a green square on the throw rug, and then puts the cow back in. Her brow indicates just how seriously she is taking her job of care-taking. Kenneth is tending to the pig, letting it graze in the same patch of pasture, his brow also furrowed. My heart swells with pride at what a good dad Kenneth is. I want Cameron to grow up to love her father and to seek his company and counsel as much as I do mine.

They are both so involved in the tending of those little farm animals that they do not hear me say that dinner is ready. I almost hate to interrupt them, and I'm also a little envious of their ability to focus to the exclusion of everything else. My mind seems to do quite the opposite, flitting all day from one thought to another, only settling down when I go to sleep. Sleep. There's another area where Kenneth and Cameron are peas from the same pod. When we were first married, Kenneth would wake me multiple times during the night with his mumbling. His words were not articulate, but his intonation indicated he was working through something nonetheless. I chalk it up to that engineer's problem-solving mind of his. And now Cameron has begun babbling in her sleep. The first few times it happened, I quickly hurried into her room to check on her and make sure she was okay. Now, even though it still wakes me up, I don't get out of bed to check. I do wonder if she has the engineer gene and cannot, like her daddy, turn off her brain.

I finally get their attention, and we sit down to a dinner of roasted chicken, rice, and green beans. Cameron is slowly developing a taste for green vegetables. My appetite for vegetables has never abated, and I reward myself for eating my vegetables by eating a double helping of rice. I am my own worst diet enemy, and we haven't even gotten to dessert yet. Sigh.

- - - - -

Fall quarter has begun, and the Emory campus is bustling with coeds in mini-skirts, frat boys in their NY State license-plated cars, and students of every stripe plastering the campus with Dooley-themed posters. I feel so dowdy when I see all those well-dressed, slender young women. While I do love being a mother, I wish I had not so wholeheartedly embraced the African admiration for full-figured women. Cameron and I go visit Dad, aka Papa Don, aka Dr. Donald Gardner, in his office. Two years ago, he received a plum appointment to serve the Carlos Museum as one of the resident experts on antiquities while also being permitted to continue teaching Arabic and World history, now part-time. He is in professional, professorial Nirvana. When Kenneth and I first declared our intent to sign up for the Peace Corps, he desperately wanted us to serve someplace in the Middle East, or at least an Arabic-speaking African nation, like Morocco, but we had our hearts set on Cameroon. I guess you could call it the National Geographic effect. Their infrastructure needs matched what we could offer—well, Kenneth, anyway. It's funny, though, how providing one's parents with a grandchild can offset any previous slights, perceived or real. Once Cameron arrived, Dad stopped trying to convince us to change our assignment. And once I wrote to my parents about our intent to move back to the States, the only idea he pushed was for us to please consider the Atlanta area. As if I would have picked anywhere else.

Dad whisks Cameron out of my arms and takes her around, showing her off to the secretaries and his other colleagues, reveling in their compliments about how darling she is. He's always had a way with young children, and when he's around them, his demeanor changes from regal Mr. Chips to goofy Mr. Green Jeans. It's one of the many things I love about him. He simply does not care what anyone else thinks about him. Then, when we're alone in his office, he lets Cameron toddle around, pointing at and touching many of the items he has spent a lifetime collecting. "Whassat?" she asks, touching an antique urn. He gently takes her hands into his and demonstrates how to hold an item that is of inestimable value.

"This, Cameron, is an urn. And this is how we hold it. See?" I marvel at this man and his instinctive ways. They repeat this routine until they have completed a tour of his office, including all things that are visible to a small child. Then, while Cameron rests in my arms after a small snack, Dad and I sit on the sofa in his office and talk.

"Enjoying your house?"

"Yes, we are. The house needs a lot of renovation, so I don't know if we'll make an offer to buy it or not, but it suits us for now. I do love the quirky neighborhood and how close we live to you and Mom and to the Fields."

"Met any of your neighbors yet?"

"Funny you should ask. Just today I was debating whether or not to ring the doorbell and introduce myself to the lady who lives across the street. I see her from time to time peeking out of the curtains, but when I look again, she's gone. I think she lives alone, and she looks fairly elderly. Do you think I should try to meet her? Surely she's harmless, if a little nosy."

"You already know what you're going to do, don't you? And if you take Sugar Foot with you," he nods towards Cameron, who is now asleep between us, "how can she help but be neighborly?"

"Think I should take something with me? Mom's Blonde Brownies, maybe."

"That would be nice." Then, "Did you know, when your mother was a coed, she would take Blonde Brownies and chilled Coca-Colas to the work crew on the Channel 5 television tower? She and several of her classmates rented a house on Emory Road, and they could see the construction of the tower from their backyard."

"I never knew that. How come I've never heard that story before?"

"I suspect it's because I later teased her about either trying to nab a handsome construction worker or sticking close enough to the construction site in case her Florence Nightingale skills were called for."

My father, the elegant expert in antiquities, had fallen quickly—and hard—for the beautiful, young School of Nursing student enrolled in his World History course. Ever the gentleman, he waited until after the final exam to express his feelings for her. As it turns out, she wasn't trying to woo any construction workers but, instead, had been pining away over her handsome professor, never guessing their feelings were mutual.

"When the crew finished the tower, they offered her the opportunity to climb to the top."

Again, I'm flummoxed that I'd never heard this story from their early days of courtship. "Did she do it? Did she climb to the top?"

"No, Meredith, she did not. And if you ask her about it today, she'll say it's because she's afraid of heights. But I think she regrets not taking them up on their offer. And I regret teasing her about the muscled workmen."

There is a lull in our conversation as Dad revisits those days in his mind and while I try to picture Mom, in her nursing school uniform, carrying a tray of brownies and iced bottles of Coke to a sweaty, lascivious work crew. Dad breaks our reverie. "Have you noticed any young children in your neighborhood? Any potential playmates for Sugar Foot?"

"If there are, I haven't seen evidence of any. I have met a few of the locals at Sevananda, and one of them has a little boy. We've talked about scheduling a play date."

"Good. And Kenneth? How is he? Does he like his new job?"

"I'm not sure what he likes anymore, Papa Don. He's not himself these days. Oh, he still dotes on Cameron." I smile down at my sleeping daughter. "He really is a good daddy, but he seems so, I don't know, distracted, I guess. Remote. I ask him about his work, and I get very short answers. I hope I didn't make the wrong decision, bringing us back home."

"Give him time, Meredith. Some people have a more difficult time with reverse culture shock. My guess is that some of the things you love the most about being back stateside are exactly the things he is struggling with."

"Like what, for instance? Maybe I can be more patient if I have an idea of what he's thinking and how he's feeling."

"Well, for one thing, once you've seen extreme poverty up close and had to work hard for every resource, hearing people complain about having to wait in line to fill out a permit could be grating."

"Yeah, I guess. I can see that."

"And he's used to seeing real results every day in the field. Making a difference in the lives of others. And now... "

"Are you saying I made a mistake by moving back?"

"No, Meredith. That is not what I'm saying. Just give him time to adjust to his new normal. And make sure he stays involved in Cameron's life. Nothing grounds a man more than taking a part in the upbringing of his child."

Then he winks at me, and the world is, once again, orbiting on the correct axis.

- - - - -

Cameron falls asleep while I'm walking back from Sevananda. I have the little wagon we take on our walks outfitted with a soft blanket and a small pillow for those times when she gets tired of walking. In Sevananda, she'd snacked on a few carob-covered raisins, which will, no doubt, appear whole in her next dirty diaper, and chattered throughout the store, charming our cashier with her dimpled smile and the coy fluttering of her eyelashes. As soon as we put our groceries in the wagon, though, she starts whining. "We'll be home soon," I tell her. "Can you be a big girl and walk?" Selfishly, I'm thinking if she walks most of the way home, she'll take a longer nap. At which point her lower lip begins to quiver, and I can see a meltdown in the making. I squat down and hold her carob-sweetened, chubby little hands. "Cameron, do you hurt anywhere, baby? Tell Mommy what's wrong." One enormous tear plops on my pants leg. I nod at the wagon, where our groceries are piled up toward the front. "Mr. Whiskers looks lonely. Maybe you can cuddle with him while Mommy pulls both of you in the wagon. Would you like that?" She wordlessly nods. I lift her into the wagon, and within a minute, she's conked out. At the corner of Euclid and Austin, I decide to go right on Austin, a much longer route home. Not one to waver from an established routine, my decision surprises me, but before I talk myself out of all I could accomplish while Cameron naps if I get home sooner, I allow myself this little detour. I'd overheard someone in Sevananda talking about the yard art near Sinclair. Why not?

The art isn't so much in someone's yard as it is at the edge of the greenspace, attached to a stand of trees. I stop at the first one. The artist has taken discarded items, likely from some of the local house renovation dumpsters, and created a person. Hubcap head with painted-on face, dumbwaiter door for the body, a twin bed slat for the arms, and fire grate legs, dressed in old denim, a grate prong poking through the holes in each knee. The shoes have been constructed of grapevine and moss. Where the left hand would be is the circular light bulb from an old kitchen fixture; the right hand is a large X made from two paint stirrers. And on the chest, the artist has painted Joe loves Margaret, February 14, 1973. Precious. The installment next to it is equally whimsical. The artist— Joe? —outdid himself last year. He'd taken the springs from an old baby crib and threaded a cast-off flannel shirt and corduroy pants through the left side and a long dress on the right. "His" head was a rusty bucket topped off with an Atlanta Braves baseball cap. " Her" head was a still-intact globe from an old light fixture, and it, too, was wearing an Atlanta Braves baseball cap. Where they were holding "hands" was an old silk flower arrangement. In addition to Joe loves Margaret, February 14, 1974, he'd added Home Run! Something stirs in me, and a sob rumbles up from somewhere deep inside me, catching me so off guard that I must steady myself on the adjacent tree. Good grief. Get a grip, I chide myself. While I am touched by Joe's devotion to Margaret, I cannot imagine what has shaken loose in me. And just like flipping off a switch, as I hurry home, I focus instead on all of the chores awaiting me.

- - - - -

I linger a bit today in the parking lot after shopping at Sevananda, chatting with my new friend, Willow. Her little boy, Kai, and my Cameron noticed each other a few weeks ago as Willow and I were doing our shopping. Willow's hair hangs in long, thick dreadlocks, tied back in a loose ponytail, and she has multiple piercings and tattoos. Today, she is dressed in a long batik-print dress, and, despite the fact that it is a late fall day, she is wearing Birkenstock sandals, and her feet are caked in dust. She also, it seems, has an aversion to using deodorant. I grew used to body smells in Cameroon, and I understand that masking body odor is not an obligatory American custom. I just didn't expect it here now.

But she is a mom, and she is friendly, and our children have taken to each other. Willow and I sit beside each other on a concrete ledge at the far end of the parking lot, chatting and watching our kids sit together in our wagon, jabbering and playing with Mr. Whiskers. It's sweet to see Cameron share her best bunny with Kai and to see him handle Mr. Whiskers with such tenderness.

Willow is also a native of Atlanta. She went to Euclid Elementary, but dropped out of Bass High School when she was 16, leaving home to join a traveling Renaissance Fair. She is not married to Kai's father, Gabe, whom she met at the Fair. After Kai was born, she continued to travel with the Fair and perform, but life on the road with a baby became too difficult, never quite knowing what their accommodations would be from town to town or where their meals would come from. So, while Gabe still travels and performs as a sword juggler, Willow moved back home and lives in her parents' basement on Elmira Place. They provide grocery money in exchange for light housework and yard work. Gabe comes home when the fair isn't touring—more in the winter months, less often in the warm months.

Willow tells me all of this in a very matter-of-fact way, as if all couples who are raising children begin parenthood on the road and then go home to live with their parents. As much as I love mine, I cannot imagine living with them again. Not after establishing myself as an adult, a spouse, and a mother.

I ask Willow what she did at the Renaissance Fair. She, too, is a juggler. I wonder how in the world she managed to do that when she was pregnant. In her soft, little girlish voice, she tells me, "I got used to each gradual change in my body and just adjusted." Then adds, "The last month was hard, though." She smiles. Willow is the epitome of understatement. And the ease with which she talks about her body makes me envious. I can't even bring myself to say "my body" without feeling self-conscious and awkward.

Kai and Cameron become restless. Nap time for both, it seems, so Willow and I part ways. As she walks away in one direction, holding her grocery sack in one hand and Kai's hand in the other, Kai turns back and waves. Cameron holds up Mr. Whiskers and wobbles him back and forth, waving in return. And something settles in me. Something I didn't realize wasn't quite settled until just now. In the years we were in Cameroon, I was never idle long enough to notice the lack of friendship. Kenneth and I had each other, and then we had Cameron, and that felt like enough. I'm in a new phase of my life now. I need a good old-fashioned girlfriend, although Willow is anything but old-fashioned, and I want Cameron to know friendship, too. Willow and Kai are an answer to a need I didn't know I had.

- - - - -

There is a vagrant who has begun lingering in the neighborhood. He perches on the ledge in the front yard of a nearby house, one of several properties that have seen better days. There's not a For Sale sign out front, and I don't think anyone lives there. He doesn't seem menacing, but what do I know? He could be an axe murderer. Just to show him that I see him and that I mean him no harm, I nod to him when Cameron and I are outside, and he nods back in acknowledgement. It looks as if every item in the world he owns is in the tattered duffel bag he carries, and that apparently does not include a razor or a comb. I'm guessing he sleeps in one of the nearby parks. At any rate, I don't think he has access to a hot shower very often. Occasionally, I notice him looking up at the front of Mrs. Across-the-Street's house, and I think, "Good! Now she'll have someone other than the Fields to spy on." It's not very charitable of me, I know.

The conversation with my dad from months ago comes back to me, and I determine to bake a batch of my mother's famous ice-breaking, friend-making Blonde Brownies. The recipe makes two rich, heavy 13x9-inch pans. We'll share one pan with Mema and PopPop Fields and my folks, and the other I'll divide into two: one half for Mystery Man and the other half for Mrs. Across-the-Street. I knew I was saving those empty Folger's coffee cans for a reason. My mission is to try to be neighborly and learn their names. I also hope Mrs. A-T-S will decide, after meeting me and Cameron, that we are entirely ordinary and not worth her curiosity. And that Mystery Man will see that we're decent people, so if he has axe murdering on his mind, he can direct his impulses elsewhere.

The house smells butterscotchy and delicious. As the brownies bake, I picture the aroma as a scout for Team Adipose, searching for somebody (me) that it and its fellow members can inhabit. They truly are so rich, they should probably come with a warning label. While they cool, I'm certain the fat scout sends out an all-clear signal for an extra inch or two to take up residence on my stomach and thighs. I knew I shouldn't have licked the spatula and the bowl! I am sure my resolve to eat only one brownie will be tested by those subversive goodies.

After the brownies have completely cooled, I cut one pan into squares that will fit neatly into the empty coffee cans. While I do this, Cameron sits at the kitchen table, coloring. Who can resist a batch of brownies, a homemade greeting card, and a cute nearly two-year-old kid all in one visit? Then Cameron and Mr. Whiskers climb into the wagon—yes, she actually has him go through the motions of climbing into the wagon—and Cameron holds on tightly to our neighborly offerings. Wouldn't you know it? Mystery Man is nowhere to be seen. Still, on a mission, I trudge up the steep driveway to Mrs. A-T-S's front door, glancing back every once in awhile to make sure both Cameron and the cans are still secure in the wagon. I arrive at my neighbor's front door a little out of breath, and before I can steady my breathing, the front door cracks a little. The screen door between us remains closed.

"Vat d'you vant?" I hear it through the crack, accusing.

"I, uh, it's . . . um, we're your neighbors from across the street. I'm Meredith, and I have my little girl, Cameron, here with me. We've brought you something."

"Vat ist?" her suspicious reply. We've yet to see her face.

"I made some Blonde Brownies. They're from a recipe my mom made up. They're really g---"

"No have. Am diabetic." She says this "dye-BET-ich," and the "ich" is extra phlegmy.

"Well, um, we'd still like to mee ---."

"Ahm goink now. My program, it's on," And with that, she shuts and locks her door. And dispenses with my concern that her television set is broken, as well as my neighborly intentions. I can feel my face reddening, and tears well up. I want to hurt her back the way she has just hurt me. How dare she act so uncharitable, so unneighborly in front of my daughter!

As I pivot around to turn the wagon in the homeward direction, Cameron hands me the card she has colored for Mrs. Shuts-the-Door-in-Our-Faces. Her face and her heart are as innocent and sincere as mine are wounded and angry. Chastened, I take the card from her and slip it into the latticework of the screen door.

Later, while Cameron plays quietly with her Fisher-Price

farm, I'm again consumed by anger. I eat my humiliation's weight in brownies, alternately condemning myself for caring about that woman and for my lack of willpower. Score another win for Team Adipose. And the FearGuiltShame Triplets. When I am nauseated from so much sugar, I pack the remaining brownies into the can we'd already prepared for Mystery Man, less out of charity and more out of the need to remove further temptation. I put the card Cameron made for him and the can of brownies into a paper sack, folding the top closed. I walk the sack over to his favorite watching spot and leave it there. On the outside of the sack, I've written Dear Mr. Watcher, please enjoy these homemade brownies. From Your Neighbors, The Fields.

- - - - -

My in-laws are coming to brunch tomorrow, and I am at Sevananda with Cameron, looking for just the right ingredients for a healthy, tasty meal. They hosted a Thanksgiving meal for us and included my parents, and everything was just perfect. I know I cannot measure up, but I will try extra hard to make Kenneth proud of me and to please the Grand Fields. At Thanksgiving, I was aware that Mema was watching what food I put on my plate and how much of everything I ate. I could feel her disapproval when I politely accepted her offer of pecan pie for dessert, and I could practically hear her critical thoughts when I, along with everyone else, talked about how full we were after the meal. So I feel pressure to serve something wholesome and delicious and to prepare just enough food so there won't be even the temptation of seconds. A quiche, I think.

I'm looking at the fresh vegetables as Willow and Kai round the corner. She's holding a can of soup in one hand and Kai's hand in the other. With her head down and taking rapid, staccato steps, she appears to be a woman on a mission, but Kai says, loud enough for everyone in the produce department to hear, "Cam-win!"

Cameron stops fondling an acorn squash I've put in her hands to preoccupy her, and her eyes light up. "Kai!" If Willow had hoped to zip through the store quickly and unnoticed, our children have foiled her plan. She stops her speedwalk and reluctantly looks up at me. There is a noticeable bruise on her cheek—that greenish color they get as they're fading.

"I haven't seen you in weeks! Are you okay? What happened?" I nodded toward her cheek.

Avoiding eye contact, she mumbles, "I'm fine. Her voice and eyes are flat, not their usual exuberant quality. While we occasionally get together at the park to talk and to let the children play, I do not feel as if we are close enough for me to pry any further. So, instead, I try to keep things light. While Kai and Cameron have made themselves at home sitting on the floor of the produce department, v-legged, feet touching, rolling the acorn squash back and forth—I guess I'll be buying it now—I proceed to tell Willow about my recent encounter with Mrs. A-T-S and Mystery Man, whom we now refer to at home as Mystery Mike. She gradually relaxes and becomes engrossed in my story, interjecting appropriate commentary like "you're kidding!" and "she didn't!" I may embellish a little under this type of encouragement. And soon she is telling me that Gabe is home for a few weeks, what they did for Thanksgiving, and what their plans are for Christmas. I tell her how much I'm looking forward to brunch already being over and about the cloud of disapproval that my mother-in-law carries with her as far as I am concerned. She tilts her head to one side as she nods, that universal gesture women use to indicate understanding. Then, in that typical wispy, childlike voice of hers, she says, "Well, we gotta go," and looks at Kai, saying, "Daddy's waiting, isn't he?" Kai rolls the squash back to Cameron one last time, then stands up, taking hold of Willow's hand again.

I impulsively lean over and give Willow a quick hug. "If I don't see you before, Merry Christmas." And I cannot be sure I don't hear her voice crack just a little when she wishes me a Merry Christmas, too, as she walks to the front of the store with her son and that one can of soup.

- - - - -

If there is ever any question of my ineptitude, my mother-in-law will fill you in on the myriad details of my shortcomings. For example, over the past several months, I have managed to kill all four of the houseplants she's given me: first a potted geranium, then a ficus, and an Easter lily. And now I've killed the aloe plant. Who kills an aloe? Me, that's who. Mema and PopPop are over for Sunday brunch and to bring Cameron her Christmas present. They'll be on their usual cruise to the Bahamas during the holidays. The conversations during the meal are cordial, if a little stiff. Even though Kenneth's mother has told us she is "not a little people person," their attention to their granddaughter is tender. After we eat, while the menfolk are relaxing in the living room, entertained by the impromptu pas de deux of Cameron and Mr. Whiskers, Mema and I are cleaning up the kitchen. I wash; she dries. She looks at the empty clay pot on the window sill where, just a few weeks ago, there had been the healthy aloe plant she'd given me. Earlier, I'd seen her not-so-surreptitiously glancing around for the ficus. Until now, I've been able to hide the fact that the aloe's plant siblings are all deceased, but when she asks me point blank about the aloe, I have to confess. "I forgot to water it, and then I over-watered it. It's dead. I'm sorry."

"And the geranium? Did you manage to keep it alive?"

"No, ma'am."

"Can I assume, then, that you've also killed the Easter lily and the ficus?"

"Yes, ma'am. I'm so, so sorry."

"Can't you keep anything alive?" she asks, not disguising her irritation.

While I am extremely tempted to say, Well, I do somehow manage to keep your son and granddaughter alive, I warble, "I guess I didn't inherit my mother's green thumb." I alternate between shame, feeling I should be sentenced to the gallows of plant killers, and indignation. Did I ASK you to give me plants? Do you even SEE that your granddaughter is thriving? Can I at least get credit for the things I do right instead of condemnation for the things I don't?

Just as the FearGuiltShame Triplets are summoned, as my emotions wrestle between groveling or standing up to her, we hear a crash and then a pitiful wail from the living room. Expecting to see the Christmas tree on its side, we rush in to see that Cameron's sidekick, the sly Mr. Whiskers, has twirled her into a bookcase, knocking an African elephant statue off and onto the floor. PopPop distracts the weeping Cameron by picking up the elephant and asking it if it's okay, then putting its trunk up against his ear as if listening. They carry on this make-believe conversation for some moments, and Cameron's weeping becomes sniffling, and her sniffling turns into a little grin when PopPop air-gallops the elephant over to Cameron and says, in his best elephant voice, "I have a little headache. Do you have a little headache, too?" She nods. "So shall we all sit together on the sofa and read a book?" Again, she nods. She selects a Babar story—how apt—and climbs with Mr. Whiskers into PopPop's lap, and we all listen to him read.

In no time, Cameron has dozed off. Kenneth carries her to her room, and then we say our goodbyes to his folks. There's nothing quite like a good cry to lull one to sleep, and now that they've left, I think I might do just that.

Chapter Two: 1976

IT'S SNOWING. Fat flakes that make a soft "poof" sound when they land. Cameron is mesmerized, and I am mesmerized watching her expression as she stands at the living room window. Nothing we experienced in Africa would have prepared her for this. I have the television on in the background, listening to Guy Sharpe discuss school and business closures in and around Atlanta, and I am grateful I stocked up ahead of the chaos that now grips the city. When Kenneth gets home and changes out of his wet clothes, he sits beside Cameron at the window, and they watch the swirling flakes together. According to Guy, this beautiful white stuff will become ice some time during the night. Power outages are expected, and Atlantans are urged to stay off the streets after nightfall. We are encouraged to hunker down at home with emergency supplies—canned goods, candles, flashlights, extra blankets, transistor radios, extra batteries, and other winter whatnot we Southerners are not accustomed to. Since we lived our everyday lives in Cameroon with just two hours of electricity a day, we are used to such primitive conditions, except for the cold. And yet, I'm delighted for the shift in our normal routine and to have an excuse for us to be together as a family for an extended time.

I remember camping out in the living room with Mom and Dad during a snowstorm when I was about six years old. We dined by candlelight—corned beef hash eaten straight out of the can—and we slept in sleeping bags with extra blankets piled on top. The next morning, Mom made oatmeal on a Coleman camping stove, which was kept in the pantry for just such emergencies. The snow was so white that, even though we had no electricity, the sun reflecting off of it brightened our breakfast room. No candles are needed. After we finished breakfast, all three of us put on extra layers of clothes and tromped through the snow to the Emory campus. There, students had taken metal serving trays from Dobb's Hall and were sledding down the steep hill in front of the Fishburn Building. If we currently lived closer to campus, that's what I'd do with Cameron and Kenneth. We'd walk to campus, and we'd borrow some trays and sled. But we make our own fun before the ice arrives. We make snow angels and a snowman and throw snowballs at each other until dusk. I notice Mrs. Across-The-Street is watching us, but I don't care. Let her watch. We are enjoying being a family. Then we come inside, dry off, and drink hot chocolate with extra marshmallows. And even though we still have electricity, we camp out together in the living room. After Cameron falls asleep, I attempt to crawl into Kenneth's sleeping bag with him, my intentions obvious. He tells me how tired he is and kisses me on the top of my head, just as he kissed Cameron good night. It's hard not to think I repulse my husband. And equally hard not to think I'm being too sensitive. I honestly don't know what to think.

- - - - -

"Uncle G" is dead. He didn't crash his car on an icy road. He didn't slip and fall on black ice. He was killed by a limb that fell from a tree. If he'd left home one minute earlier or one minute later, one of Dad's dearest friends and colleagues would still be alive. Atlanta is still recovering from one of the worst ice storms in decades, and since the worst of the ice had been cleared from most major streets, Uncle G was walking to his office on campus to grab some materials for a textbook he was collaborating on. Mrs. G said he'd gotten restless after being cooped up in the house for so many days, what with all his notes and reference materials in his office. He promised her he'd gather some materials into his old Army-issue rucksack, stop at Kroger in Emory Village for a few items, and come right back home. He told her the short walk would clear his head and lungs. Now he's dead, and Dad is helping Mrs. G with funeral arrangements, trying to be strong for her sake. Mom says that when he hangs up the phone or returns home from helping Mrs. G, he is quieter than she's ever seen him. The worry lines on his forehead are deeper. He not only misses his friend, but he also has to arrange coverage for Uncle G's winter quarter classes and take on Uncle G's advisees. Uncle G had five doctoral candidates up for their dissertation defense in April. Out of respect, maybe I should call him Dr. G, but he's been Uncle G to me my entire life. One minute earlier or one minute later.

- - - - -

Uncle G wasn't the only one who's been restless. Kenneth has been more wound up than usual, extra antsy and edgy. I know the jokes about snow babies born nine months after a storm, and yes, I fantasize about presenting Cameron with a baby brother or sister in September, but Kenneth has rebuffed my overtures again. Has my weight gain of the past few years really made me that unpleasant to touch? Oh, he apologizes the next morning, and I make some joke about how much more relaxed he'd be, but he just makes another one of his excuses. Is he trying to spare my feelings? It's not working.

And Cameron. I swear she is a barometer of her dad's moods. If he's happy, she's giddy. If he's distant, she's sulky. If he's distracted, she's off in la-la land, in a world I'm never invited to join. The edgier Kenneth gets, the crabbier Cameron becomes. I'm sad about Uncle G dying but grateful for the excuse to leave them alone together while I help Mom, Dad, and Mrs. G.

- - - - -

My baby is officially a two-year-old toddler and has mastered many words, "no" and "why" among them. Am I crazy to want another child? Maybe so, but I do want a baby brother or sister for Cameron.

- - - - -

It's springtime once again, and I have now developed the habit of always walking the long way home from Sevananda, just so I can keep up with the lives of Joe and Margaret. We've lived in our little rental house for over a year now, and I'm inextricably drawn to these art installations, which Joe adds to several times a year. One day recently, Mema and PopPop both had a rare day off from work and invited Cameron and me over for lunch. I'm betting it was PopPop's idea. Although we don't live far from them, they so rarely get to spend time with their only grandchild, or their only child, for that matter. Kenneth wasn't exactly a latchkey kid, for they had "household help" while he was growing up. So, while he doesn't have many memories of meaningful interactions with his A-list parents when he was a child, he knew they thought he was the perfect son. Mema is a much-in-demand interior decorator with a high-profile Atlanta clientele, and PopPop is in corporate real estate. I'm certain Mema has never really approved of me, and my lack of style doesn't exactly endear me to her. It only confirms her opinion that I'm all wrong for her precious Kenneth. I can't get a real read on PopPop. He's always been cordial to me, and he has a sweet way with Cameron. So either he's a good actor or he actually thinks I'm okay.

Anyway, while driving home after lunch, I went by the green space near Sinclair to look at the yard art again. Lo and behold, there is a newsworthy addition to the most recent installation. It appears Baby makes three for Joe and Margaret. Why didn't he tell us they were expecting? Judging from the tattered blue blanket wrapped around the baby doll that is propped between them, they have a son. The next time Cameron and I walk to Sevananda, we take the short route there and the long route home. I slow down to look more closely at the addition to this junkyard family. The baby doll was no doubt thrown in the trash because its facial features and hair are nearly worn away—I hope by a child who took that doll everywhere, loved its face and hair off, and is now too old for dolls. I also notice that, while Joe identifies himself and his beloved Margaret, Baby has no name. This fascinates me. At first, I chide myself for taking such an interest in these people I'd never met—people? Are they real? —but I justify my interest by telling myself that at least I don't watch soap operas every day like someone we do know. Those people on the soaps are definitely not real. So, this is my new Sevananda routine. I walk the short way there and the long way home. And Cameron is usually either asleep or so preoccupied talking to Mr. Whiskers that my slower pace in front of the Joe and Margaret Show escapes her notice. Or does it? I sometimes play out a little fantasy of Willow, Gabe, and Kai joining Joe, Margaret, and Baby for dinner at the home of Meredith, Kenneth, and Cameron. I snicker, too, when I imagine shaking hands with Joe's X hand made from two paint stirrers and observing Margaret changing Baby's diaper with one hand that is made from a garden glove and the other a small trowel.

- - - - -

Cameron and I have another new ritual on our almost daily walk to Sevananda. There's an old, three-story Victorian-era house on Waverly with a turret that's painted purple. The house is in serious disrepair, but I imagine it was quite a showplace at one time. I wonder what the original color was. I cannot imagine that the original owners painted the turret purple. But maybe they did. Maybe they were wealthy Atlantans who didn't give a fig about whether or not purple was the "right" color for the exterior of a home in what was then one of the classiest neighborhoods in Atlanta. Sometimes, especially if you're very rich, you can fly in the face of convention. I remember when I was in college and Mom and Dad hired painters to strip the walls in the house and repaint them a neutral beige. There were seven—yes, seven—layers of different-colored paint, including one layer that was purple and one that was flat black. The flat black must've dated from the early fifties, but when was purple in vogue? And I decide right then that the original owners of the house on Waverly chose purple, that their descendants have always lived in that house, and that it's in disrepair only because the current descendants are really old and unable to do more than the minimum upkeep to prevent termites from squatting and taking over. I picture an elderly spinster and her equally elderly widowed brother puttering around in the

43

house. What must their daily routine consist of? One day, I must have slowed down a bit more than usual to contemplate Mr. and Miss Turret's goings-on because Cameron stopped her chatter with Mr. Whiskers and looked up where I was gazing. Okay, I was gawking. I had no choice but to tell her about the two old people who live in that house.

So now, each day, as we pass, we discuss what the Turrets—Tilly and Tommy—must be up to right then. Today, I start by conjecturing, "She is probably washing up their breakfast dishes. What do you think they had for breakfast?"

"Eggs. Eggs, toast, and coffee."

"And while she is washing dishes, what do you think he's doing?"

"Um," she considers, "reading the newspaper."

"What will she do when she's finished washing the breakfast dishes?"

"She will feed the kitty."

"Oh. They have a kitty now?"

"Uh-huh. Her name is Lady Whiskers."

"I see. I didn't know that. Did Mr. Whiskers tell you this?"

She nods.

"And after she feeds Lady Whiskers and he reads the newspaper, what will they do?"

"They will have a piece of candy."

Busted! How long have I been sneaking a piece of candy after cleaning up the breakfast dishes, thinking my secret was safe with me? I will either need to become more covert or find a better way to reward myself for completing my domestic duties. At any rate, I love sharing my active imagination with my daughter and listening to her equally imaginative ideas. Even if she believes everything we say about Mr. and Miss Turret, there can't be any harm in it, can there? I wonder what we will learn about the Turrets on our walk tomorrow. Meanwhile, she is expanding not only her vocabulary but also her worldview, for, even though we do not know them personally, she is learning what it is like for people to be very, very old and be responsible for a very, very old, very, very tired, and very, very big house.

- - - - -

Georgia's very own Jimmy Carter has been elected President of the United States. What a great way to close out our country's bicentennial! From humble peanut farmer to President. Amazing!

Chapter Three: 1977

WE RING IN 1977 by making an offer on the house and becoming homeowners. And despite the cold temperatures outdoors, there is a discernible thaw in Kenneth's frostiness. He has joined a men's chess club and seems to be enjoying the intellectual challenge as well as the camaraderie. Many evenings, he stays up late working on his game strategies after we've put Cameron to bed, and I can no longer keep my eyes open. So maybe the "for worse" part is behind us now that we're settled and Kenneth has a hobby. We are discussing home improvement projects, too, which provides us with some much-needed closeness. We have a long list of projects that includes renovation jobs we will need to hire out as well as smaller ones we think we can manage on our own. I also hope to kindle a little more romance in our renewed closeness by losing some weight.

Yes, I'm on yet another diet. This is the one where you eat eight hotdogs one day, eight bananas the next, and eight boiled eggs the third day. You keep repeating the cycle for a few weeks, and the weight is supposed to just fall off. If I can whittle myself down in size, maybe Kenneth will consent to let me keep my diaphragm in the box, and we can conceive another child. Or at least enjoy trying. Maybe all that's been holding him back is that he's afraid I'll gain even more weight without having lost the original baby weight.

Kenneth says he knows of an independent contractor who can take on some of the large renovations. We just need to decide in what order to tackle them. We both know we're looking at years of small and large jobs, especially on just one income. But I have to say that the dreaming out loud together, the planning, and the discussing help me see in Kenneth the things that made me fall in love with him in the first place.

I smile as I remember the first time we met. We were at a regional youth conference in Savannah for high school students who worked on their school newspaper. There were students there from all over the southeast. Turns out Kenneth attended Cross Keys High School, not far from mine in Druid Hills, and both of us were in the Class of '68. We ended up being put in the same small group for all of the conference sessions, and what impressed me most was his sincerity and his passion for getting the facts correct. He was so methodical and analytical, a counterweight to my off-the-cuff approach to writing news articles. The yin to my yang. We hit it off immediately, and I was so smitten that I cannot remember most of the other students who were in the group with us that weekend. What I do remember is that the news article we wrote as a team won the Best Journalism competition.

We hung out together between sessions, sat together for all of our conference meals, and exchanged phone numbers before getting into our respective club sponsors' cars for the ride back to Atlanta. Afterwards, we talked almost every night on the phone and met at the Dekalb Mall nearly every weekend. That continued throughout our junior year of high school, but then the demands of my summer babysitting gig, Kenneth's after-school job, and my volunteer work during our senior year ended our courtship. Courtship? In all that time, we never did more than hold hands and talk for hours on end.

Then, surprise, surprise, we ran into each other—literally, at the beginning of our sophomore year at Emory. I was a legacy , and the Fields are huge donors. I was in the English education program, and Kenneth wanted to major in civil engineering. Their plan was for him to transfer to Georgia Tech after completing his first two years at Emory. I was leaving Dobbs Hall after lunch one day, just as Kenneth was entering. I was so busy yakking with a girlfriend that I bumped right into Kenneth, knocking the entire stack of books he was carrying onto the ground. And that was the year our friendship blossomed into a full-blown courtship, including, this time, kissing in addition to hand-holding and talking for hours on end. We loved to joke about how it was meant to be for a Gardner, me, to be with a Fields, him.

Since we both still lived at home with our parents, we spent a great deal of time at each other's houses, doing homework together, watching television, and sharing meals. Meals at our house were typically casual, with lots of conversations about many topics. My parents were so fond of my serious, intellectual, and well-read boyfriend that they invited him into their hearts. I cannot say the same about his parents. The Fields are just cut from different cloth. Mealtimes with them were more formal affairs, and the conversations were mostly about their interactions with the Who's Who of Atlanta society. Occasionally, I'd be invited to dine with them at the Brookhaven Country Club, and while they and I knew I was out of my element, Kenneth seemed unaware. Unaware or unaffected.

At any rate, our conversations about our dreams for our home and our lives together have renewed my hopes for our future together, including more hand-holding and kissing and whatever else those lead to.

- - - - -

We now have a three-year-old. Some days, it feels as if time drags by so slowly and on purpose, just to aggravate me, but at the same time, the years since Cameron was born have passed quickly. We have a little cake with three candles in it for dessert tonight, and then Kenneth leaves for his chess club after Cameron has had her bath and he has read her a story. He promises her we will all go to Piedmont Park on Saturday and have a "proper celebration. She doesn't even ask what he means by a proper celebration; she just accepts his pronouncement. It's me who's pouting. Actually, I'm not pouting; I'm furious. If I want to go to Rich's and buy myself a new pair of shoes, I have to ask Kenneth if he'll be available to watch his own daughter, whereas he gets to tell me where he's going. Do I really want another child with this man?

- - - - -

I am married to an escape artist. Even when he's at home, he's not all here. Oh, he still gives Cameron his undivided attention when she is speaking to him or showing him something, but when it's just the two of us, he's brooding and temperamental. Distant. If I want to attempt our first home improvement project by upgrading the smaller bathroom, he wants to try his hand at putting more insulation in the attic. The only thing we can currently agree on in the home improvement arena is to fly the butterfly flag, that widely recognized symbol of urban renewal, off our front stoop.

I don't know if it's out of spite or to prove a point, but without asking Kenneth, I transplanted a small oak seedling from the backyard to the front yard. I wonder how long it will take him to notice, to comment, to compliment, or complain. Maybe I'm doing this so he'll have to talk to me instead of engage with his mistress, that stupid chess board.

Oh, and add another failed diet to the failed diet tote board. I never even made it to the eight bananas day. Instead, I vomited soon after choking down the eighth hotdog. Ever hopeful that this was a sign my diaphragm had failed, I didn't even mind that horrible lingering aftertaste of processed meat. And then I started my period several days later.

Who am I kidding? I cannot seem to lose weight, no matter what diet I try. What I want is for my husband to tell me I'm beautiful and desirable and that he would very much like to have a second child with me. Maybe I should take up chess lessons so I can compete with his mistress for his attention. Meanwhile, if I am going to get any serious small home improvement projects completed while we save up for big ones, I know I cannot keep Cameron occupied all day, so I have enrolled her this coming fall in Glenn Memorial's nursery school program. I'll start with the Mothers' Morning Out program first and, if that goes well, consider the all-day option, at least a few days a week. As cute as she and Kai are on our park play dates with him and Willow, I think she'd benefit from having a few more playmates. And I'd benefit from a little peace and quiet and an occasional nap to recuperate from Cameron's nighttime dream-babbling.

- - - - -

I feel so foolish. Foolish, afraid, and crazy Somehow Willow and I get on the topic of having another child, and that conversation leads to birth control and the bedroom. Willow really knows how to spice things up when her man is in town, and she's very forthcoming about it. I wish I could talk as naturally about my sex life—what sex life?!—as she does.

While she does not want a baby brother or sister for Kai, I would very much like another child. She recommends I just "forget" to put in my diaphragm and not tell Kenneth. I cannot do that. I will not do that. Maybe one reason they can keep the embers of passion alive is that Gabe is home so infrequently. Still, she is shocked to hear how seldom Kenneth and I make love. So she helps me devise a date night plan, a belated Valentine's Day celebration.

I make reservations for us to eat dinner out at Petit Auberge and then to see Camelot at the Fox so that, afterwards, Kenneth and I will come home "in the mood." Cameron's sleep-talking won't pose a distraction, as she's spending the night with Willow and Kai. Willow suggests I surprise Kenneth, and she even tells me something that gets Gabe turned on.

So, even though I feel a little silly doing it, I also get excited—okay, horny—preparing my surprise. I buy a box of red jello and dye my pubic hair bright red. Willow warns me I'll need to wear a mini-pad in my underwear while we're out, and I'll need to cover the surface "where you take him" to keep from dying everything else red. She promises me it will wash out with a shower if Kenneth doesn't wear it off in the throes of passion first. So, after he gets home from work, our date night begins.

I am giddy with excitement. Kenneth keeps asking me if everything is okay, and I keep saying everything is great and is only going to get greater. He might have groaned a little

53

bit. Was that in anticipation? I can't tell.

The meal is wonderful, and the show is very romantic. They both definitely put me in the mood. I feel nervous about how he will respond to making love to a redhead. Well, not a redhead, per se, but definitely a change. Isn't red supposed to be the magic color that makes all bulls ready to charge? Let's hope so. I am ready for him to be ready.

When we get home, Kenneth wants a glass of wine. I take that as a good sign. That he's really getting into our romantic evening. And that he doesn't automatically set up a chess board to practice his latest strategy. While he's in the kitchen getting the bottle opener and two wine glasses, I go to the bedroom and insert my diaphragm, put on my negligee, and take the extra sheet I'd left folded on the end of the bed with me to the living room. I plan to "take him" right there on the living room floor. Kenneth walks into the living room from the kitchen as I'm entering from the bedroom, and he stops, staring. I can't read his expression, but my heart is thumping so hard that I imagine he can hear it. I drop the sheet and ask, trying to be coy, "See anything you like?" Kenneth sets the wine and the glasses down, still staring. Oh, this is going to be good. Worth the wait, I think. And he just keeps staring. And, yes, he is staring there, through my deliciously sheer negligee. His hands are trembling. We aren't going to sleep a wink tonight, I think. So I pour on the coy.

"Come here often, sailor?" I ask. Kenneth blushes. And so do

I. This is not our usual repartee. If I'm to be totally honest, we don't have repartee.

"What are you doing, Mer?" he asks.

"What do you think, Big Boy?" I continue the act. "You look lonely. Like you could use some company. How long have you been out to sea?"

Kenneth stammers. "I, uh . . . Jesus, Mer, what's gotten into you?"

My first impulse is to say, Well, certainly not you, but I don't. "I just thought I'd spice things up a little, is all. You know, since we don't seem to, uh, connect as much."

Kenneth hangs his head, his hands still twitchy and trembling. Then he takes a deep breath and lets it out slowly. I reach over and remove his glasses, setting them beside the wine bottle. I start to unbuckle his belt. He flinches, then looks up at me, at my determined expression, and he lets me undress him. Is this sexy? I don't know, and Kenneth provides no indication, but he also doesn't resist.

Once he is naked, I spread the sheet over the floor rug, grab a few throw pillows off the sofa, then take his hand and pull him down onto the floor with me. I kiss him tenderly, and he doesn't respond, but neither does he pull away. So I straddle him and kiss him harder, rubbing his chest with my breasts while I do. With my hands, fingernails painted red to match my pubic hair, I stroke him—on his face, his chest, his arms, his legs, his belly, and then his penis. It takes quite a lot of stroking and coaxing to get him hard. Maybe because this is new to us—me on top, looking into his face—we usually do the missionary position, with him gazing just beyond or above me. So now I'm the one determining what's next. I guide him into me and gauge his reaction to this new, red-haired dominatrix. Well, not a dominatrix in the strict sense, but in charge. Kenneth's face relaxes, and he lets me rock my hips on top of him. I grab both his hands and place them on my breasts. He doesn't move them away, but neither does he seem to know what to do with them. I'll show him next time, I think, not wanting to completely blow his mind this time.

Then Kenneth closes his eyes, and he seems to go somewhere inside his mind, somewhere I'm not sure I'm allowed. But he lets me continue to decide what we do next; he lets me move over him and on him. Maybe the red hair was just too much. But here we are, making love for the first time in countless weeks. I erase those thoughts and concentrate on just us, on reconnecting with my husband, on pouring some glue on the cracks in our relationship. I will see to it that all is mended and that we are stronger than ever. I already know what I want to ask him and what I want to say to him in our post-love-making pillow talk before I let him take me for round two.

And then, all too soon, Kenneth gasps as he climaxes. He opens his eyes and seems genuinely surprised to find me there, still riding him. He doesn't seem to know what to do. Even though I didn't reach climax, I smile at him. I take one of his hands and kiss his palm. I stroke his face. He seems lost. I slide off of him and lay beside him, my head on his chest. I take his free arm and wrap it around me and I listen as his breathing returns to normal. I look up at his face, and he's staring at the wall behind his head. So I wait. Wait for our pillow talk, for him to meet me halfway across the bridge that connects his life with mine, the bridge that was us before we had Cameron. And the next thing I know, he is sobbing. His whole body is convulsed with his weeping. I've only ever seen him cry like this one other time, the night before we left Africa.

I ask him, "What's wrong? Honey, please tell me what's wrong. What can I do to help you?" And he shakes his head, mute except for the sound he makes crying. I wait again, and when his crying has subsided, I ask, "Did I do something wrong? Kenneth, please talk to me."

He shakes his head again and opens his mouth to say something, but no words come out. He sighs and rolls to his side to sit up. He takes one of the throw pillows and places it in his lap, rubs his hands through his hair, then looks at me and says, "I'm going to bed.". He kisses the top of my head as he stands, gathers up his clothes, and then walks into the bedroom. The questions and the confusion bounce off of each other inside my brain, which suddenly feels like it will explode. And I conclude the evening by sitting on the sofa, wrapped in that stupid red-stained sheet, alone with my fears, drinking far too much of that bottle of wine.

- - - - -

I can't say that, growing up, I gave Memorial Day much thought. I was aware of the sacrifices our armed services made to insure our rights and freedoms, and I knew or knew of veterans from World War II, but Memorial Day has become more personal to me after Vietnam. It's been just over two years since the fall of Saigon, and it seems every week I hear of another high school classmate or the spouse of a classmate who died in Vietnam. People are still wearing MIA and POW bracelets. And I now see so many men living on the streets, some with just one leg or one arm, all with hollowed-out eyes. Much like Mystery Mike. It has not occurred to me until just now that he might be a veteran. I feel so dumb. And now this morning, as I am going to the curb to get our *Atlanta Constitution*, I notice Mrs. Across-The-Street has not one but two American flags planted in her front yard. I am humbled by this. It never occurred to me that she could be in mourning, and I resolve to try once again to meet her.

My plan is to do a little reverse spying. I need to figure out when each day she goes down her steep driveway to her mailbox, and I will just happen to be on that same schedule to collect our mail. I am determined this time to befriend her and let her know how much I appreciate the sacrifices represented by those two flags. So, tomorrow, as soon as I hear the mail carrier's Jeep making its stops in the neighborhood, I will watch out the front window for Mrs. A-T-S and hope that she is a creature of habit, as tethered to the mail carrier's schedule as she is to her "program" on the television.

- - - - -

The mail carrier usually delivers in our neighborhood during Cameron's nap time. During her nap, I'm typically in the back part of the house folding laundry, doing dinner prep, or ironing Kenneth's shirts, but today, I set up the ironing board in the living room so I can look out the front window, directly in line with Mrs. A-T-S's mailbox. I have already determined that her "program" comes on after Cameron's nap, so unless she watches several soaps, I assume she collects her mail soon after it's delivered.

I have ironed two shirts since the mail delivery when Mrs. A-T-S, walking cane in hand, carefully shuffles down her steep driveway to her mailbox. After collecting her mail, she hobbles back up to her house. It is painful to watch her walk. I wonder if, on top of having diabetes, she also has arthritis. Something in me softens when I consider the loss represented by those two American flags on Memorial Day as well as the loss represented by her need for a walking cane. I have let her short-tempered response to my brownie overture take up too much space in my head, so I will try, once again, to be neighborly. I just need to have a plan and be patient. Until then, I will begin collecting our mail when she collects hers.

- - - - -

There is something unusual happening at the Turrets'. As Cameron and I round the corner from Elizabeth Street onto Waverly, we are already discussing what Tilly and Tommy are doing at this precise moment. Cameron conjectures that Tommy is setting up the chess board while Tilly is fixing them a snack. Kenneth has, on occasion, pulled Cameron onto his lap while setting up his chess board, patiently explaining what each of the pieces is called and how each one may move. I admit to being secretly pleased when she insists on calling the knights "horsies" and the rooks "castles." My precocious daughter seems to understand that chess requires two players and that when her daddy is at his chess board, he's "prattising" for his chess club nights, where he squares off against his opponents. But Tommy and Tilly Turret play chess at home. My clever child. At any rate, Tommy and Tilly might not be playing chess right now because there is a lawn maintenance truck parked in their driveway, and while one straw-hatted workman is wielding a weed-whacker, another is pruning the Turrets' overgrown shrubs. And if that were happening at our house and we couldn't be outside to watch, we'd have our noses smooshed up to a window to watch. I don't know how enthusiastic the Turrets are about this activity, but I think Cameron and I are eager to walk by here again tomorrow to see the improvements to their property. Likely, we'll see more of the front of their house than we've ever seen now that the bushes are finally getting some much-needed attention.

- - - - -

I realized today that I haven't seen Mystery Mike for awhile. Has he found a place to live? Or maybe he is spending his days in a different neighborhood. Or he really is an axe murderer and has been arrested. I wonder if Mrs. A-T-S realizes that, while she has continued to spy on the Fields family, Mystery Mike was spying on her. At least, that's what it looks like to me. I wonder where he is and when is the last time he had a good shower, haircut, and shave. And I wonder why I care.

- - - - -

What an interesting day! First, I casually arrive at our mailbox just as Mrs. A-T-S arrives at hers. I wave at her, and she acknowledges me with a nod of her head before tucking her mail underneath her armpit and climbing back up her driveway, leaning heavily on her cane. Later in the afternoon, I notice Mystery Mike back at his usual perch. Have I conjured him here? If I have those kinds of powers, why can't I conjure myself back into a size 8? Still, I'm bemused by my relief at seeing Mystery Mike back in the neighborhood, and I decide that Cameron and I will have our afternoon snack outside today. We'll spread a blanket on the front lawn and have a picnic, and I'll take extra snacks with us, just in case. It's the middle of June and nearly the hottest part of the day, but that doesn't deter me.

Cameron wakes from her nap fussy. No, she doesn't need to go potty. No, she doesn't want a drink of water. No, nothing hurts. No, she cannot tell me what's wrong. No, Mr. Whiskers won't tell me, either. When I announce that we are having snack time outside if she can stop whining, though, she stops in mid-pout, intrigued. Then we bargain. If she will go potty like a big girl, I will let her choose our snack. Soon, we are outside on our blanket—me, Cameron, and Mr. Whiskers— with a jar of ice water, some Dixie cups, napkins, and enough Ritz crackers and cheese slices to make an entire meal. Then, conjurer that I am, Mystery Mike appears, walking down the street, heading our way. I decide that instead of merely waving, I will speak to him.

"Hello."

He stops walking, a look of confusion on his face, as if questioning whether or not he's really heard someone speak directly to him. I wonder if people who live on the street are used to being visible but not really seen. More like avoided. He cocks his head in our direction, and I smile at him and wave, again speaking, "It sure is a warm afternoon. Could I offer you a cup of water?"

He hesitates, scratching his scraggly face, then takes a few tentative steps toward us. I pour a cup of water and hold it out for him. He downs it in three big gulps.

"You must've been really thirsty. Would you like more? And would you like some crackers and cheese?" I point toward our snack.

He again hesitates, then holds out the cup for me to refill. After I refill his cup, I place several cheese-and-cracker sandwiches on a napkin and hold those out to him. He does not speak, but he accepts the crackers with a polite nod, not quite making eye contact with me or Cameron, then turns to continue walking down the street.

Cameron has been watching all of this without any real curiosity, as if it is the most normal thing for folks to do: have a picnic on the front lawn in the heat of June, offer a vagrant a cup of water and cheese-and-cracker sandwiches. And as he continues on his way, she says, "Bye, Mister!"

Mystery Mike turns around and lifts his free hand in a subtle wave. I cannot be sure beneath all that stubble, but I think he may have been smiling.

- - - - -

I'm on a roll. So far this week, I've managed to time my arrival at the mailbox to coincide with Mrs. A-T-S's. If she suspects this is intentional on my part, she doesn't indicate it with the slight nod of her head and the index finger wave from the hand that holds her cane. Still, I do not want to be obvious, so I must think of other reasons for being out in the front yard at mail time. Like maybe watering the little oak seedling I transplanted, which Kenneth, by the way, still has not noticed. Or if he has, he has not commented on it. Fine. Maybe by the time it is a full-grown tree and Cameron makes us grandparents, we can hang a swing from one of the branches for our grandchild. So it's settled. Next week, I'll mix things up a bit. One day, I'll fetch the mail at the same time she does. One day, I'll be watering the seedling. One day I'll be wiping the remnants of pollen off of the front stoop railing.

- - - - -

Cameron and I saw Willow and Kai again today. We don't seem to run into them as much as we used to. We stick to a pretty consistent Sevananda run during the warmer months, heading out soon after breakfast to avoid the midday heat. It seems like they used to be on the same schedule we were, but now it's rare that we run into each other, and the past few times I've called about a playdate, Willow has been evasive. Today, I can't help but notice she has a large bruise around her upper arm. So I ask about it.

She tries to make light of it. "Oh, that. I bumped into a wall while vacuuming my parents' living room. For someone who used to juggle swords, that's pretty clumsy of me, huh?" Then she forces a laugh, but the usual twinkle in her eyes isn't there.

"Willow, I'm your friend. I hope you know you can tell me if something is wrong."

She glances around, then at Kai, who is absorbed in an animated discussion with Cameron. Something about what Mr. Green Jeans was telling Captain Kangaroo on the television There is desperation in her eyes, and she starts to tell me something in a hushed voice when a dreadlocked dude walks up beside her and places his hand at the small of her back.

"Daddy!" Kai yells, excited. "You came to the store, too?"

"Hey, Bud." He grins and scoops Kai up, plopping him on his shoulders in one swift motion, revealing arm muscles that are large and ropey.

"Meredith, this is Gabe. Gabe, this is Meredith and her daughter, Cameron. I've told you about them—about our playdates at the park." Gabe nods and extends a hand.

"It's nice to meet you, Gabe." I take his hand and look up into his face, searching for signs of fatherly kindness and not arm-bruising menace. I cannot read what I see there, but I notice Kai is enraptured.

Then Willow takes Gabe's hand and says, "Well, we don't want to keep you. See you soon." And with that, she steers the father of her child around, heading in the opposite direction of where our shopping cart is pointed. I'm not hurt by this. I understand it means something that I'm not supposed to know about, but what exactly that is, I cannot say. But I will find out.

- - - - -

There are painters at the Turrets'. There is scaffolding set up across the front of the house, and a crew is scraping away at the flaking purple paint. Cameron supposes that Tilly is up in the tower at this very moment, watching the action. That's where we'd be, for sure. She also supposes that Tommy has set up his chess set in the back of the house and is "pratissing," away from the commotion. I must get her to share that tidbit with Kenneth at dinner tonight and gauge his reaction to her matter-of-fact assessment of what an obsession with chess looks like to the rest of us. For the time being, though, I'm very curious about the goings-on at the Turrets' home and, since we are soon to embark on our first fairly large renovation project, how much the Turrets are paying for their home improvements. I can only imagine how many thousands of dollars it will cost for their entire house to get a new paint job. Cameron and I both hope they don't change the color scheme.

- - - - -

Joe and Margaret must have gotten a puppy. It appears Joe is responsible for walking their new acquisition, as there is a leash made from grapevine extending from his "hand." The puppy's head is made of a pitted foam-rubber ball with two magnolia leaves for floppy ears. The body appears to be an old t-shirt stuffed with pine straw. The arms of the t-shirt form the front legs, and two sticks form the back legs, while an old television vacuum tube is the puppy's tail. That Joe is really clever.

I wonder if Margaret wanted another baby, and Joe said they could get a puppy but that he didn't want another child right now. Kenneth and I discussed another baby just last night, and his response was that we couldn't renovate the house and have another child and that we needed to renovate the house now while we had one child. I suspect he'd say the same about getting a kitten or a puppy, but he did, at least, make it sound as if having another child isn't totally out of the question. Good. For now, though, I'd like for him to hold me close on occasion, tell me he's glad he married me, that I'm still beautiful, and that he thinks I'm a good mother to our child. Does Joe say those things to Margaret? Am I jealous of Margaret? Of an art object or of an ideal? I'm not sure, but I do wonder sometimes if I'm a little too obsessed with the lives of Joe and Margaret, the Turrets, Mrs. A-T-S, Mystery Mike, Willow, Gabe, and Kai, or if my obsession is evidence that I need a hobby. Or a psychiatrist. Maybe I'll talk with Dad about this.

- - - - -

I scored a victory with Mrs. A-T-S, but I need to qualify that. We have our first curbside conversation as we both collect our mail. I just so happened to be watering the seedling before she started the long trek down her driveway. When I see her start her descent, I turn off the water hose and time my arrival at our mailbox with her arrival at her mailbox. Today, rather than the nod and the finger wave, though, she informs me that I have been watering a weed.

"I believe it's an oak seedling," I counter.

"Is weed," she replies bluntly, in her Slavic-soaked English. "I am sure."

"Well, thank you for telling me."

She merely nods and turns to start the climb back up her driveway. I'm stunned. Either she is far more impolite than I previously thought, or it is hopeless that I might inherit even a smidgen of my mother's green thumb, albeit too late for all of the poor house plants I've managed to kill.

When Cameron wakes from her nap, I tell her we are going to the library. We often go on Friday afternoons to load up on books for the weekend and return the previous week's haul. While I prepare her snack, she gathers up all of last Friday's books. She has little concept that today is Wednesday and not Friday, but that's okay.

At the library, after Cameron selects five books—that's our limit; it helps her narrow her choices and learn to count—I settle her in a chair beside the card catalog while I look up books on trees and weeds. Then I settle her on the floor in the stacks where the books on botany are located. Both times, she "reads" aloud to Mr. Whiskers, which never fails to melt my heart. She is a born teacher.

After searching through several books with detailed descriptions and photographs, I find the definitive source and am awash with embarrassment. For the past however many weeks, I have been watering an oak leaf weed. My mistake is understandable, given my lack of horticultural know-how and the shape of the leaves, but I want to cry when I think that the only green thing I've managed to keep alive and, yes, grow, is a daggum weed.

When I have finished my research, I take Cameron back to the children's book section and find A Child's Guide to Botany. Not for her. For me. Apparently, this is where I must begin if I am ever to keep the right sort of plants alive and correctly identify them in the first place.

- - - - -

I take a shovel out of the carriage house in the back, where we store all of our lawn implements, and proceed to dig up the oak leaf weed. Today, I do not care if Mrs. A-T-S and I have an exchange at the mailbox or not. I need to remove from the world's view the evidence of my ineptitude. Cameron sits on a blanket nearby, playing with some of her toys, while I dig. Even though it is morning, the day is already hot, and I am soon sweating. All my careful tending has caused the root system to become well developed. I don't know diddly about plant care, but I do know enough to take out the entire root if I don't want any more weeds sprouting up.

I have just laid the shovel down to wipe off my face with my t-shirt when Mystery Mike appears beside me. Without saying a word, he picks up the shovel, and in two or three well-aimed jumps on the top edge of the shovel, he has dug out the entire root system. He then picks up the black Hefty lawn trash bag with one hand and deposits the weedling (my name for this weed-in-seedling's-clothing) into the bag with the other. As he holds the bag, he looks at me and shrugs his shoulders, arching his bushy eyebrows.

"Oh, you can put it over there." I point to the side yard, where we keep our garbage cans until pick-up day.

He returns after stashing the trash bag beside the cans and picks up the shovel, gesturing again. His silence is a little unsettling. Is he mute, or does he choose not to speak?

"I'll put it away later. Thank you." And I reach over to take the shovel from him, hoping he doesn't think that I think he cannot be trusted to see the contents of our carriage house. Just to make sure I haven't awakened the rage of an axe murderer, I switch the shovel handle to my left hand, look him in the eye, and extend my right hand. "I'm Meredith, by the way."

"Ron." So he can speak after all!

"Well, thanks again, Ron."

"No problem, ma'am." He turns to walk away, and I make an impulsive, feels-right decision. "Um, Ron?" He stops and turns around. "We'll be having snack time outside again this afternoon, about 3:00, if you'd like to join us."

He nods, noncommittal. "Thank you, ma'am." He smiles at Cameron, who has observed this small weedling drama play out with the quiet, dispassionate objectivity of children, turns around again, and walks off in the direction of Euclid.

- - - - -

I think Mrs. A-T-S took pity on me, having seen my humiliation with the weedling. Today, she lingers at her mailbox as I approach ours.

"Hello," I say, as usual. And instead of the typical nod and finger wave, she speaks to me.

"Gut afternoon."

This is the day I have been hoping for, and yet I find I have nothing to say to keep the conversation going. Why didn't I think up discussion topics, questions, or comments? Stating the obvious, I respond, "I dug up that weed." I point to the small crater in the front yard. "Thank you for letting me know. I am embarrassed at how little I know about plants."

"You are velcome. I am sorry it vas not a tree."

"Yeah, well, the sad thing is I kept that weed alive longer than any house plant my mother-in-law ever gave me." She smiles at this. She actually smiles. "My name is Meredith, by the way. Meredith Fields."

"I am Magda." She doesn't provide her last name. "I vill go inside now," she informs me, and she turns to climb up her driveway to the sanctity of her home. Still, this feels like a genuine breakthrough. I cannot wait to tell Kenneth at dinner tonight. Mrs. A-T-S has a name, and it is Magda, and I, Meredith Fields, have befriended her. I will leave out the bit about the weedling, I think.

- - - - -

Kenneth and Cameron are watching the 6:00 news while I wrap up dinner preparations. I walk into the living room to tell them "five minutes," which is code for "Kenneth, work with Cameron to pick up and put away her toys." At that moment, there is a story about Anita Bryant's Save Our Children campaign. Kenneth walks over to the television and snaps it off, muttering angrily, "She should stick to selling orange juice." What could be wrong with saving the children? I wonder, but the kitchen timer calls me away.

Kenneth seems extra distracted at dinner, and I so badly wanted to share my Magda story with him. I know someone who will listen, though, so after dinner, I call Willow and invite her and Kai over for a lunch date tomorrow. If the weather permits, we'll eat outside. For some reason, it matters to me that Magda sees me interacting with people my own age.

- - - - -

Cameron and I get our front lawn picnic ready. All Willow and Kai have to do is show up. I have two large blankets spread out on the lawn. There are PBJs, apple slices, Kool Aid, and carob-coated rice cakes on one, and Mr. Whiskers and a few other toys on the other. Since they are walking here from their home, I am not concerned when they are fifteen minutes late. When they are thirty minutes late, though, and the apple slices have begun to brown and Cameron has begun to whine, I become worried. I leave everything set up outside and take Cameron inside so I can call. I'm not certain what I'll do if Willow doesn't answer, other than leave a message. I halfway hope she doesn't answer, though, as that will mean she and Kai are on their way. Willow picks up on the second ring.

"Hey, Willow. It's me, Meredith. Are y'all coming?"

"Oh, sorry," she slurs her words. "I forgot."

"We can wait if you still want to come over."

"Um, I don't think we'll be coming." She sounds far away.

"Willow, is everything alright? Are you okay?"

"Yeah, sure. I just forgot. Kai is upstairs eating lunch with my mom. I'm sorry."

73

"Oh, okay. Rain check?"

"'Kay. Um, I gotta go."

"Yeah. Are you sure you're okay? You sound a little, I don't know, not yourself."

"I just have a really bad headache. Sorry. Um, I really gotta go."

"Okay. Talk to you soon." I try to keep my voice steady. I'm both irritated and concerned, and I don't know which I hope is the better of the two. I'm irritated because this friend who has never forgotten a play date before has not only forgotten but has sent her son upstairs to eat with his grandmother, and now I will have to explain to Cameron why Kai is not coming over for lunch. I'm concerned because she sounded so out of it. Maybe she is using drugs, and that accounts for the mysterious bumps and bruises and this new slurring of words and forgetting, in which case I'm glad Kai is with his grandmother. "Let's get together real soon. Bye."

Cameron intuits that Willow and Kai are not coming, and her bottom lip begins to quiver. Truthfully, I feel sad, too, but to ward off a total meltdown—hers and mine—I propose an alternative. "Let's go ahead and have our picnic—you and me and Mr. Whiskers. And, if Mystery Mike, er, Ron, is out there, we'll invite him to join us. Would you like that?"

Her lower lip trembles just one more time before she nods,

and moments later, we are back outside, seated on the food blanket, eating our lunch.

Cameron has finished her sandwich and apple slices and has just taken a bite of her rice cake when we both spot Ron walking down the street toward his watching spot. Before I can say anything, Cameron stands and waves. "Hey, Mister Ron. We have lunch for you."

Ron slows his walking, and his eyes flit back and forth. He looks like he feels trapped, so I pour some Kool Aid and take the cup to him. "You don't have to eat with us if you don't want to, but we'd like to share. I made this picnic for four people," I point back at the blanket, where Cameron is still standing, waving, "but my friend... The truth is, she forgot. You'd be doing me a favor if you'd take some of the leftovers. It's nothing fancy. Just PBJs and apple slices." I realize I'm rambling, so I pause. Ron takes a sip of the Kool Aid. "Anyway, you're welcome to some of it." I turn to walk back. And wordlessly, Ron follows. I can tell because Cameron's smile is brighter, and she gives a little jump of joy. Something tells me, as he accepts a CARE package of lunch leftovers, that Ron is not an axe murderer but a very wounded soul.

- - - - -

Elvis Presley is dead. I know his many fans are bereft, but all I can think about is little Lisa Marie now being fatherless.

- - - - -

I got lost yesterday. Lost of the turned-around, completely disoriented variety. Feeling the need to work my muscles and think without interruption, I convince Mom to pick Cameron up from Glenn Memorial when nursery school is out and keep her until I get back. My plan is to drive to Tallulah Gorge and walk for awhile, then return home in time to cook supper. Hopefully invigorated and with greater clarity. Maybe a pound or two lighter.

I park the car and identify a trail that will take me to a knob where I can see for miles in all directions. I need that vantage point and the inspiration that I hope will come with it. What is it about those art installations that so consumes me? Makes me sad and angry at the same time? Why do I feel drawn to them, despite how they make me feel?

I set out with a canteen of water, a handkerchief, and a map provided by the gift shop. The knob, according to the map, is 1.2 miles from the parking lot trailhead. My plan is to walk to the top, mulling over my thoughts on the way up, and then to let the vista speak to me. I have, frankly, become weary of living in that little room inside my head, trapped by my thoughts, impulses, and failures. I hope the vista will provide a key. Yes! I'd like a key to unlock that little room and release me to return to my life unencumbered. I feel my family deserves this. They need me to be me again. As I set out, my first thoughts though, are actually questions. Does Kenneth even realize how distracted and remote I've been? Does he know I've been wrestling, and he's just too kind or too intimidated to ask me about it? Or are we both distracted and remote—from ourselves and each other? I must sort this out.

The hike is pleasant enough, despite walking straight into several spiders' webs. I seem to destroy most of them with my face, never my chest or my neck. How long has it been since someone walked this particular path? Are there any snakes lying in wait for my juicy ankles? If I get bit by a rattlesnake, how long before I'm found? Would I be dead or alive? I refocus on the questions I'd come all this way to ponder, listening to birds calling each other and the breeze rustling the leaves at the treetops. In the solitude of nature, I am astonished at how much sound one leaf makes when it loses its anchorage to the mother tree and drifts down to the forest floor, bouncing on its way down from branch to branch. How many different bird songs there are. How the shift in terrain alters the vegetation and rocks that line the blazed path. All of these observations seem to mean something, but what? What am I meant to do with these observations and these ruminations? If I put them in a blender with the thoughts that live every day in that little room inside my head, what would that puree look like? Would I be more at peace and less distracted?

When I reach the knob, I am panting. Hard. I have at least accomplished one of my objectives, and my muscles are quivering from the exertion. The view is spectacular, just as I expected it to be. It is breathtaking, and not just because my legs and my lungs aren't used to this type of exercise. I feel kind of proud of myself for having walked steadily uphill without stopping, and I reward myself with the opportunity to rest and look. As my breathing returns to normal, I feel an unmistakable urge to return to the classroom. Just like that. I hadn't come on this little day retreat to contemplate returning to the workforce, but there it is. Clear and strong. I wait a bit more, bringing forth in my mind the images of the art installations and my developing reactions to them, as well as Kenneth's chronic moodiness. How is going back to teaching an answer to those deeper questions? I turn my body by degrees to see how the view changes at due north, due east, and due south, to see if the answers present themselves when the view changes. And that's when I see what looks like an extension of the path. It loops around the edge of the knob and appears to run parallel to the path I'd walked up on. Amazed at myself, the rule-follower and risk-avoider, my feet seem, of their own volition, to step onto the alternate path. Surely, I think, this path will peter out just down that slope, and then I'll turn around and retrace my steps. The path continues, though, as do I, reminding myself that I am walking parallel to the blazed trail and that I can turn back once this path ends. Apparently, I am wrong on both counts. The path seems to just taper off. I look to the ridge on my left, where, I assume, the blazed trail is still running parallel, and, foolhardy as it now seems, I plunge into the woods toward the ridge so I will not have to backtrack. I keep that ridge in my sights as I scale a hill that is littered with fallen trees and thorn bushes. And once I reach the ridge, I discover it is but a plateau, and there is another ridge beyond it. That must be where the trail is, I think. And I push on. At one point, the incline is so steep that I have to crawl up on my hands and feet, grabbing at roots and footholds to avoid falling backwards. That's when I notice a fallen tree to my left and determine I can use it not only to help me reach the ridge up ahead but also as a reference point. Wrong again. I do, in fact, use that fallen tree trunk to help me climb up toward the ridge, all the while quelling thoughts about snakes. Once I reach the next ridge, though, I see another ridge and what looks like a path. Finally! I work my way up and over to it, only to discover it is not a path, and I am now staring at another knob on the face of the mountain. The parallel path is nowhere in sight. By then, I am not sure in which direction to walk. According to my map, which is of little use to me since I don't have my bearings, there is a creek that runs near the original trail. I have no choice but to either try to retrace my steps or walk straight downhill until I find the creek, and then follow the creek. Which direction, though? Right or left? I walk down one ridge-side, looking for the fallen tree I'd used just minutes before. Nope. Nowhere to be seen. I stop, leaning on a small oak tree, and listen, look, and think. I decide to just keep walking downhill until I find a creek bed or get killed by a timber rattler, whichever occurs first. I am nearing a cleft between two hills, where I hope to hear water, when I see an old logging road. I see tire tracks embedded in the dried mud, so I know it has been used fairly recently. I follow it. First, though, I find a small fallen limb, which I carry like an acolyte carries the candle lighter down the aisle, obliterating every spider web on the way. I keep expecting to pick up the white blaze of the trail I started on, but I never see another trail branching off of the logging road. But follow that road. I do. Many minutes later, I hear a rooster crowing. I round a bend and see an old house with wild turkeys pecking in the yard. I know civilization cannot be too far away. Shortly, I hear highway sounds. At about the same time, I hear a small creek to my right. Where have you been? The only response I get are the vocalizations of the fowl behind me. I walk a little further, and there is the highway. Phew! Almost there. All I need to do now is walk on the highway back to the parking lot where I left my car. A walk that takes me a good thirty minutes.

After I use the gift shop restroom, I look again at the map to see where I'd walked intentionally and where I wound up on the highway. I am stunned at how turned around I'd been, at how quickly I'd lost my bearings, and at how far from my original plan I'd deviated. Maybe those art installations are rooster calls and turkey gobbles bringing my attention to where I am in relation to where I thought I was or should be. All I know for sure is that I need to polish my resume. I also know that getting lost resets something in me. I don't quite know what it is, but my internal compass for what I want and what I need finally seems to be pointing back toward true north.

- - - - -

It's official. We have begun our first large do-it-yourself renovation. Kenneth and I decide we can manage refinishing the hardwood floors ourselves. One room at a time, we will move all of the furniture out, tape up plastic sheeting, sand the floor, and apply varnish. We will likely spend the next four or five weekends doing this, but while Cameron is at nursery school, I can at least move most of the items in each room to the living room and tape up the sheeting. We will do Cameron's room first and the living room last in case we make mistakes in our maiden voyage with the sander. Both of our parents have agreed to take turns occupying their granddaughter's attention at their houses while we are sanding and varnishing. The other tricky part will be keeping her out of each room we've worked on until the varnish dries completely. While I have doubts that we know what we're doing and concerns that we'll start but not be able to finish, Kenneth seems confident we can complete the project without hiring someone to help, as if we could afford to do so. Our goal is to have this project completed in time to put up our Christmas tree in our newly painted living room. I so want to see the look of admiration on Mema Fields' face when she realizes I am a good helpmate for her precious boy and that, while I am not great at keeping green things alive, I'm pretty darn good at tending to the humans in my life.

Chapter Four: 1978

WE BARELY FINISHED the floors before Christmas, and the Fields had already left to spend their holiday before we completed our project, but when they stop by today for a little New Year's visit, I could tell Kenneth's mother was impressed. I can barely contain my glee. The talk soon turns to our next project. While Cameron shows PopPop some of the loot Santa brought her, Kenneth and Mema sit on the sofa, and I sit on the floor, wrapping ornaments and putting them back in the box. "I want to renovate the carriage house, but Kenneth wants to retile our bathroom." I smile a self-deprecating smile. "And that makes sense—to do something on a smaller scale and something we can afford." Mema is obviously pleased that my irrational project didn't get the Kenneth Seal of Approval. I'm probably the only thing he's ever decided on that she doesn't agree with. Oh, well. Just wait until I tell her my plans to apply for a teaching job. I can see the thought wheels turning already. Now she'll NEVER have time to water the houseplants!

- - - - -

Cameron and I are at my parents' house, talking about her upcoming 4th birthday. I swear the years are flying by. I remember when they used to say the same thing about Christmas arriving so quickly, as if a week, not a year, had passed since the last one. I thought they were crazy and that Christmas would never get here. Now I get it. The subject turns to our next renovation project and then to Kenneth. I tell them about Kenneth's big assignment for the City of Atlanta, that of an expansion of MARTA services. It seems Atlanta's infrastructure cannot keep pace with her growth, and now bus and rail service need to move beyond the perimeter. Kenneth is excited about these additional responsibilities, and on the nights he isn't at his chess club, he has county maps, surveys, plats, and copies of deeds spread out all over the dining room table. I am proud of my husband, that his civil engineering expertise is recognized, and that he is tapped for duty. I explain all of this to my parents while Cameron plays with a puzzle on the floor of their living room, absorbed in getting the pieces in the right places. Then I decided to come clean about our next home renovation and my anxiety about it. "While we were working on the floors together, I enjoyed our being a team. I can't help but wonder if he picked retiling the bathroom because it's more of a one-man job. There's not much need for my help, and I feel like he's avoiding me. Am I being silly?"

My dad, ever the sage, asks, "Are you? Is it possible that

Kenneth's decision has less to do with avoiding you and more to do with taking on a project that you can not only afford but also won't require disrupting the whole house again?"

"I guess you're right. I'm just feeling like we're going through more than our fair share of marital doldrums. He's so preoccupied—with work, with the bathroom project, and with his chess club." I don't mention how infrequently Kenneth and I make love, but I am curious whether or not my expectations are realistic. "Do all couples go through these phases? Did you? Do you?"

Mom takes Dad's hand in hers and smiles sweetly. "Of course, darling. Every couple has its ups and downs. But you get through them, and you come out stronger because you did. Right?" She looks up at Dad adoringly, and he nods.

I wonder, though, if their doldrums are like mine and Kenneth's. I wonder if Mema and PopPop Fields have had their ups and downs, or if he just learned to keep quiet and agree with everything she says. Do Willow and Gabe have their ups and downs, as infrequently as they are together? Do Joe and Margaret? Did Tommy and Mrs. Turret? If only there was a book in the children's section of the library titled A Child's Guide to a Happy Marriage.

- - - - -

My daughter is a four-year-old. A Dr. Seuss-reading, question-asking, sleep-talking, Go Fish-playing four-year-old.

On the Saturday after her birthday, we meet Willow and Kai at Euclid Elementary School's playground. Kenneth is at a chess tournament. Of course. Until today, Cameron has been content to let me push her on the swing, satisfied with going only as high as I can push her. That all changes today. She watches as Willow launches Kai with one big push and then steps back as he furiously pumps his legs, going ever higher.

"Mommy, higher!" my daughter commands.

"I'm pushing you as high as I can. See how Kai is pumping his legs? If you do that, you can go as high as he does," I say with a lump in my throat. Do I really want her sailing so high?

Cameron moves her legs back and forth rapidly and just as rapidly loses momentum. I stop the swing altogether and squat down beside her. "Watch. See how he leans back and pulls on the chain when he's moving up? And he's sticking his legs out, right? What happens when he's comes back down? Watch."

Cameron studies Kai intently, then synchronizes the index and middle fingers on her right hand, like miniature legs, with Kai's legs, scrunching up her face just like Kenneth does when he's concentrating. And while she studies Kai, I surreptitiously study his mother for any signs that she may not be okay. And I am relieved that the old Willow is here today. The Willow who is bright, funny, and alive "Push me, Mommy," Cameron demands. I give her the bug-eyed reminder face, which must be the universal Mom face for use

86

your nice, asking words. "Pleeeeease." And in very short order, she and Kai are soaring together, punching the clouds with their feet and piercing their mothers' hearts with their giggles. I am so proud of my daughter and so sad that her daddy is not here to see this little victory over gravity.

- - - - -

While Cameron is in nursery school today, I go to the Dekalb County Board of Education and put in an application to teach ESOL. Although I don't have the required certification to teach English to Speakers of Other Languages, my experience teaching in Cameroon should certainly give me an advantage. It doesn't hurt that I have several letters of commendation from the diplomats whose children I taught, thanking me for my service while Kenneth and I were in the Peace Corps. I do not know when I will hear back from today's application. I think I will give it a few weeks and, if I hear nothing, I will apply to Atlanta Public Schools, maybe Fulton County. I'd rather stick closer to home, though. I won't even worry about babysitting logistics until I get a job offer. For now, though, I am beginning my umpteenth diet in case I am called in for an interview. Otherwise, I'm going to need a new wardrobe for work since I'm probably two or three sizes larger than I was when I left for Africa. Mastery of English, I've got. Of my own appetite, I do not.

- - - - -

Cameron and I are just returning home from our weekly trip

to the library as Magda is fetching her mail. Even though it is still springtime, the weather today is unusually muggy, and Magda labors to get up her driveway with a small parcel tucked under her left arm.

"Let's see if we can help Miss Magda, shall we?" I say this to Cameron, who enthusiastically agrees. I unbuckle her seatbelt and help her out of the car. Holding hands, we look both ways before crossing the street, then walk rapidly towards Magda.

"Magda," I say, using my outdoor but neighborly voice. She turns around, precariously balanced on the walking cane in her right hand. "Let us help you, won't you?" I can tell she's not sure about accepting our help. I gently nudge Cameron in Magda's direction, and, in our unspoken mother-daughter language, she understands, reaching for the parcel. Magda relents, and I take the rest of her mail and then hook my arm through her now-free left arm, and, together, the three of us slowly climb her steep driveway.

I attempt to make small talk while we're walking. "How long have you lived here?"

"Long time." She ponders. "We move here when Junior is a baby," which she pronounces bebby. "1946, I think. Long time," she repeats. Indeed. Thirty-two years is longer than I've been alive.

"What did your husband do, Junior's father?"

"CDC. Research," this neighbor of a few words cryptically replies. I'm impressed, though. That must have been a plum job, being appointed to the newly-formed CDC after World War II. While I'm curious about what he researched, I don't want to push my luck, so I change topics.

"If it's this warm in April, I wonder how hot we'll be in the middle of summer."

"Very hot. Too hot."

"Would you let Cameron and me bring your mail to you so you don't have to get out in the heat? We don't mind, do we, Cameron?" My doe-eyed daughter eagerly nods, grinning in that cute and winsome way she has.

Magda considers, but before she can come up with a reason to refuse our offer, I announce, "It's settled, then. We'll bring your mail to you, starting tomorrow." I say this as we arrive at her front door. Magda lets go of my arm, opening the screen door and then, ever so slightly, the front door. She turns around to face us, reaching for her mail. It's very clear that we will not be invited inside.

"Thank you, young lady," she says to Cameron, and to my ears it sounds like yunklady.

"You're welcome, Miss Magda. Bye bye."

"We'll see you tomorrow," I say, and as I do, Cameron begins skipping down the driveway, hurtling toward the street so quickly that I have to run to catch up to her. I don't know that she wouldn't have stopped to look both ways, but I don't want to take that chance.

At dinner that night, I let Cameron tell Kenneth how we helped our neighbor today, and in the telling of it, I am stunned not only by the purity of her heart but also at how accurately she can mimic Magda's accent. I now have two new curiosities: what does the inside of Magda's house look like? Does it resemble Miss Havisham's home in Dickens' Great Expectations, and that's why we're not allowed in? And where, exactly, is Magda from? The first is admitted nosiness on my part. The second is in the interest of linguistics and, I hope, honing my ESOL skills.

- - - - -

Apparently, babies can be made in a test tube. I wonder how Louise Brown's parents will explain to her how she came into the world. Will she understand that she was still conceived in love, but not in the way we typically consider it? Will she be okay?

- - - - -

Cameron and I visit Mama Jo and Papa Don for lunch. While Dad is in his study with Cameron, showing her his arfacs, Mom confides that she is worried about him. Here is what I know from our conversation. He, this man with meticulous routines, has been misplacing simple items, like his wallet or his car keys. When they finally locate the missing items, it's usually by accident, and they are in strange places, like behind an antique pot on the kitchen window sill or tucked away in the placemat drawer. He has no memory of putting them there and seems just as mystified as Mom about how they got there and why. What I also know is this: if Mom is worried enough to voice her concern, it's probably worse than she describes. She typically spares me the worst details about any situation, whether it's a toddler with cancer she is taking care of at Eggleston or a squabble amongst some ladies at church over the color of the new sanctuary carpet that almost, she told me years later, resulted in a second Civil War. So I wonder. What is she not telling me?

When I push her for more details, her hands flutter as if she wishes to swat away the fact that she has given utterance to a mere passing concern. She attempts to minimize my worry— her worry, too?—saying, "I shouldn't have said anything. It's only happened a few times. He's fine. He's still sharp as a tack. I'll bet it's just overwork." Then, the deflection, the laying of blame "You know, they just take advantage of him, of his expertise, and of his goodness. Anything Emory asks him to do, he'll say 'yes,' He didn't have to teach this summer, but they wanted him to. He didn't even ask if there was anyone else who could do it. He just agreed to do it." Then the gotcha "How about you and Kenneth bring Cameron by for dinner more often, give him an excuse to leave work early, to say 'no'?" As if I need more fuel for the fires of daughter guilt. As if the FearGuiltShame Triplets need an excuse to come calling. As if I need a reason to describe how "off" Kenneth and I are lately. Oh, if only the fluttering of my hands could swat away that observation. Still, I must make a better effort with Kenneth and with Mom and Dad.

- - - - -

It is a blistering hot day. The heat today has overridden my endless curiosity about Magda, so I try to dispense with our mail delivery as quickly as possible. I usually attempt to engage her in conversation at her door while trying to sneak peeks into her home, but this day, as we trudge up her driveway, I am fantasizing about cooling off with one of the ice cream sandwiches stashed away in our freezer. Then I scold myself; surely I can restrain myself until after dinner tonight. Still, I need to get inside and out of this heat. Meanwhile, Cameron is chattering away at Mr. Whiskers, describing our neighborly mission in detail, as she does most days we're climbing Magda's driveway. Out of the corner of my eye, I notice that Ron is watching us. I try to imagine what it's like for him to live out of his duffel bag. Where does he go to escape the heat? To shower off the buildup of perspiration and body odor? How fortunate I am to have a house with beautifully stained hardwood floors and a recently retiled master bathroom. And how hard Kenneth worked to complete the project. I suspect it was, in part, because he was missing so many chess club gatherings, but also in part because we all had to share the smaller "children's" bathroom. Still, we are a family. We have each other. Does Magda have anyone to call family? If so, I am unaware of their existence. She has a lawn crew take care of her yard, and I assume she has her groceries delivered. We now deliver her mail. That does not constitute family.

By the time we reach Magda's front door, I am awash with emotion. Pity for Ron. Gratitude for Kenneth. Tender love for Cameron. Compassion for Magda. And irritation at my self-centeredness. So what if my t-shirt will have sweat circles under the armpits by the time I get home? And in that instant, I decided that we will not escape the heat inside our home. Instead, I will hook up the sprinkler in the front yard and let Cameron put on her bathing suit and leap through the water to her heart's content. Who knows? I might just join her in our improvised rain dance.

- - - - -

Just as I am beginning to believe that all three of my applications for teaching positions have been filed in the proverbial circular file, I get an interview at Euclid Elementary, followed by the phone call I have been hoping for. I have been asked to teach ESOL part-time in a pull-out program. My students will remain with their class most of the time, and I will work with small groups of them a few days per week. I am elated! I am also scared out of my mind. I'll be teaching with a provisional ESOL certification, pending completion of graduate coursework at Georgia State to get the actual certification. I'm not sure what makes me more nervous, going back to work or going to graduate school. As for logistics, even though it's in the opposite direction of where he works, Kenneth will be taking Cameron to Glenn Memorial on the days I teach since he has more flexibility in his work hours. I'll pick her up when I'm finished. Dekalb County has given me one year to begin the graduate program, so at least I have a reprieve in the evening childcare department, which will also buy Kenneth time to reconsider his obligations with that infernal chess club. I think this new job will be good for all of us, and with the extra income, we can take on a few of the larger renovation projects. Kenneth still does not want to restore the carriage house, even though I thought I made a pretty compelling case for renting it out for yet more income. When he listed out for me all that would need to be done to make it habitable, I had to concede that finishing the many projects in our current living quarters made more sense. The new school year is just weeks away and I have so many things to get done before then that I am a little overwhelmed. First, though, I feel the need to reach out to Willow and Kai and schedule another play date. Once school starts, we will not be able to meet much during the week, if at all.

- - - - -

Willow is skittish when we meet up at the Euclid Elementary playground. Kai, too, which is unusual. He is not his usual chatty self, which puzzles Cameron. She continues to try to draw him into conversation and play, but he will not leave Willow's side. I have never seen this adventurous little boy be clingy, and it worries me. I try to make conversation, ask

Willow how things are, and she glances down at the child who has glued himself to her right leg, then answers evasively, "Oh, you know..."

Well, no. I don't. That's why I asked. I understand that, while Kai is within earshot, she will not tell me what's wrong. And I know something is wrong. I must do something to help her if she will let me, but first I need Kai to let go of her leg. I squat down and take one of Cameron's hands, place my other hand on Kai's shoulder, and ask, "Who knows how to spider swing?" That gets their attention and they both look at me, eyes wide, as if I were the Oracle of Playground Mysteries. "First of all, who knows how many legs a spider has?"

"Eight," Kai replies immediately. He gots eight legs."

"Right. And how many legs do you have?"

"Two."

"Yes! And two arms, too, right?'

At this point, he looks at me as if I'm several crayons short of a full box, so I explain how spider swinging works. "One person sits on the swing first; usually it's the bigger person." I look at Kai when I say this, and some sparkle returns to his eyes. "Then the other person," I look at Cameron, and she is clearly intrigued, "sits on their lap with their legs in the other direction, like this." I use V fingers on both of my hands to demonstrate. "And when you add up the arms and the legs, how ma--?

"Eight! Just like a spider!" Kai announces and lets go of Willow's leg.

"Wanna try it?" I ask them. They respond by clambering to the swing. Kai climbs onto the swing, and I lift Cameron onto his lap. Their faces are about a foot apart, and they are grinning eagerly. "Ready?"

"Yeah!" they yell in unison. I pull back on the chain of the swing, just below where their hands are clutching tightly, then give Cameron's back a gentle push when I let go. In moments, they are spider-swinging like pros, giggling and chattering.

I step over to Willow, who has been watching with detached fascination. She whispers, "Thank you."

"For what?"

"You know. For calling. For caring. It's so good to see him happy again."

"Of course." Then, "I know something's wrong. You don't have to tell me anything, but I want you to know that if there's anything I can do to help..."

"Yeah. I know. I appreciate it."

I wait for a moment to give her the chance to tell me what's going on while debating whether or not to tell her about my new job, afraid that if I do, she will think she cannot ask me for help. We both start to speak at the same time, her "I might have to" crossing over my "I wanted to tell you."

"You first," I say.

"You sure?"

I nod, and she starts over. "I might have to go away for a little while—Kai and me. It's no big deal, and I'm not even sure. I haven't said anything to my parents yet. But I wanted you to know, in case you call and I don't - -"

"Daddy! Look at us!" Kai's voice breaks in. Willow stiffens, and her eyes widen. Gabe is approaching his son and my daughter, and Willow's and my gaze are drawn to the scene. He looks at the spider swingers with amusement.

Gabe's voice booms, "Look at you go!" And Kai beams. Cameron, too, because her friend is so happy. And because she is so happy.

Willow whispers, as she pulls away and begins walking their way, "I'll talk to you later, okay?"

I nod, following.

Gabe says, more to Kai than to Willow, "I've finished packing for my next trip, and I came by so we could spend the afternoon together before I have to leave. Okay, Buddy?" As he is talking, the swing has slowed almost to a stop. Gabe places his hand on Kai's back.

"Okay." Then, "Can we get ice cream? He looks at Willow for approval. She nods, a smile on her lips, but the faraway look in her eyes tells a different story.

We disentangle the children and say our goodbyes. Willow, Kai, and Gabe head off in the direction of their home while Cameron and I stand there watching. Then I look down at her and say, "Guess what? In a few weeks, Mommy will be teaching at this school while you go to your school. It's going to be great."

"Mommy?"

"Yes, Love?"

"Can we have ice cream, too?"

"Why not? Let's go home and see if Mystery M-, if Ron is hanging around. We can invite him to our ice cream party. Want to?"

"Yeah!"

Her enthusiasm and the prospect of sharing our ice cream sandwiches with Ron help blunt my concern for Willow.

- - - - -

The next time we drop Magda's mail off to her, I tell her

about the upcoming changes in routine. "I'll be teaching part-time at Euclid. We'll still deliver your mail, Magda, but it might be a little later in the afternoon. Is that okay?"

She nods and replies, "Is okay." Then, "And while Mother is teaching, where will you be, young lady?" she asks Cameron. To my ears, my new job sounds like teechink, and Cameron is still yunklady. Hearing her speak only increases my eagerness to get back into the classroom.

"I go to Glenn Memorial," Cameron says.

"Nursery school," I elaborate. "At Glenn Memorial United Methodist, near the Emory campus."

"Ah," Magda replies thoughtfully. "We did not have such things when Junior a little boy."

"I understand. When I was little, my mother hired a babysitter for the few days she worked. Did you have a babysitter for your son?"

"I not work after Junior is born. My husband, he tell me I am not work. I tell him, 'Take care of baby is work, hard work!'" She smiles a little when she shares this.

"If you don't mind my asking, what did you do before Junior was born?"

"I am pastry chef in my Papa's bakery in Poland. Is where I meet my husband. His army comes to my village after war is over. When we move here, I cater parties. Big parties, small parties."

"A caterer. Wow. You must be a wonderful cook. Do you still bake?"

"No. I not make cake after Junior go to Vietnam and no come home. Who I am baking for?"

I have an idea then that I hope is not ludicrous and will not offend Magda but, instead, will please her.

"Would you consider baking for Cameron's next birthday? Don't worry; you don't have to answer now. It's six months away."

"Maybe. We decide later."

"Okay. Fair enough. Well, we'll see you tomorrow. I know you don't want to stand here with your door open, air conditioning the whole neighborhood."

"Goodbye," she says to us. Gootbye. "Goodbye, Little Miss," she addresses Cameron.

"Bye, Miss Magda. See you tomorrow."

As we are walking down the driveway, Cameron looks up at me and asks, "Mommy, what is ceck?"

- - - - -

The school year has begun, and Cameron has adjusted beautifully to having two working parents. I, on the other hand, am having a little trouble making re-entry into the classroom. Every day I drive to Euclid, I question my decision to return to work and my fitness for the job, and yet almost every day I teach, the experience proves to be rewarding. My students are so interesting—and interested; they absorb everything I say, and do all that I ask them with earnestness, a desire to please, and an even greater desire to learn. And thanks to the educational environment at Glenn Memorial, Cameron is blossoming into a precocious, talkative child who can hold her own at the dinner table as Kenneth and I discuss work and school—hers and mine—and home remodeling projects. Kenneth seems to be more relaxed and content and is genuinely interested in my work, as I have always been in his. He lingers after dinner a little longer, too, the siren call of his chess club meetings less urgent. Given a bit more time, I think we're all going to settle into our new family routine just fine. I take to heart Mom and Dad's counsel about weathering the marital doldrums and can see the promise in it.

My students are from countries in Central and South America, Europe, Asia, and Africa. Many of their families have experienced dire hardship in their home countries. Some have not, though, and are here because their parents have been hired to teach at Emory or Georgia Tech or Georgia State. A few of my students are the children of parents who are in Atlanta to work on post-graduate degrees, and a few have parents who work in the private sector. Regardless of their background, I am astonished at their resilience and their willingness to immerse themselves in a new culture. I try to keep all of this in mind when I give them assignments to complete at home. I try to think of ways that will help the parents acclimate just as much as it will help their children, ways that will not seem intrusive or complicated and that will allow the parents to be a part of their children's education, regardless of their mastery—or not—of English. Two things I am experimenting with to improve their communication skills are English-only Tuesdays and watching one episode per week of Sesame Street. On English-only Tuesdays, I encourage all my students and their families to try to get through an entire day speaking and reading only English. They are permitted to look up words in a translation dictionary if they have one, but they are encouraged to speak the English version of the words they look up. I ask them to create a list of new words they learn as well as words they hear or see but cannot decode, even given context clues. We work on those mystery words in class. I ask my students where they heard the word and what other words were spoken or written with them, and, in their small groups, they work on spelling them correctly and defining them. I assigned watching Sesame Street with a little trepidation. After all, some of my students are already ten or more years old. Since many of them have younger siblings who are not yet in school, I tell them that watching Sesame Street as a family will help them—my students—help their younger brothers and sisters learn English, and will make learning easier for their siblings when they start elementary school. Portraying my students as teachers in the family has, so far, resulted in eager compliance with what could be seen as a ridiculous homework assignment. I hope that continues to be so. I believe, though, that I am the one learning more each day than these dear children are, at least from me. And I do have so much to learn!

- - - - -

It is the Saturday before Halloween, and I have been trying to think of ways to introduce this strange mix of pagan and orthodox traditions to my students. If I had been more on top of things, I would have researched similar traditions in their cultures for comparison, but as Halloween is just days away and I have only now thought to consider how weird it might seem for many of them, I must make do with what little I have at my disposal. I have a children's book with lots of pictures of the most common images we associate with Halloween: witches, goblins, ghosts, scarecrows, bats, and skeletons—how macabre! Well, not the scarecrows, but the rest. I decide not to try to teach them about the origins of Halloween but, instead, to talk about what they might expect to see and do. How did I explain all of this to Cameron when she was younger? I ask her.

"Mommy's students might not understand what Halloween is. What should I tell them?"

"We dress up, and we get candy."

"Right. Anything else?"

She thinks for a moment. "Yes! We carve a pumpkin and put a candle in it!"

"Oh, right. Do you remember what we call the pumpkin after it's carved?"

"Um," she closes her eyes, trying to retrieve the word, "a, um... I know! A jackal lantern."

"Right, a jack-o-lantern," I pronounce the word slowly and distinctly, thinking a jackal lantern might be a more appropriate term, given their toothy, menacing grins. Then I have an idea. "Would you help me make a jack-o-lantern for my students? We can make one for our family and one for me to take to work."

"Oh, goody!"

"If we walk to Sevananda, two pumpkins might take up the whole wagon. Do you think you can walk all the way home if I let you ride there?"

"Yes, Mommy. Yes, yes, yes. When can we go?" She is jumping up and down. "I even want to go the long way home so we can say 'hi' to the Turrets."

"It's a deal. Let's go potty and get Mr. Whiskers and go."

"Yea!" My sometimes reluctant shopper is enthusiastic about this project.

We select two medium-sized pumpkins at Sevananda and

place them carefully on top of the old towels we have put in the wagon to prevent them from rolling around. On the way home, Cameron and I, with Mr. Whiskers' input, discuss what kind of face we should carve into the pumpkin for Mommy to take to work.

"Should it be scary, you think? Or silly?"

Cameron thinks about this, taking her consultant role seriously. "I think silly, so they won't be afraid."

"Silly it is, then. And when Daddy gets home from work this evening, we can carve our Fields jack-o-lantern and make it as silly or as scary as you want to. How about that?"

Cameron nods, grinning. "Okay!" Then, "Mr. Whiskers, don't be scared if we make a mean face. It's only make-believe."

"Yes. Make-believe." How does one convey that concept to budding English language learners?

I am mulling that over as we turn the corner to the Turrets' street, but the For Sale sign in their yard stops me mid-thought. For Sale? How can that be?

Cameron sounds out the words. "For. Sale. For Sale. Mommy, are Tommy and Tilly moving away?"

"I guess so, honey." Make-believe, indeed. And I am suddenly ashamed that I have allowed this fantastical fascination with these make-believe people to become all too real for my daughter. And to myself, for a curious thought occurs. I will miss them. What, precisely, and who, exactly, will I miss?

Before I allow myself the opportunity to answer that question, I say to Cameron, "Let's hurry home so we can carve a silly jack-o-lantern for Mommy's students!" And with that, I shoved a lingering shadow-thought out of my mind.

- - - - -

I learned my lesson with Halloween about teaching non-native students about American holidays and celebrations. I am more than prepared to help my students understand Thanksgiving. I have spoken with all of their teachers and created age-appropriate supplemental assignments to help them grasp the meaning behind Turkey Day. If their culture has any sort of harvest celebration, I have incorporated that into our lessons, too, for comparison's sake. And I have co-opted some of the clever activities Glenn Memorial uses with their nursery schoolers, tailoring them for English-language learners ages six and older. Their eagerness to appropriate our culture into theirs is gratifying. I do hope they will be discerning, though, in what they accept, and not mindlessly follow along. I wonder if the parents of some of Jim Jones' followers are now questioning what, if anything, they could have done differently when raising their children.

Meanwhile, Kenneth and I have offered to host the Thanksgiving Day meal at our house. The closer we get to the day, the more I believe we may have made a huge mistake.

Even though Mema and PopPop Fields, my parents, and I are divvying up the dishes we'll each provide for our meal, I am overwhelmed at the thought of playing hostess. The Fields' Thanksgiving meals are usually quite lavish and formal. And stilted, if I'm to be honest. I tell Kenneth that the Triplets—FearGuiltShame —are back, and his answer is to make this family celebration our own. We do not have to be formal; we do not have to make certain there are three meats, five vegetables, two kinds of dressing, and four different desserts. And he is right. When I ask him if he will defend me if—scratch that, not if, but when—his mother expresses her disapproval of me, out of earshot of my parents, of course, he assures me that he will, but that he doesn't think it will come to that. My request and his assurance were so easy that I cannot believe I never thought to ask before now.

While he is being this agreeable, I broach with him inviting Magda to join us and he approves. If she does come, sharing a meal with the five Fields and the two mild-mannered Gardners could either solidify our neighborly affections or completely undo them. I don't ask Kenneth this, but in the back of my mind, I consider inviting Ron, too, if I see him out and about.

When Cameron and I deliver Magda's mail later that day, I invite her to our Thanksgiving Day meal. "Please say you'll join us."

Magda wavers for a moment, giving me hope she'll say yes. I

am not surprised, though, when she says no. "I spend day with my memories," she declares.

"But you still need to eat, and we always have so much extra."

"Thank you. My husband, he die on Thanksgiving four years ago. I go to the cemetery on Thanksgiving. I spend day with him and my Junior. He die in Vietnam in November ten years ago. Is how I spend my Thanksgiving."

Tanksgivink Day, Magda style, sounds like a downer to me. "Well, if you change your mind or the weather is bad, please come over, even if it's just for part of the meal."

The day arrives, sunny and mild. During the meal and throughout coffee and dessert, I kept watching out the front window for signs of Magda and Ron. I also wonder how my students are celebrating today. I am eager to hear all about it Monday when we're back at school, just as I am eager to learn more about how one spends the day at the cemetery, how a vagrant can disappear and reappear so often, and where he goes when he's not here. And I wonder where the Turrets are moving to and how they are spending their last Thanksgiving in their for-sale home, how Joe and Margaret and Baby Makes Three are doing, and if Willow and Kai are upstairs with her parents or downstairs with Gabe. As I look around the table in my own home, I am thankful for my family, for my job, and for the many certainties in my life.

- - - - -

Christmas has come and gone in a blur. Kenneth's parents go on their usual trip to warmer climes while we scramble to get a tree, decorate it, buy and wrap gifts, and play Santa Claus. I get a little wistful realizing Cameron will not always believe in Santa, and the stirrings to have another child, if only to keep the magic alive longer, cause me to be a melancholy Mrs. Claus.

While Cameron is enjoying some of her new loot and I am taking the decorations off of the tree, Kenneth asks me what's wrong. I tell him only half of it—that I am sad thinking about not experiencing Christmas through the eyes of a believer in Santa. He responds with the typical analytical nature of an engineer. "Mer, think about it. We won't have to hide some of Cameron's gifts and pretend that Santa has wedged himself down our fireplace to deliver them. We'll be able to wrap all of them and put them under the tree. Let's just enjoy watching her figure it out, okay?" Then, "I don't know why you have to make such a big deal out of our daughter growing up."

I am stunned by that last comment. I open my mouth to argue, but I have no words. He can tell by my expression that his words stung, that I am struggling to articulate what I am feeling, to rebut. He offers no olive branch, no apology for, if nothing else, wounding me. My silence and his silence provide me an opportunity to ask myself if I am, indeed, making a big deal out of Cameron growing up, if I'd prefer for her to stay forever the age she is now, and how I might have given him that impression. Kenneth's assessment is like a breaking cue ball, sending my thoughts bouncing in all directions at once, and I quickly determine that, no, I am not opposed to Cameron growing up. I delight in each phase of her development. There is just something blessedly magical about the pretense of a jolly fat man delivering our heartfelt desires under a glittering tree while we are all sleeping. I lay the ornament I am cradling in my hands on the floor beside the half-naked tree and walk out of the room. "I'll be in the kitchen making supper," I tell Kenneth. "I need you to finish packing up the ornaments." And it is Kenneth's turn to be stunned, for I have never before assigned him a chore, but he can tell that I mean business. The Grinch has officially stolen Christmas this year.

Chapter Five: 1979

THE NEW YEAR begins with my application to Georgia State for their Master's in Applied Linguistics program. If I'm accepted, this coming fall I will start graduate school at the same time my daughter begins Kindergarten. If I think too much about it, I drive myself crazy with worry; I feel I'm barely keeping all my spinning plates aloft as it is. Ever since our Christmas tiff, Kenneth has redoubled his efforts to be supportive of me. He talks me away from the ledge at least once a week, expressing his great belief in me as a wife, a mother, and a teacher. What would I do without his steadying presence?

- - - - -

My little girl is no longer officially little. She is five years old and has become a whip-smart kid who is, by turns, sweet and sassy, agreeable and intractable, happy and pouty. I don't know if this is her true nature coming into fullness or if she's picked up some unsavory habits from her playmates at Glenn

Memorial. Kenneth swears she will outgrow the sassy, intractable, pouty stage. I want to hope so, but in all honesty, I think she inherited these particular tendencies from him. Well, not the sassy part, as Mema Fields would have brooked none of that when he was growing up, but definitely the dug-in and moody parts.

When I ask Cameron about having a little birthday celebration at home with her grandparents and Kai and some nursery school friends, complete with cake, ice cream, presents, and balloons, she insists I provide cupcakes for her at nursery school instead. It seems that is the in thing now, getting recognition at school and being queen or king for the day with one's peers. So, rather than ask Magda to bake a birthday ceck from one of her recipes, Cameron and I together make cupcakes and frosting from box mixes, saving three cupcakes for us to have a little celebration at home. Her grandparents still shower her with gifts, but she revels most in the attention she gets at school.

That night after dinner, before she blows out the single candle on her cupcake, Kenneth and I remind her to make a wish. She informs us, "I already made a wish at my school party," which is true. I saw her close her eyes and then blow out her candle. "—for a baby brother or sister. And that's what I am going to wish for with this candle." Then she blows out the candle with one big puff of air. As she does, I notice Kenneth secretly trying to assess how I respond to Cameron's very matter-of-fact declaration. Do I tell her the old tradition that if one says their wish out loud, it won't come true? Do I just nod and smile? Pretend I didn't hear her and make no comment? Tell her that having sex more frequently is typically a requisite activity. I secretly check Kenneth out, too, to see his reaction, but this master of stoicism is unreadable. We haven't discussed or argued about another child for months. There have been too many other things for us to center our attention on, and I can see how my applying to graduate school would tend to make Kenneth believe that I've come around to his way of thinking—that Cameron is the only child we will have. Yet with that simple, out-loud declaration over her birthday candle, Cameron's wish kindles the little spark in me that, despite all we have going on with two jobs and multiple house renovations, I very much want another baby, and not just because of Christmas. I decide to wink at Kenneth and gauge his reaction to that minor flirtation. I get the same reaction as if I'd winked at the refrigerator, which is to say, no reaction at all. I have gone so many weeks without being resentful of Kenneth, and in one puff from my daughter's lungs, the hurt and resentment are back. If there had been an extra cupcake, I know I would have eaten it to soothe my feelings. I also know the FearGuiltShame self-recrimination that would have ensued tomorrow when I still could not fit into my pre-Cameron clothes. I would have thought taking a part-time job would lend itself to losing a few pounds, but instead, late-night lesson plans and potato chips have resulted in weight gain. How I loathe being back in that ping-pong head game of want-a-baby-but-need-to-lose-weight!

- - - - -

Spring is just around the corner. I see evidence of it nearly everywhere. Ron is back from wherever he wintered. Azalea buds are popping out in the Turrets' front yard. (And the For Sale sign is still there, which, for some odd reason, is comforting to me.) And most days, Cameron's sweater comes home in her little school satchel instead of on her. Springtime also means I should be hearing any day from Georgia State about the fall quarter. I have even taken to going to the mailbox twice some days in case the postman realizes he forgot to deliver a very important piece of mail to our home. Kenneth and I have also settled on our next project, and it's a big one. We are replacing all the kitchen cabinets with new, custom-built ones. Since our kitchen will be in disarray for some time, we will need to rely on our Webster charcoal grill for cooking when I cannot get to the stove. There's no way I was going to do that in the winter. I plan to prepare and freeze a lot of casseroles and then warm them up on the grill while the meat is cooking.

In mid-March, I deliver Magda's mail to her on a day when my parents have picked Cameron up from Glenn Memorial for some granddaughter time at their house. On her front stoop is a small rosebush, the bottom wrapped in burlap and sitting in a Pike's Nursery bucket. "Is for you," Magda announces, pointing at it.

"Oh, Magda, that's very kind, but I don't know anything about tending roses."

"You take," she commands. "I teach you."

Touched, I say, "Are you sure? What if I kill it?"

"It lives, you will learn. It dies, you will learn," is her simple but profound reply.

"Okay. If you're sure, would you mind if I planted it in the backyard so I can see it while I'm doing dishes?" My request is a half-truth. I also don't want to live through the embarrassment of my mother-in-law monitoring my skills at keeping a green thing alive. I simply won't draw Mema's attention to it when we're in the kitchen together, but if it's in the front yard, she's sure to see it.

"Is a gift. You plant where you want. Where it will get sun."

"Yes, ma'am. I will. And you will remind me when it's time to fertilize it or prune it, right?"

She nods. "Is good," she says as she begins to pull her door to.

As I descend her driveway, I am cautiously optimistic. How I hope it vill be goot!

- - - - -

We have hired a carpenter and handyman to do the cabinetry. He comes highly recommended by a buddy of Kenneth's from his chess club. His name is Aleksander and I have developed a bit of a crush on him. Aleksander has classical Mediterranean good looks, complete with shoulder-length dark, wavy hair, an olive complexion, and an aquiline nose. When he is in the kitchen measuring or marking the wood, I find excuses to go in there. We are paying him by the job, not the hour, so I don't mind when he stops working to chat. There are evenings, too, when he's still working as we are getting ready to eat dinner, and so we invite him to join us. Many times he does just that, and we all enjoy our dinner conversations a great deal. I would never act on my attraction to him, but a girl can fantasize, can't she? At any rate, Kenneth and I are very pleased with the work Aleksander is doing, and we plan to hire him for some additional projects as the money becomes available.

- - - - -

I have not only been accepted to Georgia State to begin the Master's in Applied Linguistics program this fall, I have been hired to teach full-time in the fall as well. All of this has transpired in the span of a week. I am wild with excitement and trepidation. Kenneth continually reminds me that I can do this and that we can do this. He also suggests, for our daughter's sake, that I project more enthusiasm and confidence about school. And he's right. We want her to be excited about starting Kindergarten this fall. Tamping down my nerves requires every iota of determination I possess.

The wrinkles of child care are, for the most part, taken care of. I have been assigned a classroom of my own, so Cameron will go with me to Euclid every morning and stay with me until the school day begins. The two afternoons a week I have class at Georgia State, one of Cameron's four grandparents will pick her up, take her home, feed her a snack, and get dinner ready. They have set up a rotation so each grandparent gets special time with their only grandchild two days out of each month. Fortunately, for Kenneth, at least, my classes this fall are not on the nights he has chess club. He will be home to spell the Grandparent-on-Duty by the time dinner is ready, and I will be home before her bedtime so I can still tuck her in. Cameron really will have the best of both worlds and her fair share of undivided attention.

This plan also suits Mom greatly. She tells me that, although there have been no more episodes of Dad misplacing things, she has been wanting him to have an excuse to moderate his work schedule. My full-time employment and his granddaughter have provided just that. I suspect that on the days Mom is the Grandparent-on-Duty, she'll coax Dad into joining her in the name of preparing his world-famous, Cameron-pleasing Papa Don hotdogs or knocking out a few household honey-do's for us. I have started a list of those quick chores to enable the conspiracy—everything from attaching the new kitchen cabinet handles to wiping grubby handprints off of light switches.

Speaking of new kitchen cabinets, Aleksander did a great job on them. He is a genuine craftsman, and Kenneth and I have agreed that we will hire him again when we need his carpentry expertise. One of the renovations we're considering is extending the pantry and adding a utility room off the back of the kitchen. I'll need to sock away many paychecks before we can do that, though.

- - - - -

Summer has come and gone so quickly. I am proud to say I have worked up a few months' worth of lesson plans for all ages and levels of English language learners. I am certain that I will feel on top of things until exactly five minutes after the bell rings on the first day of school. Still, with my own schoolwork to contend with soon, I need to be prepared. Or at least have the illusion of being prepared.

We have been able to enjoy a few family outings that were in our budget. I do love making memories! We went to Callaway Gardens for the day, and another time we went to Stone Mountain for the day, and we have been to the Atlanta Zoo several times. Cameron was intrigued by the Florida State University Flying High Circus performers at Callaway. These gifted college students put on quite a show. For days afterward, Cameron mimicked the tightrope walkers on her jump rope, performing her death-defying routine over and over for Mr. Whiskers and all of her grandparents. Of course, the rope is lying on the ground, but then that same rope becomes the vine she swings on from a low branch in the backyard while imitating Willy B, the resident gorilla at the zoo. And Cameron was quite a trooper on our climb up Stone Mountain. When we got to the top, Kenneth pointed in the direction of our home and then in the directions of "where Daddy works, where Mommy works and Cameron will go to school, where Mommy will go to school, where Mema and PopPop live, and where Mama Jo and Papa Don live." Despite his overly analytical ways, it is helpful to have a husband with a civil engineer's sense of direction. So now, after pretending to be Willy B's simian cousin, Cameron points out to Mr. Whiskers (in random directions) all of those landmarks. We conclude the summer, Cameron and I, with a shopping trip to Rich's to buy school clothes for her and work outfits for me. We are ready for the school year to begin.

- - - - -

I have a new boss at Euclid. Actually, he is in charge of the ESOL program for the entire school system. So, rather than reporting to the principal, Mr. Staley, I technically report to Mr. Carlisle. We meet weekly to discuss my Euclid students and how I am serving their needs. He is fluent in Spanish and French and understands a lot about the cultures many of our students come from. He has been doing this long enough, though, to understand the difficulties of acclimating to a new country, even if he is less familiar with some students' native countries and their customs.

Mr. David Carlisle, who prefers to just be called Carlisle, also takes an interest in my studies. And not merely to find out what courses I'm taking and the grades I'm earning. He wants to know what topics we're covering in my coursework and how I am applying that knowledge as a teacher. He has encouraged me to establish my Master's thesis topic early on and incorporate what I am learning at Georgia State and in the classroom into my research topic. He swears I'll thank myself during my final semester. Such wise counsel! I don't yet know what the topic will be, but I am now intentionally casting my net for a research-worthy idea. Carlisle thinks it's great that I assign my students, even the older ones, to watch Sesame Street, and asks me to consider researching that assignment from a linguistic and pedagogical standpoint. I'm not sure about that, but because I respect him so much, I will at least entertain the thought.

- - - - -

The phone is ringing this late fall afternoon. Cameron and I have just finished delivering Magda's mail to her and are coming in our back door, juggling school bags and our own pile of mail. I pick up, out of breath, moments before the answering machine clicks on.

"Hello?"

"Hello," a cultured, clipped voice on the other end responds. "This is Mrs. Butler. Do you have a moment?"

I mentally searched my class rosters for a student with the last name Butler and came up empty. As this voice has no discernible foreign accent, I then search my mental Rolodex for another teacher or a school administrator named Butler. I have worked at Euclid Elementary for awhile now, but I do not know the names of everyone who works there. Not wanting to reveal this lapse, I simply replied, "Yes."

"I'm calling to ask when the last time was that you've seen Wilhelmina. Have you seen her recently? Today, perhaps, or yesterday?"

Again, I madly searched my memory banks for any Wilhelminas I knew. And, again, I come up empty. How embarrassing. I'm fairly certain I don't have a student by that name, but maybe there is some confusion about who Wilhelmina's teacher is. I stall. "May I ask what this is in reference to?"

"I think she's missing. When I went downstairs this morning to walk Kai to school, he was still in bed, asleep. Wilhelmina was nowhere to be found. I have waited all day to hear from her, and she is still not home. She has not called, and she did not leave a note. This is very unlike her." There is a slight warble to her voice now.

Suddenly, all the tumblers mesh, unlocking the mystery. "You mean Willow! Willow is not there?" And my conversation with her last summer on the Euclid playground suddenly comes back to me. Since then, we have bumped into each other occasionally at Sevananda, and Kai's Kindergarten class is across the hall from Cameron's, so I have seen Willow dropping off or picking up Kai once in awhile. We also saw each other across the auditorium at a PTA meeting, but she has, for the past many months, declined all of my overtures to get together on the weekend. She is always polite but evasive.

That confident young woman who could make dreadlocks, underarm hair, Birkenstock sandals, and long batik dresses fashionable has gone into seclusion, replaced, it seems, by a wary stranger. How much of this do I share with her mother? Do I tell her about the mysterious bruises and Willow's excuse-making? Instead, I ask, "What does Kai say? Did she tell him when she would be back?"

"Kai is not talking. I have asked him many questions, and he just stares back at me. Wilhe-, Willow, called upstairs last night and said she was not feeling well and asked that I walk Kai to school this morning. When I tried to get him ready, he went limp. He wouldn't eat breakfast, and he wouldn't get dressed, so I kept him home. He has essentially slept the entire day on the divan in my living room. After he woke the first time, I asked him to go downstairs and get some of his things, and he balked. I am quite worried."

I have to ask, "Is Gabe in town?"

"Not to my knowledge. But Wilhelmina does not always tell me when he will be home, as she knows I do not approve of him."

This is a revelation. It has never occurred to me that Kai's grandmother would not approve of his father, and Willow has never mentioned it. "Have you called all of the emergency rooms? Have you contacted the police? Even though you and Mr. Butler are upstairs, I do not think Willow would just leave Kai by himself, do you? Something must be wrong."

"There is no record of her at any of the local hospitals, and the police will not open an investigation until she has been missing for at least 24 hours. As I have no idea when she left, I will have to wait until tomorrow morning to file a report."

"Is there anything I can do for you, for Kai?"

"I don't believe so, but if you do hear from her, please let me know immediately." Then she recites her phone number, and I realize my hands are shaking as I take it down.

"Of course. Of course. And if you hear anything, will you please let me know?"

"Yes. Now I must go. I have other calls to make, and Kai is waking up again."

Cameron has been keenly observing all of this. Not much gets past her. She is respectfully waiting for me to end the call before speaking, like we have trained her. It is only when the dial tone becomes a staccato alert that she takes the handset from me and hangs it up on the kitchen wall, snapping me back to the present. She knows something is terribly wrong. She can read it off my face; she heard it in my voice. Before she can launch into the questions she certainly has, I launch into my own fact-finding mission. "Honey, do you see Kai at school, like on the playground or in the lunchroom?"

"Sometimes," she answers warily. "Why?"

I dodge answering directly for the time being. "How does he seem? Do you two talk or play together at school?"

"Not since he hit me."

"What?! He hit you? Where? When?"

"He said he was sorry. He said it was a accident." I let this grammatical goof go, my mother's heart laden. "He said we couldn't be friends anymore."

My head is reeling. "What? Why? And you didn't answer me —where did he hit you, and when did this happen? Why didn't you tell me?"

"I wanted him to spider swing with me on the playground, but he said no, and he pushed me away, and I fell down. His teacher saw him and made him say sorry. Then she made him sit on the bench with her. It didn't hurt, Mommy. I didn't cry, but Kai did."

I work there. I know Cameron's teacher and Kai's teacher. Some of their students are also my students. How could they not tell me about this incident? I vacillate between motherly rage and concern for my friend. The urge to do something to help Willow and the recognition that I can do nothing are overpowering. An uneasy feeling settles in the pit of my stomach. I pull Cameron to me and hug her tight, and she does not protest, sensing my need to protect her.

After we put Cameron to bed that night, I relate the phone call to Kenneth and my sense of unease. I berate myself for not speaking up to her mother about Willow's bruises.

"You tried, though, did you not, to find out if she was okay? Kenneth asks.

"I did. I probably should've said something, though."

"Let's think about that for a minute, Mer. Let's say you get a phone call from someone you've never met, telling you they are concerned about someone mutually known to you. Let's say Mr. Carlisle. You see Mr. Carlisle every day, but the other person sees him only occasionally. But they are worried about him because he has a bump on his head, a bump that he explains away. Who are you going to believe, a stranger or your companion?"

"Maybe you're right. I don't know. I just wonder why Kai said he couldn't be friends with Cameron anymore. Not that he didn't want to, but that he couldn't. Why didn't she tell us he'd said that? Why didn't Kai's teacher tell me about what happened on the playground? I just don't understand people sometimes."

Kenneth takes my hand and kisses it. "And yet, you still go out there every day," he points toward the window, "and you try. You try your best to make a difference. Isn't that all we can really do?"

Good question. Sweet response. So why do I feel so helpless and defeated?

- - - - -

Between teaching, parenting, and going to school, I can barely keep my days straight. I'm so glad I created those lesson plans this past summer, as I rely heavily on them during the weeks I have research papers, midterms, or final exams due. I am enjoying my studies in linguistics and am especially intrigued to learn how the English language as we know it became the English language as we know it. There are certain constants in our written and spoken languages, but, for the most part, language is fluid. I wonder sometimes what influences this wave of immigration will have on American English, as well as what subtle clues to their own heritage many immigrants will find as they pick up our language. I mean to ask my favorite professor, Dr. Thomas, which languages that are far older than ours have appropriated our bastardization of theirs. How universal, for example, is "hot dog"? Where are all the places on the globe where I can order one?

Speaking of Dr. Thomas, I must admit to being somewhat surprised that one can actually earn a doctorate in linguistics. If one does not want to teach, where else could one ply her trade with a Ph.D. in linguistics? Not that I am the least bit interested in earning a doctorate after completing my Master's. I truly think it would kill me; it is not, after all, called a terminal degree for nothing. All of the Ph.D. candidates I have met already look like zombies from overwork and lack of sleep. I do not wish to join their ranks.

There is still no word on Willow. I call Mrs. Butler about once a week to see if she knows anything and to check on Kai. The

Butlers have transferred him to Paideia School, a private, very reputable, very expensive school off of Ponce de Leon. They feel he will fare better in an atmosphere where nobody asks him too many questions about his parents, both of whom are reportedly missing. Mrs. Butler says Kai is talking again but is not his typical inquisitive, outgoing self. He goes to school, comes home, watches cartoons, dutifully does his homework —oh, yes, Paideia gives their Kindergarteners homework! — eats dinner, takes a bath, and goes to bed. He doesn't ask to go places, and he doesn't ask for ice cream, his favorite. Mrs. Butler says he seems oblivious to the approaching holidays. He is compliant, but not his usual happy self. Oh, poor Kai. Poor, sweet Kai.

During one of our phone conversations, I relate to her what Kai said to Cameron on the playground the day he pushed her down. "Do you know why he would say he couldn't be friends with Cameron anymore?"

"I think Gabe tries to control both of them. The more he travels with that, that Renaissance Fair," she spits the term out, the words bitter in her mouth, "the more he seems to care about who Wilhelmina and Kai are spending their time with. You've seen him, haven't you? He can be a very imposing presence."

"Yes, ma'am." Suddenly, I understand Willow's gentle rebuffs of my overtures. My fears about her whereabouts redouble as I imagine her a prisoner in the clutches of her son's father, unable to run or hide. Or maybe she is hiding somewhere. I don't speak these thoughts out loud to Mrs. Butler. She has enough on her mind without me fueling her anxiety. Instead, I send a thought message into the ether. Willow, wherever you are, find a way to call me and tell me how I can help!

- - - - -

I've just gotten home from watching Kramer vs. Kramer with my mom. I know it's just a movie, but I cannot fathom walking out on Kenneth and Cameron to find myself. I am so sad for little Billy.

Chapter Six: 1980

MRS. BUTLER CALLS on New Year's Day to say that police have found a body they believe to be that of Willow. Some New Year's Eve revelers were drinking and setting off firecrackers by a railroad trestle in an area that, for safety reasons, is marked by the City of Atlanta as a no-trespassing zone. They are the ones who actually found the body and, despite their worries about being arrested for trespassing and setting off firecrackers, they reported it to the Atlanta City Police Department. I hardly know what to say to Mrs. Butler. Of course, I am curious about how long the police think the body has been there, and if they know the cause of death, but I will not ask her these questions. In the background, I can hear Kai whining for juice. I thank Mrs. Butler for the call and reiterate that I am willing to do anything for her, for Kai. I suspect that when she hangs up, she puts on a brave face for Kai. I, on the other hand, ring in the new year weeping.

- - - - -

The new quarter at Georgia State coincides with my gaining a few new students in the Euclid ESOL program. My head is spinning, and I continue to question how I will get everything accomplished. Kenneth is so supportive, as are all four grandparents. Despite Kenneth's MARTA project ratcheting up, he makes sure he is on Daddy duty the evenings I have class. And Carlisle continues to be supportive as well. If I crash and burn, it will not be due to lack of help and encouragement. Just the thought of the FearGuiltShame Triplets returning to taunt me if I fail, especially considering the support I receive from the family and my boss, is the engine driving me forward. I cannot attribute it to self-confidence, but to panic.

Carlisle and I continue to meet weekly, and it feels to me like we are more colleagues than boss and supervisor. He seems genuinely interested in me, my teaching, my studies, my family, and even our home improvement projects. I have learned that he is the devoted only child of his elderly widowed mother, often taking her to the theatre or to the movies in addition to spending every Sunday afternoon with her. He is not married, and I cannot figure out why. He is such a nice person. If I knew a 50-ish woman interested in languages and fine arts, I would gladly introduce her to Carlisle. It seems like a waste to me that he is not sharing his life with someone.

Even though I have plenty to keep me busy, I have become quite active in the Euclid PTA. Not only am I the parent of a student there, and not only do I teach there, but I also feel duty-bound to speak up for the unique needs of my students. I occasionally catch a whiff of condescending attitudes towards them and feel the need to confront misconceptions. I have also heard implications that "too many resources" are devoted to the program, my program, so while the school and county administration are supportive of ESOL, I think they rely on the ESOL teachers to articulate why investing in "those children's" education is beneficial to us all. Despite how much I detest confrontation, I surprise myself sometimes at how vocal I can be in advocating for my students.

- - - - -

The Iran hostage crisis is over. I can only imagine family members' relief at their loved ones finally coming home, alive and safe, and how Mr. and Mrs. Butler hoped for the same outcome. But the world feels like a tinderbox. Has it always been so, and do I think this more now because I am a mother and a teacher?

- - - - -

We have a six-year-old. Six going on sixteen some days. This delightful, willful, helpful, stubborn, sweet, and sassy child is sometimes too smart for her own good. Or maybe she's too smart for my own good. I try to remember what I was like at six. Did I read as much as she reads, and as eagerly? Was I interested in as many things as she is? One thing I am certain of is that I didn't argue with my parents, as she sometimes does with us. Well, mostly me. I'm also certain that I was not as moody. I need to ask my parents what they remember about me at six years old. I dare not ask Mema if Kenneth was a moody boy. And if I did, she'd just tell me he is a brooder, that he thinks a lot, about a lot. Which is true. I don't believe, though, that thinking a lot about a lot gives one license to be surly and impatient with those of us who don't spend more of our time navel-gazing. Am I being unfair? I don't think so, for while it is a tender sight to observe Cameron engrossed in a book near her daddy, who is engrossed in MARTA maps and city plans, it is also galling when they ignore my call to come to the kitchen for dinner. Getting their attention is a genuine challenge. Once I do, you'd think from their reaction that I have asked them to walk barefoot across hot coals instead of walking to the kitchen to feed their bodies the food I have so devotedly prepared, even if loving preparation occasionally means I merely open a can and stir the contents in a pot on the stove. If I had sucked my teeth at my mother as Cameron (and sometimes Kenneth!) do with me, my father would have put me over his knee, I'm certain.

Meanwhile, the Kenyan consulate has asked Kenneth to go to Kenya for ten days in a consulting role. The dates are somewhat flexible, so we try to arrange his trip for the days when both Euclid and Georgia State are off for spring break. Part of me wants to go with him, but the other, wiser part of me realizes how much reading and preparation for the remainder of the school year I can accomplish if I stay stateside. I can get ahead in my reading for Georgia State and in my lesson plans, and that thought alone brings me comfort. While I will miss Kenneth and Cameron terribly, we will fill our days with purpose so that, when he returns, we will be able to heap attention on him.

- - - - -

March has roared in like the proverbial lion, with much wind and rain. I curse at the wind mostly out of fear that the few tender buds on my rose bush will be blown to smithereens. Under Magda's botanical mentorship, I have lovingly tended that rose bush to get it where it is, and I will be so disappointed and sad if I lose all of the buds.

The rain has revealed what our next renovation project must be, that of expanding and enclosing the back porch. We need a larger laundry room, but we also need a place to enter the house and leave our muddy shoes. We've become quite protective of our refinished hardwood floors. Plus, we'll be able to take off our dirty clothes after working in the yard instead of tracking dirt and grass clippings throughout the house. Kenneth and I got an estimate for the renovation job from our handyman, Aleksander, and I had to sit down after reading it, but Kenneth thinks his consultancy job in Kenya plus some of my salary this year should cover it without our having to borrow money to pay for the job. I hope so. I'm tired of wiping muddy footprints off our floors.

- - - - -

Kenneth flew out to Kenya this morning, several days before spring break begins. We've got everything worked out, though, so that when I stay late tomorrow night for Euclid's PTA meeting and attend class on Thursday evening, one of the grandparents will be with Cameron. There is no class on Friday because it's Good Friday. I'm kind of looking forward to having an all-girls week with Cameron, just as I'm sure I'll be looking forward to the return of reinforcements. Cameron has asked her dad to bring her an elephant. A real one. I do believe she was serious. Until he returns, though, we can have cereal for dinner if we want to, or popcorn. We can sleep on pallets on the living room floor or build a fort under the dining room table using sheets, blankets, and the sofa cushions. We'll read books by flashlight in our fort, eating our popcorn. It will be great. So long as she likes the idea.

- - - - -

I've gone and done it. I think I may have lost my job, not because I cannot adequately teach my students but because I cannot adequately control my temper at the PTA meetings. This PTA meeting starts with the usual recap of the previous meeting and voting those meeting minutes into the record. Then the end-of-school-year plans for the fifth grade trip to Six Flags are discussed, as is the combined band and chorus concert. Pretty boring stuff, especially because I have a Kindergartener, and they are not invited to participate in band or chorus. So boring, in fact, that my mind wanders—to the Turrets and how they're doing; I must check on their home to see if it has sold; and to Margaret and Joe and Baby Makes Three; are they expecting another, I wonder?; and to Ron and where he's been the past several weeks; I hope he's okay. I am snapped back to the Euclid Elementary cafeteria and the real world when Mrs. Headlee, the current President of the PTA, starts in on the strange customs and religious practices of "those children" and on how financially impractical it is for Euclid to serve them. "Those children" are my students! She is proposing that "those children" be served at another school, not this school. It is her sneer-lipped, Wild Turkey-slurred, cold-hearted pronunciation of "thooose chull-drin" that brings me back from my flight of fancy. How dare she rank them as less important than any other student at Euclid!

"Madame President," I say, raising my hand and speaking over her, intentionally interrupting her diatribe. She pauses, and I do not wait to be recognized but, instead, launch into my own diatribe. "As many of you know, I am the full-time ESOL teacher at this school, a role I am extremely proud of. And there are some things I think you should know about my students. Our students." My voice warbles at first, but as I continue to speak, my protective instincts provide an authoritative edge to my words. "First of all, 'those childre' are people, just like any other children at this school, in this county, in this country, in this world. And they deserve our consideration and respect. Secondly, Madame President, if you had taken the time to get to know them and their stories, you would soon realize that many of them have endured more hardship in their short lives than most of us will endure in our entire lifetime. I defy any parent or educator sitting here tonight to say that, if their family's lives were in peril, you would not do anything and everything within your power to give them a better, more secure, life. And finally, if we all had just a portion of the courage they and their families had to start over in a new country, sometimes knowing very little English, we would all be better human beings. I give you Feliks as an example. Did you know his father was trained as a physician in Poland? But he cannot get a job as a doctor here without navigating through a maze of red tape, all of which takes time and money. In the meantime, he works as a janitor—yes, a janitor—cleaning the bathrooms and offices at Grady Hospital, where he hopes, one day, to serve the citizens of this state as a doctor. So, when you talk about 'those children' with such disdain, Madame President, I submit that you are really dressing up your personal hatred in robes of moral outrage, impugning your own character, not theirs."

I sit down, and my knees suddenly feel like Jello. There is a roaring in my ears, likely due to my elevated blood pressure, and I cannot hear anything other than the pounding of my heartbeat. I stare into my lap, for I cannot bear to see Mrs. Headlee's face, twisted with contempt—for me and for "thoose chull-drin." And I will remain here until the meeting is over. A few parents come over to shake my hand afterward and offer a few words of encouragement, and I smile weakly at them, but it seems most of the attendees are going out of their way to avoid me. I consider looking around for Mr. Staley, the principal, but think better of speaking to him before I skulk out. I feel certain I will be summoned to his office first thing tomorrow morning. I also feel certain I did the right thing by speaking up for my students and their families. Maybe I should not have said everything I said. I only hope he will give me the opportunity to justify my actions and that he will let me finish out the school year.

- - - - -

Mr. Carlisle is waiting in my classroom the next morning. I have arrived early in the hopes that I can avoid seeing Mr. Staley or any other administrator. I lead Cameron to the small round table at the back of the room and ask her to color a Welcome Home picture for her daddy while Mr. Carlisle and I talk up at the front of the room. My knees, once again, are Jello, and my heart is pounding.

"Heard about your performance last night," he starts, even before we can sit down. I cannot read his voice or his expression. "Staley called me the minute he got home."

"I'd like to expla-"

"You do not owe me an explanation, my dear." He cuts me off, smiling. "I just came to congratulate you and to say that I wish I'd been there, if for no other reason than to witness Mrs. Headlee's reaction. That woman should come with a warning label stamped on her forehead. You know she's an alcoholic, don't you? And the only reason she got elected president of the PTA is because her wealthy father donates a boatload of money to the school. Nobody really likes her, but most people are afraid to stand up to her."

"I didn't know that about her, no. Maybe I shouldn't have said some of the things that I did. I just get so defensive of the kids in our program, you know?"

"Yes, I do know, and that's another reason I am here. I've been offered the position of Coordinator of Language Programs with Atlanta City Schools, including the ESOL program. There'll be an ESOL opening at Bass High School this fall. Would you consider taking it?"

The roaring in my head is back, and my thoughts are having trouble catching up with what Mr. Carlisle has just said. I'm sure I misheard. "Wait. What? You want me to teach ESOL to high school students?"

Mr. Carlisle nods. "I should tell you that the program there is not as large as the one here at Euclid, so the job will include two days a week at Mary Lin Elementary. Still, it's a step up, and there's a bit of a pay increase that goes with it. When you've completed your Master's degree, you'll be eligible to earn even more money, and the program at Bass should be full-time by then as well. What do you say? Will you consider it?"

"I'd be foolish not to, but please tell me what will happen with the children here at Euclid? Do you have someone in mind to take my place?"

"Staley assures me he's had numerous inquiries about teaching ESOL here. You aren't, after all, the only linguistics student at Georgia State, you know?" He winks at me at the same moment I redden with embarrassment. Of course, I'm not the only person qualified to teach in this program. How silly of me.

"You've already spoken to Mr. Staley about this? I'd like to discuss this with Kenneth when he gets back. He's in Kenya for a short-term consulting job, you know. I don't think he'll have a problem with it, but –"

"I understand. You think about it. We have some time to discuss the particulars. Mainly, I just wanted to come by and give you a big Atta Girl for standing up to Horrible Headlee. You probably drove her to partake of an extra swig or two of whatever it is she puts in her soda."

"Do you think I should apologize? I'd hate for her daddy to stop writing checks to the school."

"Don't you dare," he says, light-hearted but with just enough sternness to indicate he means it. "I'll be in touch after Spring Break. Will that give you and Kenneth enough time to talk it over and come up with a list of questions?"

"Yes, Sir. And thank you."

"You're welcome. And no more of that, Sir or Mr. Business. Call me Carlisle, remember? I mean it. All my favorite teachers do."

He winks again, and with that, he leaves the classroom. From the back of the room, I hear Cameron humming Frere Jacques to herself as she colors the Welcome Home picture for her daddy. She stops humming, crayon posed above the paper, and looks up. "Mommy?"

"Yes, Love."

"Is Horrible Headlee Collier's mom?"

When will I learn that this child hears and understands far more than I give her credit for? Collier is one of the Kindergarteners in the class Kai used to be in. "Yes, Honey, Collier Headlee's mom is Mrs. Headlee, but we will not call either of them horrible, okay? Mr. Carlisle was just joking. It was a grown-up joke, and we will not repeat it. Okay?"

"Okay, Mommy." And she returns to her coloring.

- - - - -

I blinked, and I missed it. I haven't walked or driven by the Turrets' house in weeks, and now the For Sale sign has been taken down. Cameron and I started this Saturday with an impromptu trip to Sevananda. We've been going on the way home after school, but it is now Spring Break, and we decided this morning we wanted to dye Easter eggs and we will need supplies. We plan to draw on them first with crayons, then dye them all red with beet juice, so we determined we would walk to Sevananda for our eggs and a can or two of beets. When we finish buying our supplies, Cameron asks if we can walk the long way home and "see Tommy and Tilly's house." Now we are standing in front of their rambling mansion and see no signs of life—no moving in, no moving out, no Tommy, no Tilly.

"Where did they go, Mommy?" Cameron asks earnestly.

I am torn. Do I tell her I do not know? Do I make something up? Remind her the Turrets are pretend? I decided to be a grown-up about it. I kneel down at eye level next to my daughter. "You know Tommy and Tilly are make-believe, right?"

"But Mommy, that's a real house." She points emphatically. "Why would pretend people live in a real house?"

How do you answer that logic? That her mommy makes people up? Because she has an over-active imagination or - ? Not for the first time, I wonder why I created such elaborate stories about the inhabitants of that purple-turreted house. I cannot fathom why I allowed myself to get so caught up in the imaginary lives of this imaginary brother and sister, nor can I put my finger on why I am so sad. Is it the reckoning with my daughter and this loss she will experience due to my vivid imagination, or is there something else lurking behind the sadness? Am I really so lonely that I must invent people to inhabit my life?

"Honey, you're right. The house is real. But Mommy made up

that Tommy and Tilly live there. I don't know who lived there. But we can keep checking to see when the new owners move in. Maybe they'll have kids around your age. Wouldn't that be great?"

"Okay." She hangs her head, a little dejected. She misses Kai, and I have unwittingly added to her misery by letting our make-believe world become too real and occupy too much of our real world.

"Let's go home and get started on those eggs, okay?"

She perks up a little. "Alright." And I try to guide our talk on the way home to very real things in a very real world.

- - - - -

Kenneth has returned home. Cameron colored several more Welcome Home pictures for him, including one of him leading a baby elephant into our backyard. We tape the pictures up all over the house for him to discover as he resumes his normal household routine, and we prepare one of his favorite meals—pork roast, mashed potatoes, and Brussels sprouts. As we sit around the kitchen table, eating dinner and listening to his travelogue stories, as well as his explanation to Cameron about how unfair it would be to a baby elephant to separate her from her mother and how unlike Africa our backyard is, I cannot help but feel that his absence from us only made his heart grow fonder of his daughter. Maybe I am looking too closely for signs that he missed me, too. I remember the words my Daddy said after we arrived back in

Atlanta about how reverse culture shock sometimes takes awhile to process. I should be more patient and let him re-acclimate more, but how do you explain that he seems genuinely glad to see Cameron but ambivalent about seeing me? I didn't expect a passionate kiss—not that I wouldn't have gladly reciprocated—but I did expect more warmth and more professed feelings of having missed me. Surely some of the sights he saw in Kenya reminded him of the happy times we spent together in Cameroon. Are we entering another season of marital doldrums, or is my husband just very tired and using his energy reserves for his child? Would he be more responsive to me if I'd eaten salad every night for dinner instead of cereal and popcorn?

- - - - -

The Monday after Spring Break ends, Cameron and I arrive home after school, and after taking Magda's mail to her, we find Kenneth home. He and Aleksander are measuring the back porch and discussing the expansion and enclosure of our future laundry room. I think the popular interior design magazines refer to it as a mud room, which is apropos for our home. I am pleased, surprised, and a little irritated. I am surprised and pleased to see Kenneth home so early, and I am irritated that he has proceeded with the project without our having recently discussed it. This impulsivity is unlike him. Despite our periods of marital inertia, we still discuss big decisions. Just last night, after giving him a full day to recuperate from his trip and after putting Cameron to bed, I told him about the PTA episode, then broached the subject of teaching at Bass.

"I actually used words like 'impugn.' Can you believe it? I never use words like that, but I was fired up. Maybe," I say jokingly, "my command of vocabulary is one reason Mr. Staley agrees that I'm suited to teach high school." Then, "So, what do you think of Mr., -er, Carlisle's offer?"

"It's great, Mer. Mr. Carlisle wouldn't have offered the job to you if he didn't have such confidence in your ability. Mr. Staley, too."

"The job comes with a pay raise, but it'll also complicate getting Cameron to and from school."

"We'll manage. I may be able to work it out by taking her. Let me talk to my boss about it. You do want the job, don't you?"

"Very much. Especially knowing that Mr. Staley will look after my kids at Euclid. He even offered today to introduce all the candidates to me so I could give him my assessment of how well they'll fit with—what did he call it? —the Euclid Fold."

"Then it's settled. You can let Mr. Staley and Mr. Carlisle know you'll take the job. We have all summer to work out the logistics."

And so now, Cameron and I are standing in the kitchen, slack-jawed at these two men, engrossed in their discussion of drywall, dimensions, and the duration of the project. Three of the Dreaded Ds of Home Renovation. When you throw in the fourth D, the dollar amount, you can just expect that some of the D estimates are too low and that the aggravation will increase exponentially. Still, we need to get this project underway soon. Lawn mowing season has already arrived, and I'm looking forward to cleaner, drier hardwood floors.

- - - - -

There are sawhorses in the kitchen and plastic sheeting across the back wall and entrance to the back porch. As Aleksander bends over to saw a piece of lumber, I catch myself daydreaming about him. In that way. His personality is more gregarious than Kenneth's, and he is extremely handsome, in a lumberjack sort of way. Kenneth is handsome, more in a bookish sort of way. They're both handsome men, but Aleksander always seems glad to see me, even as I'm clearly in his way as I get dinner preparations underway. He again works many evenings, right up until dinner is ready, and accepts our invitation to stay and eat with us. He generally leaves at the same time Kenneth does on his chess club nights. I have no idea if Kenneth invites him to dinner the two nights I am in class. All I know is that dinner is usually waiting for him and Cameron when he gets home, courtesy of the Grandparent-on-Duty. I'll have to ask Cameron if dinner includes said grandparents, Daddy, and Aleksander. If so, I secretly hope he prefers my cooking to theirs.

Speaking of class, I am very much looking forward to having

the summer off from teaching and from taking classes. I will obviously need to do a great deal of preparation for my three days a week at Bass, but I will also indulge in reading a few novels for a change. As fascinated as I am with linguistics, one can only read so many peer-reviewed journals before going a little batty. Cameron and I are in countdown mode for the last day of school. We have fashioned a paper chain for each day left of the school year, and each morning she tears one of the links off the chain, counting the remaining days of her Kindergarten career. I suspect we will need to go to the library at least twice a week to keep her occupied. I thought I liked to read, but my child surpasses me in her enthusiasm for the written word.

- - - - -

The police have arrested Gabe for Willow's murder. I have not known hate before now. I have all summer to nurse my hatred without the distraction of teaching and being in school.

- - - - -

Cameron and I take one of the first full rose blossoms to Magda on our daily mail delivery. It is a beautiful coral color, and I feel nearly as proud of it as I did after giving birth. Won't Mema Fields be impressed to learn that I can actually cultivate something other than lesson plans and excess adipose tissue? Of course, the rose bush would not have thrived were it not for Magda's botanical coaching. She reminds me when it is time to fertilize, prune, and mulch. Still, I am so pleased to present her with this lovely gift.

"Thank you, yunklady," Magda says, accepting the rose from Cameron. The stem is wrapped in a wet paper towel and aluminum foil. And to me, "You did goot."

"The rose bush did what it was designed to do, but only because you helped me keep it alive. Thank you."

"You are willing student, that is why." Yes, I am quite villing to prove my mother-in-law and those FearGuiltShame Triplets wrong!

"Well, we make a good team. Would you like for us to put it in a vase for you?" I look inside the house, as if to enter.

"I will put in vase after my program. You have wrapped it well."

I know this is our cue to skedaddle, and I reconcile myself to the fact that I will never know what the inside of Magda's house looks like or why she will not allow us in. Still, when I consider how much progress we have made as neighbors, I dare not complain. She refuses our invitations to share meals at our home, just as she denies us access to her home. If those are the rules to maintain our neighborly relations, so be it, curiosity be hanged.

The next day, as Cameron and I are getting the mail out of Magda's box, an old-model Mercedes pulls into her driveway, driven by none other than Magda. Mystery solved about how she gets her groceries and goes to doctor's appointments and to the cemetery to visit her husband and Junior. I don't know why I am so surprised to learn she still drives, but I readily admit I made assumptions. I am chastened to realize I have jumped to conclusions about Magda just as Horrible Headlee does about the ESOL students. The car idles at the bottom of her steep driveway, so Cameron and I walk over to the driver's side. Magda rolls the window down to accept the small stack of mail, then points in the back seat at an azalea plant. 'You take," she orders. "If you can grow rose, you can grow azalea."

I am lost for words at her generosity and feel even worse about my many wrong assumptions. I also feel a bit of panic, not wanting to press my luck.

Seeing my hesitation, she suggests, "Will look good under the bay window," and her suggestion definitely sounds like marching orders.

I open the door to the back seat and lift the potted azalea out. "It's lovely, Magda. This is really so generous of you. Are you sure you trust me with this beauty?"

"Am sure."

"Thank you. Thank you so much. We'll plant it today."

Cameron pipes up, "Thank you, Miss Magda."

"You are welcome, yunklady. You will help your mama, yes?"

"Yes, Ma'am!"

Magda puts the car in gear and slowly drives up her driveway, leaving Cameron and me dumbfounded. Dumbfounded and grateful. And while Cameron is enthusiastic about this new project, I am cautiously optimistic that I have finally broken my horticultural curse.

- - - - -

I can hardly believe my summer has ended. While I am in a week of in-service and pre-planning, Cameron is at Camp Gardner, enjoying being spoiled rotten by Mama Jo and Papa Don. I'm not sure what all they do throughout the day, but they must be keeping her very busy. She mentions helping Mama Jo pull weeds and bake cookies. And, judging from the contents of her pockets, walks through the neighborhood are involved. She also says she helps Papa Don count and catalog some of his newest quidgins, which I finally determine are acquisitions. What I do know for certain is that we can barely keep her awake long enough to bathe after supper.

On the homefront, the creation of our utility room from our back porch is progressing, as is, it would appear, Kenneth's project with MARTA. The City of Atlanta is expanding rail and bus service to more and more Atlantans. On one of the final days of our summer break, Kenneth escorts Cameron and me on a ride on the MARTA train from its farthest point south to its farthest point north, then back again. We top off the adventure by eating dinner out at the Pleasant Peasant downtown. We are a bit overdressed for riding the train but dressed just right for our swanky dinner. How I wish I could bottle Cameron's awe for the entire day. I could make a lot of money selling her appreciative expressions, her oohs, and her aahs. Several times, Kenneth and I look at each other over her head, both of us grinning at how such a seemingly simple experience can induce such joy.

- - - - -

The school year begins with new routines for all of us. I teach Mondays through Wednesdays at Bass High School and Thursdays and Fridays at Mary Lin Elementary. On Mondays and Wednesdays, I go straight to Georgia State for class. I do not have an ESOL classroom at either school, but Carlisle promises that will change once I am full-time at Bass. For now, a small storage closet has been outfitted as a makeshift classroom at Bass, and I take small groups of ESOL students to the library at Mary Lin. There is a conference room there that I am able to set up as a classroom. What this also means is that I have a bag or two of supplies that I take to Bass and a different bag or two that I take to Mary Lin. The increase in pay makes up for the itinerant work week.

Cameron adores her first grade teacher, Mrs. Broward, and seems to be thriving. Kenneth takes Cameron to school each day on his way into work and shaves a few minutes off of his lunch break to compensate for arriving at work a little late. The grandparent rotation continues for after-school care.

Papa Don picks Cameron up from Euclid on Mondays, as he does not teach a class after noon. Instead, he sets her up to browse through the many encyclopedias in his office or color while he conducts office hours, then takes her home. Those nights, Kenneth warms up a can of Campbell's Chunky Soup while he makes grilled cheese sandwiches, which Cameron still calls girl-cheese sandwiches. Mema and PopPop Fields provide child care, individually or together, on Tuesdays and Wednesdays. Kenneth and Cameron get a nourishing home-cooked meal on Wednesdays. We'd likely get them on Tuesdays as well, but my pride will not allow me to accept their offer, especially because I know there will be strings attached. Mama Jo has arranged to have Thursdays off from Eggleston hospital, so she takes Cameron home after school. On Fridays, I am able to leave Mary Lin a little early, and I pick Cameron up from school. While the pace is exhausting, I am grateful to be able to teach, to have four involved grandparents pitch in, to be able to further my education, and to have a supportive husband. I am also grateful to Carlisle for offering me the opportunity to teach high school students, as this is where I feel I truly belong. I'm also grateful that Magda understands why, most days, Cameron climbs her steep driveway alone to deliver the mail while the Grandparent-on-Duty waits on the sidewalk. I was afraid she wouldn't hear of these strangers taking her mail out of the box to hand it to Cameron, but it seems she has come to rely on this daily delivery, however it occurs.

- - - - -

The holidays are upon us, and I am not ready. I am behind in everything—making lists, shopping for presents, gift-wrapping, creating lesson plans, reading for Georgia State, and doing laundry. Everything. I'm also annoyed, but not surprised, that the home improvement project is taking longer than we'd anticipated. To make matters worse, Aleksander occasionally stops working at our house and takes on a side job that he finishes in only a few days. I understand he does this, in part, because he will get paid immediately and, in part, because he needs the stimulation of a different task. Still, I had hoped to have my kitchen back by Thanksgiving. Now it appears we'll be lucky to have it back, with the job totally completed, by mid-March. I just had no idea it would take so long, but I'm not sure what I would have said if I had known. Until then, I continue to dodge sawhorses and myriad tools, many of which I cannot name.

Also, I have seen Ron again after a long spell of not seeing him. Perhaps he's been around, and I just have not noticed because of the pace of our lives. I don't think so, though, for every time he returns from who knows where, he has clothes that appear to be clean, his hair has been cut, and his beard and mustache have been trimmed. I need to ask Kenneth how he'd feel about my inviting Ron to Christmas dinner. Thanksgiving will be at the Gardners, but I insist on our immediate family continuing to have Christmas in our own home, despite the chaos. I will, of course, invite Magda, knowing what her response will be. Who knows? Maybe I'll also invite Aleksander. If he sees how difficult it is for us to operate around his construction mess, perhaps he'll hire someone to help him finish up earlier. I do hope my sour mood about all of our inconveniences doesn't spoil the holidays.

Chapter Seven: 1981

THE HOLIDAYS COME and go in a blur—thankfully, mostly a happy blur. Cameron is elated with all of her gifts from Santa, her parents, and her grandparents. This new year, I resolve to no longer make resolutions. My track record is deplorable, and the FearGuiltShame Triplets always show up when I break my resolutions, so I resolve not to resolve. I feel a burden lifted with this decision, a burden I was not actually aware of before. If I cannot shed weight by dieting, I can at least shed imaginary weight by reordering my priorities.

- - - - -

We have a seven-year-old. In many ways, I feel as if I have been a mother for my entire adult life, and in other ways, I feel as if Cameron just entered our lives. As soon as I think I know my child, she surprises me. When those surprises are delightful, I nearly cry with joy, like her announcement in early February that she wants to learn Arabic "like Papa Don speaks." This new hobby of hers is entirely without suggestion from any of the adults in her life, and I can tell it pleases my dad immensely, especially because I never showed an interest. We can only assume that she has overheard Papa Don speaking with his advisees on the days Cameron is holding office hours with him, and she has become intrigued. I am grateful that Papa Don is willing to tutor her on the days he is the Grandparent-on-Duty, and I am also grateful knowing that he will not be angry or disappointed if this is merely a passing fancy of hers. In addition to learning conversational Arabic, Cameron is also learning to ride a bike. She insists she will ride her bicycle to school, and she pouts when Kenneth and I tell her that isn't going to happen. I do not recall pushing my seven-year-old limits, as she continually does. Part of me is proud of her for her fearlessness and varied interests, and part of me wonders why she cannot be content being interested in what most seven-year-old girls are interested in.

- - - - -

Ron is at his watching spot on a Friday afternoon. Cameron and I notice him after we have delivered Magda's mail and had our after-school snack. He was not there when we got home, but as Cameron and I head out to explore the neighborhood, she on her bicycle, me on foot, we see him sitting on the ledge where we first spotted him.

"Hi, Mr. Ron," Cameron greets him, slowing her bike. He nods, smiling shyly, and Cameron stops her bike entirely, waiting for me to catch up to her. When I do, she remains there instead of getting back on.

"We haven't seen you for awhile, Ron. You doing okay?" I ask.

"Yes, ma'am. I'm doing okay, thank you." He pauses, mouth partially open, as if to continue. Whatever internal debate he has with himself, the decision to continue the conversation wins. "How about y'all?"

"I'm learning to ride my bike, Mr. Ron! I want to ride it to school, but Mommy and Daddy say no." She pokes her bottom lip out.

At this, Ron smiles broadly, enchanted with my daughter, as most people are when she is being enchanting. I sometimes secretly think to myself that they should all see her when she is definitely not being enchanting. For now, though, it is a wonder to see Ron smile so widely that even his eyes crinkle. "Maybe one day, when you're older, though, huh?"

"Yeah, maybe."

"So, Ron, you don't have to answer this, but I've noticed when you're gone and then you come back, you've had a haircut and you've got new clothes. Do you mind me asking where you go?"

He hesitates, again seemingly debating with himself. I'm afraid I've made him regret continuing our conversation.

"That's okay. You don't have to tell me. I'm sorry I asked. I just sometimes wonder if you're warm enough in the winter and cool enough in the summer, you know?"

Again, a shy smile. He seems genuinely touched by my concern. "If I need a place to go during the day, I usually sit in the Ponce de Leon library and read."

Both Cameron and I perked up at his mention of reading. "That's great," I say. "What do you like to read? We," and I motion to Cameron, "love to read."

"Yeah, Mr. Ron. Mommy and Daddy call me a Read-a-saurus."

Again, he smiles unguardedly. "I like almost anything, but especially books about history. I'm reading now about World War I and the bombing of London." He checks himself, looking quickly at Cameron to gauge her reaction.

"It's hard to imagine, isn't it?" I try to put him at ease. "And then they got bombed again in the Second World War."

"Yeah. Hard to imagine."

Cameron is now getting antsy, so I wrap up our conversation by making Ron an offer. "Listen, if you ever need a place to stay when the library is closed, we have a carriage house in the back. It isn't air-conditioned or heated, but at least it's enclosed." As soon as I say these words, I wonder if I should have discussed this offer with Kenneth first. Then I remember that he started the renovation-from-hell project without first consulting me, and I absolve myself. Sort of. I do wonder if Ron will ever take me up on my offer and, if so, what Kenneth's reaction will be. I know what his mother's reaction would be. With that, Cameron mounts her bicycle again, and we are off to see whether or not the new owners of the Turrets' house have moved in.

- - - - -

Hallelujah! It is late March, and the mud room is finally finished—many, many months behind schedule and many hundreds of dollars over budget. But it is glorious. Aleksander outdid himself, and I could not be more pleased. I will not miss the sawhorses, dust, noise, and tools, but I do think I will miss seeing him around and having conversations with him on a variety of topics. I feel a little silly about my schoolgirl crush on the handyman and convince myself that, while my feelings are harmless, it's still probably a good thing that he will not be returning to our home until our next project, which is likely years away. I wonder if all of his female clients are drawn to him.

- - - - -

This mid-April day starts off badly and does not improve but, instead, gets appreciably worse. Cameron and I bicker about her need for a sweater due to the morning chilliness. Kenneth is of a mind to let her go to school without a sweater and be cold, thus learning that her mother might still know a thing or two. I am not willing to risk her getting sick. She has had perfect attendance so far in the first grade, and if she were to be ill, one of us would have to take a day off from work to care for her. It takes us extra minutes to reach a compromise. She must wear the sweater until Kenneth drops her off at school, and then she may take it off as soon as she is inside the building. I suspect she will take the sweater off in the car, and he will say nothing. If she gets sick, he can be the one to stay home with her.

I rush out the door to Bass later than I'd like. I can still make it, but just as the late bell rings. I work with my first two groups of students, the 9th and 10th graders, and settle in for a routine Bass High School day until I begin my preparation for my after-lunch groups of students, the 11th and 12th graders. That's when I notice that, in my haste, I grabbed one Bass bag and one Mary Lin bag. I need that second Bass bag for my afternoon students.

I am flustered, and then I remember that Carlisle is at Bass this day, thank goodness. I ask him if he would mind if I skip lunch room duty and, instead, run home during that time to get the missing bag. As usual, he is calm and understanding. He offers to fill in for me in the lunchroom. I breathe a sigh of relief and head home.

I park my car in the driveway so that I can go in the front door. This will save me extra steps, allowing me to go straight to the dining room, my unofficial office, and switch out the Mary Lin bag for the other Bass bag. I let myself in, and before I can exchange the bags, I hear a metallic clanging sound coming from the back of the house. It sounds like it is coming from the mud room, like something is bumping against the washing machine or dryer.

My heart beats wildly. I walk quietly to the bedroom and grab the aluminum baseball bat we keep in our closet for just such an emergency as encountering an intruder. With bat in hand, I inch toward the kitchen. I am positioned where I can see through the window panes to the mud room, but the intruder, if there is one, if it is not, instead, a sneaky squirrel, cannot see me. I am close enough to the kitchen phone to pick it up, pull the cord around the corner, and dial 911. What I see is so shocking that I accidentally drop the bat, which rolls toward the mud room door.

Kenneth is backed up to the washing machine, and he and Aleksander are kissing each other with more passion than Kenneth has ever kissed me. They are grabbing wildly at each other's belts and pants zippers, bumping into the washing machine. The sound of the bat hitting the floor interrupts them, and that's when they stop and look through the window and see that I am standing in the kitchen, watching them in utter disbelief.

Time slows down. Sounds muffle. Senses suddenly dull. I am aware of the two of them coming into the kitchen, both smoothing down their hair, fastening their belts, and checking their zippers in concert, as if choreographed. Neither of them says anything. Instead, they both watch me, their faces stricken.

"Get out," I say, pointing to Aleksander and the back door. My voice sounds far away in my head. "Get out of my house." And he does, as quickly and quietly as he can.

I then point at Kenneth and the kitchen table. "Sit." And he obediently sits in his usual chair, head hanging. I sit in the chair to his right and say, "Look at me." I imagine my stern tone must remind him of his mother on those rare occasions when she had to admonish him as a young boy. This is one time when I don't mind sounding like her or acting like her in her disapproval.

Kenneth looks at me, and there are tears in his eyes. He blinks them away, but more follow.

"Tell me. What's going on? Talk to me," my scolding tone continues. I must not be moved by his tears, despite how infrequently he shows emotion.

"It was... he, uh, called... Alex said he, uh, thought he, uh, left a tool here and asked if I could meet him during my lunch time."

"Alex? Since when do you call him Alex?"

"Um, that's what he said when he called. 'This is Alex. I think I left a tool I need at your place.'"

"Okay, so . . . ."

"He, um. He came on to me." Kenneth pauses. I can see his

mental wheels furiously turning now, that logical brain kicking in, tallying up the potential damage—to us, to his relationship with Cameron and with his parents, and even to the City of Atlanta, if word of this, whatever this is, gets out. "Mer, it was a one-off. Like I said, he came on to me. I don't know what happened. I swear, it'll never happen again. I swear to you." His face is pleading, and his voice is trembling.

"I need time to think, Kenneth. I need time to think. For now, though, I want you to ask for a week off from work when Cameron and I get out of school. You and I are going away somewhere together, and we are going to work on ourselves. Do you hear me? And you are not to have anything else to do with Aleksander."

Before he can respond, I stand up, walk out of the kitchen, and lock myself in our bedroom. I spend the rest of the afternoon alternately crying and fuming. I do not go back to Bass, and I do not call Carlisle. At some point, I hear Kenneth start his car and leave. He has to drive through the yard to get around my car. When PopPop Fields brings Cameron home from school, I remain in the bedroom, telling both of them through the locked door that I am not feeling well. I do not come out until late that night, after Kenneth has put Cameron to bed and is curled up on the sofa. While he sleeps, I stand over him, numb, hurt, angry, and sad all at the same time. And for the next few weeks, I did not speak of that day to anyone. Kenneth and I tiptoe around each other, going through the parental motions, speaking only when necessary, and storing away our innermost thoughts until we can be alone together somewhere.

- - - - -

School is out for the summer, and Cameron is with Mama Jo and Papa Don for four days while Kenneth and I go to Saint Simon's Island for a much-needed getaway. We tell our parents we're going on a second honeymoon, and they are likely none the wiser that I have demanded this time alone together. The conversation on the drive down is stilted and superficial. I begin to wonder if we can find our way back to being together or if this unease between us is the new normal.

Once we unpack, Kenneth suggests a walk on the beach. We have splurged and are staying at the King and Prince, and so the beach is right outside our room. Once we are walking parallel to the Atlantic Ocean, our steps perfectly matched, Kenneth takes my hand, a gesture he has not initiated in so very long that I've forgotten how much it thrills me. His touch is like jumper cables to the drained battery in my heart, and I turn to look up at him as we continue to walk.

We both start speaking at once, and in fits and starts, mingled with tears of sorrow and relief, we do find our way back to being us, the Kenneth and Meredith who share ideas and opinions and common goals, who talk about anything and everything. The Kenneth and Meredith who created a precious child together. The rest of our stay is relaxing and glorious, and I am, once again, assured of my husband's love for me, for Cameron, and for his family. I still have no words for what happened with him and Aleksander, and we do not speak of it. I also cannot be 100% certain I would not have kissed Aleksander if he had tried to seduce me, so if it took Aleksander trying to seduce my husband to bring him back to me, then so be it.

- - - - -

Summer flies by in a blur of bike rides in the neighborhood, trips to the library, visits with grandparents, excursions to the zoo, mail deliveries, short conversations with Magda, and picnic lunches on the front lawn, with Ron our occasional guest. Kenneth continues to make time for us to demonstrate his devotion to his wife and to his daughter.

Cameron catches me grinning one morning at the kitchen table, the *Atlanta Constitution* spread out before me. I love these unguarded moments, when she is still half-asleep, her hair is tousled, and yesterday's spat over something trivial has been forgotten. "You look happy, Mommy."

"I am." I point to the newspaper. "Our President, Mr. Reagan, wants a woman to be a Supreme Court justice. That's a very big deal. She will be the first mommy, the first wife, to have this very important job!" I animate my explanation to indicate just how momentous this is. And part of me is eager to know how my parents and Kenneth's parents will feel about our new president offering this plumb assignment to a woman. I, for one, think it is about time.

- - - - -

One evening, about three weeks before the start of the new school year, Carlisle calls to ask if he may come by the house with some news. "News?" My first thought is that Horrible Headlee has used her connections to get to the superintendent of the Atlanta Public Schools, and I am about to lose my job.

Carlisle obviously hears the anxiety in my voice and clarifies. "Good news."

I invite him over for dinner the next evening. It will be the first time he has come to our home and the first time he has met Kenneth. I wonder how many other teachers' homes he has been to and what one serves one's supervisor for dinner. I ask Kenneth and Cameron for their thoughts on the matter, and they both agree that I should serve cheese soufflé as the main course. Cameron and I start our grocery list for Sevananda, with plans to set out tomorrow morning before the heat is unbearable.

"Can we stop by the Turrets' house on our way home?" Cameron asks. We have continued to look for signs of life after the For Sale sign was removed, and, so far, the house appears to be vacant.

"Sure," I answer, to which Kenneth responds with a good-natured eye roll. How well he knows me and my silly interest in our make-believe neighbors, Tommy, Tilly, Joe, Margaret, and Baby Makes Three. I smile gratefully at his indulgence in my fantastical stories.

Mr. Carlisle arrives right on time, which is fortunate when serving a souffle. I have allowed a 15-minute buffer, just in case, so we give him a tour of the house and of our completed renovation projects, walking softly when we get to the kitchen. There are oohs and aahs when I bring the souffle to the dining room table, and our meal of hot French bread, steamed broccoli, souffle, and chocolate mousse for dessert is a great success. Carlisle has brought a lovely bottle of wine that we also enjoy with our meal. Cameron's wine glass has grape juice in it, and we all toast the reason for Carlisle's visit —my new full-time job at Bass, complete with a classroom of my own.

"Just think," I muse, "no more Mary Lin bags and Bass bags to lug around with my Georgia State bags. I can actually put posters and vocabulary words up in my room. And a map of the world with a pin in every country my students represent." I am beside myself with joy. Life is so very good, made even better by the camaraderie at the table, the proud smile of my husband, and the stellar dinnertime manners of my daughter, who is in an exceptionally good mood this day. Part of me wishes to freeze-frame this moment in order to savor it and preserve it, and part of me is excited about all of the unknowns that await me in this new teaching position. Life is so very good.

- - - - -

We have a second grader, and I am in my next-to-last quarter in my Master's program at Georgia State. Our days are a whirlwind, but we quickly settle back into our school day routines, complete with Grandparents-on-Duty and Campbell's Chunky Soup Night. To hear Cameron tell it, her dad makes better girl-cheese sandwiches than I do. When pressed for details about what makes his better, she states that her daddy puts more cheese in his than I do. I concede defeat, grateful that this man of mine can at least make a decent sandwich. I think of my dear father and how utterly inept he is in the kitchen, except for his ability to boil a hotdog. For all of his many assets, cooking is not one of them, and this realization makes me appreciate my mother even more.

One of the ways Carlisle was able to get my position at Bass to be full-time was to offer my services in teaching an English class to low-performing students. His assertion to the school administration was that, because I am able to help ESOL students learn English, I should be able to help native English speakers learn as well. I want to make him proud, so my confident reply to this new role belies my doubts. If Carlisle has any misgivings, he doesn't show them, for he knows that I will give any teaching assignment my best and that I will stand up for my students.

The first week of class is typically devoted to getting to know my students—their names, where they are from, their facility with the language, and how long they have been learning English. Of course, I must adapt this approach to the native

English speakers, and I must try to instill confidence in them, especially those who have continually failed their ninth- or tenth-grade English. I have grown particularly fond of one young man, Tate. The first day, instead of doing a traditional roll call, I walk down each row of desks and ask each student to introduce themselves and tell me one thing that interests them. I will attempt to use that information to create reading and writing assignments specifically for them. Most of these students are already jaded by their failures, and it shows in their faces, their posture, and their monosyllabic answers to my questions. It goes something like this, as I stop at each student's desk, the class roster on my clipboard:

"Martin. Football."

"Do you have a favorite team, Martin?"

"Yeah, the Falcons."

"Thank you." I point to the girl behind Martin.

"Belinda. I like Alabama."

"The state?" I stop beside her desk.

She rolls her heavily made-up eyes. "The band."

"Do you have a favorite song?" She looks through slitted eyes at a young man whose name I don't yet know. "Yeah, 'Feels So Right.'" Oh, mercy, what have I gotten myself into? I must have a talk soon with Carlisle.

On it goes until I stop at the desk of a hulking figure, seated at the front of the last row of desks, his body barely contained by the desk.

"Muh name's Tight, 'n' I lack animals."

A quick search of the roll reveals that this student's name is not Tight, but Tate. "Tate, any specific kind of animals?"

"Ah lack all 'o' God's critters, Ma'am."

He is the first student in that room to refer to me as "Ma'am. We're going to get along just fine. His respect gives me just the encouragement I need to continue to listen, ask, and respond to his less enthusiastic classmates.

The very last student to introduce himself is "Germy." Surely no parent has named their kid Germy! Again, a quick look at the roster tells me I am standing beside Jeremy, who apparently has marbles in his mouth.

"And Jeremy," I enunciate his name, "what is it you like?"

"Getting' blowed." He does not snicker, although several of his classmates do, and that is when I notice his eyes are quite dilated and there is a distinctive odor to his clothes.

I try to make light of this in order to move on, "Not at school, I hope."

"Wherever. Whenever," his dispassionate reply.

How in the world can I teach these students? Why are they in school? Even those who seem remotely interested seem to lag far behind in their grammar skills, and I have no illusion that I am a miracle worker. I really must have a very frank conversation with Carlisle at the earliest possible moment.

When the bell rings, signaling the end of the period, I realize I have sweat circles under my arms. Fortunately, I have brought a sweater with me, which should nicely disguise the evidence of my nerves for the rest of the day. All the students scurry out of the room as if they have been paroled and fear I will catch the clerical error that released them. All except Tate, who stops by my desk to ask, "D'ya' have any pets, Miz Fields? I have a rabbit, two dawgs, a parakeet, an' a gerbil."

"No, Tate, we don't have any pets, but I look forward to learning more about yours."

And with that, Tate grins deeply, leaving the classroom. He lumbers, really, his long arms hanging like dead weights, his steps Neanderthal in nature. This gentle giant may be the one redeeming quality in his class of academic misfits.

- - - - -

What sort of madman shows his affection for someone he admires by trying to assassinate the President of the United States? If someone said, "I did that because I love you," I'm not sure I wouldn't be forever wondering what I could have said or done differently so that some misguided soul would not leap to the conclusion that the best way to prove their love to me was by trying to murder Ronald Reagan. What must Jody Foster be going through right now?

– – – – –

I have ESOL students from nearly every continent. I will need to learn a lot more about their native customs and various holidays, helping them understand not only English words and usage but also how to make sense of some of our native customs and holidays. My respect for them and the many forces they are up against once more inspires me to help them learn, acclimate, and realize their potential. I decide to devote the month of August to the study of money—theirs and ours, and the month of September to the study of music —theirs and ours, for these are two currencies that speak volumes, no matter where one is from. I will then devote the months of October through December to the study of our various holidays and celebrations, weaving in any parallels to what they are used to. By the Christmas holidays, the map of the world with its representative pins, vocabulary words, and posters about money, music, and holidays should fill the entire back wall of my classroom. Perhaps it will also spark something in my class of misfits. One can only hope.

– – – – –

One day, Nell, one of the cafeteria workers, approaches me when I am on lunchroom duty. "I think you've got my stepson in your class. Tate?"

"Tate. Yes! I am really enjoying getting to know him. He is so respectful and attentive. He sets a good example for the others." I say this more as a wish than a fact.

"Tate's had a hard life. I'm glad you've taken to him. His mama left him and his dad when he was just a baby. His dad and I have been married for about 10 years, so I've known Tate since he was a tot. I help him in the evenings with his schoolwork. He may be EMR, but there's a spark in that boy."

"EMR?"

"That's what they said about him when he was a little 'un. Well," she smiles, "I don't reckon he's ever been little, but you know what I mean. It means educable mentally retarded. I hate that."

I am also appalled at the term. "Why did they say that?"

"'Cause the cord got wrapped around his neck while he was being born, and he was a blue baby coming out. His mama couldn't handle all the extra responsibilities, so she just up and left. Tate wasn't even two years old. How d'ya like that?"

"I'm so sorry all that happened, but I'm glad he's got you." Out of the corner of my eye, I see a potential food fight emerging on the opposite side of the cafeteria, and I excuse myself quickly. "Thank you for letting me know about Tate. I'll keep an extra eye out for him."

How do you like that, a mother abandoning her child? I try the idea on for size and cannot fathom ever rejecting my child. And it makes me wonder what kinds of stories my class of misfits might tell if given the opportunity. I resolve to try.

- - - - -

Way to go, City of Atlanta! As if there wasn't enough sprawl, the city has torn down the Joe loves Margaret art pieces as they clear the way for building an upscale shopping strip with loft apartments. I have to wonder, though, if my outrage is more about the unnecessary construction or a sense of loss. And if it is a sense of loss, what, exactly, have I lost? What is so badly missing in my life that I created these fictional friends? I do not pull on those thought threads to attempt finding their origins, though, because I am on my way to class at Georgia State. Maybe later. Maybe after the holidays.

Chapter Eight: 1982

THE NEW YEAR has begun. I'm in the Emergency Room at the Dekalb General Hospital, sitting with Mom while we're waiting to speak with the doctor. The day started as usual: Kenneth slurping down a quick cup of coffee while reading the *Atlanta Constitution*, ignoring any attempt at conversation; Cameron changing clothes three times before Kenneth threatens to take her to school naked; and me, after getting them out the door, simultaneously wiping down counters, eating toast, drinking coffee, and applying mascara and eyeshadow. Mom's day started as usual, too, leaving at 6:30 a.m. for one of her two weekly 12-hour shifts at the Eggleston. When the front office at Bass calls on the intercom that I need to come take a call, my first thought is, "Oh, no. Cameron." Then Kenneth. But not my dad. So there's the double shock of hearing Mom's voice on the line and hearing "emergency room and "your father."

So far, this is all I've been able to piece together. Mom's neighbor, Mrs. Franklin, called her at work. She'd seen Dad out taking his usual morning walk while she was driving her 6-year-old, Tina, to Fernbank Elementary. It turns out her daughter has the same teacher I did, sweet Mrs. James. He seemed agitated, she said. He'd walk a few paces, all while intently looking down where he was walking, then he'd stop and squat down to look closer at the street, as if puzzling out something. Then he'd shake his head and say, "No, no. This is all wrong. They've got it all wrong." She witnessed him do this several times while backing the car out of the driveway and inching down Clifton toward Coventry to pick up Tina's classmate. She was going to call Mom after she got home from Eggleston and just ask if everything was okay, but when she got home from taking Tina to school and observed Dad still pacing, squatting, wringing his hands, and talking out loud, she called Mom right away. Mom's afraid that maybe he's had a stroke, and the staff has whisked him off into the bowels of the hospital to run tests. I feel guilty for letting my teaching job, Cameron's Brownie Scouts, Kenneth's chess club and his moodiness keep me from being a more devoted daughter. I'm all they've got, and, by the looks of things recently, I'm not much. It's funny how once you settle into a new routine, you delude yourself into thinking, I didn't get by there this week. Maybe next. At least by Mother's Day. Or a birthday. Or a long holiday weekend. On the days they are the Grandparents-on-duty, we're basically handing off the

Cameron baton when I get home, and we rarely spend more than a few minutes together. I haven't even been good about calling. By the time I get Cameron into bed, get my lesson plans completed, and talk with Kenneth about my day and his, it's too late to call. Excuses, I now see. Not reasons. The FearGuiltShame Triplets confirm that I am not a good daughter, and now my dad is Godknowswhere having Godknowswhat being done to him. He always got a little queasy when I was a little girl and skinned my knee. He has a thing about blood, this strong man against whom I measure all others. It's ironic, isn't it, that he married a nurse? If they're drawing vials of blood, he's no doubt vomited or passed out by now. Maybe both. Poor Dad. I hold Mom's hand as we wait. If ever there was a cursed four-letter word, "wait" is one of the worst.

- - - - -

I drive out of the way after work to check on my folks, guilt and concern tugging at me in equal measure. Dad has not had a stroke. All of his initial bloodwork and x-rays have come back clear. He seems fine, if a little embarrassed about all of the attention, which he refers to as "hoop dee doo." Still, his physician wants to run more tests. For now, at both Mom and Dad's insistence, the grandparent rotation does not need to be altered. I prefer to take this as a good sign, although I do make sure Cameron knows how to dial 9-1-1. Mom puts on her brave nurse face, but I can tell she's worried. I follow her to the kitchen and ask if there's something she's not telling me. "I'm just tired," she tells me.

"You're sure. You'd tell me, wouldn't you, if you thought something was wrong?"

Mom nods, then turns her attention to the cheese souffle she is pulling out of the oven. It's one of Dad's favorite dishes, and preparing it for him on a workday is a labor of love. I learned from her how to make it. She does look tired. I look around for something to do to help and accidentally slam the cupboard door shut after getting plates out for their early dinner. Mom jumps, nearly dropping the souffle on her way to the breakfast nook.

"Mer, be careful," she chides. "It doesn't take much for this to fall. You know that. Now, please go get your father and tell him dinner is ready."

"Yes, ma'am. Sorry." I skulk out of the room, feeling five years old. Feeling clumsy, inept, and useless.

After I kiss them both goodbye and start the car, I feel the tears welling up. Whoever made up that term was truly smart. My linguistic training converges with my emotions. I am aware of deep feelings bubbling up. But all this from one scolding? Not that I didn't deserve it; she'd worked so hard to prepare a lovely meal, and I'd nearly spoiled it. But still. What is my problem?

I sniffle and wipe my nose and eyes with my sleeve, sure my

middle name, Grace, belongs to someone else. And to tamp down those loose-cannon thoughts and inconvenient emotions, as I drive home, I plan a lesson for tomorrow and decide what can of delightful goodness I can open to feed my own family for dinner.

- - - - -

We have an eight-year-old. This Brownie Scout is earning badges at a head-spinning rate. No sooner do I sew one on her sash than she is immersed in earning another. Kenneth and I call her, out of earshot, of course, a Girl Scout savant, she is so eager to learn and earn. Cameron is a sponge, soaking up information as quickly as it's presented. She is observant and analytical, just like her Daddy. And moody, just like her Daddy. Still, I would not change a thing about her, as she is her own person.

- - - - -

I have tried, in vain, to get my class of misfits to read and write without having to threaten them. Threats are fairly meaningless to those who have repeatedly flunked classes. It's like holding a tack in your hand and jabbing it menacingly at the balloon that's already been busted. The threat of school suspension if they do not pass this class is more often, for these students, a promise of days without alarm clocks and sitting through classes that are "boring." I know enough that "boring" is code-speak for "I don't understand" or "I don't care." I want to try to change that, though. My hunch is that if I can help them see themselves in a story we're reading, they will not only better understand sentence structure, but they will also find something to care about. Some of my previous efforts at having them take turns reading out loud while the rest follow along have been too awkward, so, starting this week, I am reading out loud to them from *Dibs in Search of Self*. They can follow along or not. They can doodle while I read or not. What they may not do is disrupt or sleep. Dibs may have been published almost 20 years ago, but the relevance of a sad, lonely little boy who seems to be on the outside of life looking in should resonate with some of my students. We all feel like outsiders sometimes. Can I hook them with Dibs' story? I hope so, for if not, I am out of ideas. But not out of concern.

- - - - -

Spring has arrived. The rose bush and the azalea both have buds. I am in my final quarter at Georgia State. And there are also more Ron sightings now that the weather has warmed up. He is looking more scraggly and scrawny than ever. On my way to work, I will occasionally leave a paper sack with his name on it on the ledge where he likes to sit. Inside are packages of peanut butter crackers and a box of Little Debbies. He can afford the additional calories; I cannot. I assume he is not offended, as he always tips his ball cap at me when we happen to make eye contact, usually from a distance. He's a skittish one, that Ron.

Spring also means the arrival of baby birds. One afternoon, I come home from work and am greeted by PopPop and a very serious Cameron. She has found a baby bird on the ground in our backyard. Its eyes are still closed, and it is practically naked; it is just that young. Cameron is feeding it water with an eye dropper. I get an old shoe box and line it with some rags while Cameron coos to the bird cupped in her hand. PopPop has told Cameron that the bird will have to be fed often if it is to have a chance to live, and if it lives to the point at which it opens its eyes and begins to fledge, she will need to find worms to crush up and put in that eye dropper. He may have been attempting to help her face the truth that the bird probably won't live and to dissuade her from trying to be its surrogate mother, but Cameron is undaunted. Oh, my resolute daughter. This heartache-in-the-making is not a badge you will be able to add to your Brownie Scout sash, but you will carry that badge with you forever nonetheless.

After taking shifts throughout the night to feed the bird, expecting each time to find it dead, Kenneth and I are surprised to see the next morning that it is not only still alive, but it has soiled the rags. When we wake Cameron up for school, we show her this evidence that her bird is a fighter. Just like its surrogate mother. At breakfast, Cameron insists that it will be okay to bring the baby bird to school with her and that Mrs. Mize will let her feed it several times during the school day. Kenneth and I look at each other while Cameron is dropping water into the bird's open beak. We know we have to let her try this, just as we know neither of us can take the bird with us and get a lick of work done. So it is settled, and Cameron looks triumphant.

Later that same day, as my final morning class is ending, the front office calls me over the intercom to please come take an urgent phone call. I am certain it is something about Dad, and just the thought makes my eyes tear up as I sprint down the hall. Instead, I hear Cameron's warbly voice. "Mommy, something is wrong with the bird. It opens its mouth, but it won't take the water. Can you please come get us?"

I explain to the office staff that I will be back as soon as possible and that I am taking my lunch to run an errand. Cameron is waiting for me in the Euclid office, holding the box with the baby bird. She is correct. It looks as if it is gasping for air, and she is beside herself that it will not take the eye dropper.

I squat down beside the chair she is sitting in, tears streaming down her face. "Cameron, I have a student in one of my classes who loves animals. Tate. You've heard me talk about him, right?" She nods, sniffling. "How about I take the bird back to Bass with me and see if Tate can help him? If anyone can help this birdie live, it's Tate." She again nods, handing the box over to me, reluctant to let her baby go but desperate to give it this chance. "I know you are sad and worried. I want you to go back to class now and try to think about your schoolwork. I want you to know that Tate will do everything he can to help your birdie. Okay?" She again nods, then wipes her eyes and nose on her sleeve while she stands up to head back to class. As she reaches the office door, I say words that I should probably say more often. "Cameron." She turns around. "I love you, and I am so, so proud of you." She smiles and then leaves for her classroom.

My first class after lunch is Tate's class. While I ask the class to write at least five sentences describing what they know of Dibs after the eight chapters we've read, I have a consultation with Tate over Cameron's bird. He quickly assesses how dire the situation is and looks doubtful. He asks to be excused to go to the lunchroom and seek out Nell. He wants to see if she can give him some raw hamburger meat that might entice the bird. I do not hear from Tate until the next day. All I know to tell Cameron when I get home is that "no news must be good news."

The following morning, before the first bell rings, Tate's hulking body fills the doorway to my classroom. He has the shoe box with him, but the lid is closed. I know from the look on his face that he is as devastated as Cameron will be.

"It were too far gone and too weak," he states, handing me the box. "I'm sorry, Miz Fields."

At this moment, I am more worried that he thinks he has disappointed me than I am that the bird has died. "Thank you for trying," I try to reassure him. "That means a lot to me and my daughter."

"Want me to bury it fer ya?"

"No, thank you. I think Cameron will want to do that with me and her daddy. I really do appreciate what you did to try to keep it alive, Tate. I'll see you later today, okay?"

He nods and leaves silently, hanging his huge head. As my first class of ESOL students begins filing in, my heart cracks a little—for Tate, for Cameron, for a mother bird missing her baby. Later that evening, after Kenneth gets home from work, we have a small, somber burial service in the backyard. How it touches me to see a few tears trickle down Kenneth's usual stoic face and to watch him comfort our daughter.

- - - - -

"Miz Fields," Belinda is calling my name moments after the bell has rung. "If Dibs' mother was a heart surgeon, how come she wasn't smart enough to know her little boy's heart was broke?"

This is a day I have yearned for, when these kids who think they hate school and reading, writing, and learning actually initiate a conversation about something we've been doing in class. I bounce the question to the class. "What do y'all think?"

Kurt, who rarely speaks up and rarely even looks up, volunteers, "She may be book smart, but she sure ain't people smart."

Others in the class agree, and for the remainder of the class period we have a delightful conversation, lesson plans be hanged. The gray cloud of helping Cameron work through her sorrow has lifted a little. I cling to these glimmers of hope despite knowing that sometimes those hopes are dashed into shards of heartbreak, and I suddenly wonder how Kai is doing after Willow's death and his father's arrest. I must give Mrs. Butler a call.

- - - - -

This late spring Saturday starts out as they usually do, with all of us doing our assigned weekly chores after a breakfast of pancakes, sausage, and eggs. After I put in another load of laundry, I attack the breakfast dishes while Cameron helps Kenneth finish the yardwork. She is in charge of sweeping the grass cuttings off the walkway leading up to the front door and the back door. Their father-daughter banter is the kind of music that would make us rich if we could bottle and sell it. The glow in my heart is quickly replaced by my irritation at the kitchen sink once again getting clogged. When Kenneth and Cameron come in from outside, we sit around the kitchen table drinking lemonade. I break the news to him that his chores now include once again unstopping the drain.

"I'll do even better than that," Kenneth announces. "I'll go to the hardware store and buy a disposal and install it today." He turns to Cameron. "Are you up for a ride to ACE with Daddy?"

"Yea!" her enthusiastic reply. I beam at my husband. This good daddy, good husband, is going to install a disposal!

They set off together while I throw wet towels into the clothes dryer and put clean sheets on all of our beds. After they return, we sit down for a quick, late lunch of sandwiches and chips, and then Kenneth starts on his project. The engineer in him requires that he read all of the directions first, assembling the necessary tools not only for installing the disposal but also for the electrical wiring. This will be an involved process, and my contribution will be to keep Cameron entertained while he works.

We deliver Magda's mail to her and then go for a walk. Actually, I walk; Cameron rides her bike. She is venturing further and further away from me on these outings, almost out of earshot. And now, instead of waiting for me to catch up, she doubles back and covers the same territory several times, her patience with me wearing thin. "You should get a bike, Mommy. Or let me ride by myself." I just smile and nod, not committing to either idea.

When we get home, Kenneth is not in the kitchen. Instead, he is in our bathroom with a blood-soaked towel wrapped around his left hand. Cameron screams and starts to cry. Thankfully, I have not inherited my father's squeamishness around blood. Instead, my mother's nurse gene kicks in. I asked him to let me see his wound. He has a deep gash in his left hand, and his attempts to stanch the flow of blood are not working. He looks pasty, and I quickly realize we need to go to the emergency room for stitches, maybe even a tetanus shot. He has lost a lot of blood.

I grab a pillow off our bed and another bath towel, then put my arm around his waist and hold the elbow of his affected hand steady, leading him to the car. Cameron follows, crying piteously. I know I cannot take her to the emergency room with us. She would make matters worse instead of better. I also know I do not have enough time to take her to either grandparents' house. Instead, I drive across the street, up Magda's steep driveway, and race-walk Cameron to her front door.

"You have brought more mail?" she asks, in response to my urgent knocking.

"Magda, Kenneth has hurt himself, and I need to take him to Dekalb General." I push Cameron through the door to her and say, "Please watch Cameron for me."

Before she can object, I return to the car and break every speed limit while driving to the hospital. There, it is determined that Kenneth has sliced open tendons and requires dozens of internal and external stitches as well as a tetanus booster. They keep him for a few hours, not only for observation but also to assess the extent of the damage by requesting a consult with an orthopedic surgeon whose specialty is hand surgery. Meanwhile, they pump him full of antibiotics and pain medication. By the time his color returns and his pain is manageable, it is late. Once we are home, I get Kenneth settled in bed, propping his badly damaged hand with pillows, and then I walk across the street to Magda's house.

I tap gently on her front door, and she opens it almost immediately, holding her index finger to her lips. She nods toward her sofa at my sleeping daughter, nudging the door open with her hip for me to step in. Who would ever have imagined these would be the circumstances under which I would be given permission to enter the sanctity of her home?

"How'd she do?" I whisper. "Did she cry for very long?"

"She settle down soon," she whispers back. "We eat dinner; we watch Lawrence Welk; we play tic-tac-toe; and then she sleeps."

"Thank you so much, Magda." My eye is drawn to her mantle, where a United States flag is neatly folded into a triangular frame, accompanied on either side by photographs of men in uniform. I step over to see them more clearly and stop mid-stride. I turn back to Magda and ask, "Are these pictures of your husband and your son?"

Magda nods.

"I've never asked you before, but what is Junior's given name? What was your husband's name?"

"Husband and Junior named Ronald; we call our son Junior since he is little boy." My head is awhirl, and I wonder if Cameron saw the photo and also made the connection—that Junior is Ron, "our" Ron, the skittish, scraggly vagrant who has, for so long, been a ghostly presence in the neighborhood. I can understand why Magda may not have recognized him. First of all, she thinks he is dead. Second, he is far skinnier and bushier now than he was in the photograph. And then there's her diabetic eyesight and the distance from her front window, behind the sheers, to his favorite watching spot across and down the street.

I smile at Magda. "You must be very proud of their service to our country." I motion with my head towards Cameron. "And I'll bet you're really tired. I won't keep you. Thank you again.

So much." I gently nudge Cameron awake enough to help her stand up. Neither of us says a word while we walk home, but my thoughts and questions make a lot of noise in my head.

As I am tucking Cameron into her own bed, she asks about her daddy. I assure her he is okay, and she is back to sleep in moments. She does not mention Ron. I will think of some way to find out if she noticed the photograph and, if so, ask her to say nothing to Magda until I have had the opportunity to process this knowledge that Magda's son is here in Little Five Points in Atlanta, not dead but very much alive.

- - - - -

The school year is coming to a close. I am still mulling over what to do with what I know about Magda's Junior, our Ron. I think maybe I will try to speak with him first before I say anything to Magda. Cameron is now reading at a sixth grade level, and I almost feel sorry for her teacher next school year, trying to keep my daughter appropriately challenged. She will not act out in class if she is bored, but I do not want her to be bored. I schedule a conference with her current teacher, Mrs. Mize, Kenneth, and myself to discuss our options for who her third grade teacher can be. My ESOL students have come so far this school year, and I could not be more proud of them. Some of them will continue ESOL coursework with me in the fall, and some of them have made enough progress to be in all regular English coursework. A handful of my students graduated, the first in their families to graduate from an American high school. My band of misfits has also come so far. Well, most of them. I suspect a few of them will not be returning to Bass next year, and I make a mental note to be more diligent about reading the local crime news in the paper, as I suspect a few of them are already on the wrong side of the law. For the most part, though, I think our reading together of Dibs' story has helped them. They are aware that they have opinions, valid ones—about child-rearing, about education, about wealth and privilege. And because their opinions matter and I take them seriously, they are, again, for the most part, more inclined to express their opinions on paper, with greater attention to correct punctuation, spelling, and grammar.

But then there's "Germy." Oh, Jeremy, whose main goal in life remains "getting blowed." I do not see great things on the horizon for you if that continues to be your main goal in life. I see, instead, in-school suspension evolving into out-of-school suspension, and out-of-school suspension evolving into misdemeanors and ultimately felonies. The next-to-last week of school is a harbinger. The class is involved in a lively discussion about how wealth does not automatically make one smart, only that it affords one more options for trying to fix things. Belinda and Kyle have especially strong feelings about Dibs' parents' ineptitude. Belinda is expounding on what options most people would have in that situation if they "don't have gobs of money" when I become aware of Jeremy openly, defiantly munching on candy in the back of the room. Our rule has always been no food in the classroom unless they get permission from me before class and have brought enough to share. Jeremy has done neither.

"Excuse me, Belinda. Jeremy," I interrupt his snacking. "What is our rule about food in the classroom?"

Jeremy shrugs, shoving another handful of Peanut M&M's into his mouth.

I walk to the back of the room, where he is slumped at his desk in his normal posture. I hold my hand out for him to give me the bag of candy. This typically indifferent, stoned man-child is suddenly enraged. He throws the bag at me, stands up so forcefully he tips over his desk, and bolts out of the room, saying, "You old bitch!" Fortunately, the bell signals the end of the period, giving me enough time to straighten up the mess and regain my composure.

That afternoon, when picking up my mail in the teachers' break room, I run into Carlisle. I relate the incident to him. His wry response, "How dare he call you old?" is just what I need to make me grin and put the event in perspective.

During post-planning week, after the quarter has ended and all of us are cleaning up our rooms, preparing first for summer and then another school year, Carlisle drops by to chat. "I want you to know you'll be teaching all ESOL classes next fall."

"Does this have anything to do with Jeremy calling me names? I've grown rather fond of teaching that class, and I feel like I was getting somewh-"

Carlisle puts his hand on my arm to steady me and calm me, knowing how fiercely I will speak up for my students. "This decision has nothing to do with that, Meredith, and everything to do with the need to offer more ESOL classes. Now, finish cleaning up. I'm taking you to Moe's and Joe's for a drink."

- - - - -

I am officially a graduate of Georgia State University, having completed my coursework for the Master's in Applied Linguistics. My master's thesis on literacy and the English language learner has been accepted into a peer-reviewed journal. I have also completed my ESOL certification requirements. I am feeling quite accomplished. Accomplished and relieved. On graduation day, not only do Kenneth, Cameron, his parents, and my parents attend the ceremony, but so does Carlisle. The day after, Magda sends over a lovely bouquet of flowers from FTD. It feels great to have my accomplishments acknowledged. It also feels great to be finished with the degree and not have mountains of Georgia State homework on top of Bass schoolwork. I begin the summer by making mental lists of books to read for pleasure, ways to keep Cameron entertained, and what diets I will try next in my ongoing efforts to lose weight.

- - - - -

Cameron and I are having a picnic in the front yard when she spots Ron walking our way. "Hi, Mr. Ron!" She waves. "We're having a picnic! Want some crackers and lemonade?"

Ron glances up, smiling at Cameron. He's lost even more weight, and his hair and beard are almost matted; they're so unkempt. His clothes are dirtier than usual, too.

"You look tired, Ron," I say as he approaches. "Please sit with us awhile and help us finish these crackers." I point to a nearly full sleeve of Ritz crackers. Ron glances around and then reluctantly sits down, but not on the blanket. He sits on the ground beside the blanket.

Cameron scoots closer to me and pats the blanket next to her. "Here, Mr. Ron." She seems unfazed by his body odor, perhaps a side effect of our weekly trips to Sevananda.

Ron looks to me, I guess, for my approval. I nod, and he moves on to the blanket while I pour a Dixie cup full of lemonade and pass it to him. "We have cheese slices, and we have peanut butter. What would you like for me to put on your crackers first?"

"Cheese, please."

While he eats those, I prepare some more. Meanwhile, Cameron is telling him all about how she is learning to play Parcheesi. In great detail. Ron patiently listens while eating cheese and crackers and drinking lemonade, downing them as quickly as I can refill his plate and his cup. He seems to hang on to her every word.

"What games do you play, Mr. Ron?"

"I used to play Parcheesi when I was a kid. And Monopoly, checkers, chess, Go Fish, and Battleship. My favorite was checkers."

Cameron's eyes light up. "I like checkers, too!" And as she says this, an idea forms.

"Cameron, why don't you go inside and get your checkers set? I'll bet it's been a long time since Ron has played." And she's off like a shot, which buys me a few moments to tell Ron that I know he is Magda's son and how I came to know this about him.

"I wondered when you'd find out," was his soft reply. "She thinks I'm dead, and my father warned me never to disabuse her of that idea."

"But he's dead now. Don't you want her to know you're still alive? I cannot imagine any mother not being thrilled by that news."

"Maybe. I don't want the shock to endanger her health, though. I know she's not terribly well."

"I think knowing you're still alive might actually be the best medicine in the world."

He considers. "Well, she cannot see me like this."

"No, I suppose not, but I'll help you. Will you come back tomorrow at this time? I'm going to let you take a hot shower, and then I'm going to give you a haircut and a shave. What size clothes do you wear? I'll go to Goodwill this afternoon."

Ron says nothing for several moments, and I am afraid in my enthusiasm that I have overstepped my bounds. Cameron runs out of the house with her checkers set and plops down between us. As she lifts the lid off to set up the game, Ron quietly says, "Okay."

"Okay, you'll play checkers, or okay, you'll come back tomorrow?"

"Both." And then he touches Cameron's outstretched left fist. It looks like I'll be black and you'll be red."

I'm afraid to push the point, so I guess at his shirt, pants, and shoe size while enjoying the checkers showdown happening on my front lawn.

- - - - -

Ron rings the front doorbell the following day, and I show him in. I lead him to the hall bathroom, where I have laid out two towels, a wash cloth, and the clothes and shoes that I bought at Goodwill—a short-sleeve polo shirt, a pair of khakis, a belt, and Dock Siders. "If something doesn't fit, we'll see what Kenneth has that might fit," I say. "Take as long as you like."

He emerges many minutes later, wearing the clothes and shoes and smelling significantly better. Good old Ivory soap. I had purchased new socks and underwear from Sears. Everything else is second-hand but looks great on him. "How do they fit?" I ask.

"Just right. Thank you. How'd you know what size to get?"

"You're about the same height as my husband, only a little thinner, and when you left yesterday, I measured the length of the imprint on the blanket from your shoe. Oh, don't worry," I say when he looks apologetic. "You didn't leave any dirt, just an impression."

"Well, I do thank you. It's been awhile since I had on anything this nice."

"You're welcome. I was happy to do it. This is kind of exciting. Are you ready for that haircut and shave?"

He nods, and I lead him to the kitchen, where Cameron is busy coloring a picture at the kitchen table. "Hi, Mr. Ron. You look very nice."

"Thank you, Miss. What are you coloring?"

"It's a picture of an antique urn. We are visiting my Papa Don tomorrow, and I'm going to take this picture to him. The real vase is in his office, and it is very old. He lets me hold it, even

196

though it's worth a lot of money."

I look at the picture, and she has remembered every detail about that vase. I know my father will be pleased, and I'm a little sorry that I never took the same kind of interest in his artifacts that Cameron does.

"I'm going to give Ron a haircut and a shave, and then we are going to walk with him over to Magda's house and give her a surprise."

"Really?!" Her eyes lit up. "What's the surprise?"

"It's Ron. Ron is the surprise. She has not seen him for a long time."

She accepts this without further questioning and continues to color while I drape a fresh towel around Ron's neck, fastening it with a clothespin. "How short would you like me to cut your hair, Ron? I assume the last time Magda saw you, it was buzzed short, to military regulations."

"You're right. The last time she saw me, I was on leave for a few days. Maybe just a regular haircut? Nothing too short, but not too long. She was never a fan of long hair on a guy," he smiles wryly.

"Will do." As I comb and then snip Ron's hair, we chat. "Where were you stationed when you were in the military?"

"First Fort Bragg, then Germany, then Vietnam."

"If you don't mind my asking, why does Magda believe you aren't alive? You know she goes to the cemetery every Thanksgiving, and she puts flags out in the yard on Memorial Day? Does she think you died in Vietnam?"

"Yeah. That's the way my father wanted it."

"I don't understand. Why would he want his wife, your mother, to think their son, their only child, was dead?"

"I guess he thought that was better than her knowing that her son was dishonorably discharged from the Army. Not for doing anything wrong," he adds immediately, "although I was not a great soldier. But because I'm gay."

For a moment, the air goes out of the room, and my mind returns to the scene between Aleksander and Kenneth in the laundry room. I force myself to keep cutting Ron's hair, to focus on him. "Is that why you live on the streets? Could you not get a job after you were discharged?"

"Essentially." His voice becomes even softer than usual. "The Army declared me unfit for service, and my records say I am not trustworthy. I went to Canada for awhile. Worked odd jobs. But I kept up with the news at the library there. I came back when I saw my father's obituary in the *Atlanta Constitution*. But when I saw how frail my mother had become, I didn't have the heart to ring her doorbell."

"Let me tell you something, first as a mother and then as

198

Magda's neighbor." I stop cutting and step in front of him so we are face-to-face. "If I thought my child was gone forever," I glance at Cameron, who is still intently coloring, although I know she is also listening, "and then she reappeared, I would be elated. I would not care why she disappeared, only that she was back. As for Magda, she is a lot stronger than you give her credit for. She's feisty, that one is."

Ron nods, listening. "I guess I hoped she would recognize me at some point, and then I would know if I was welcome. Now we're about to find out, huh?"

"She will be glad. She will probably also want to fatten you up a bit," I say, smiling, then return to finish the haircut.

"That reminds me. Thank you for the peanut butter crackers and Little Debbie snack cakes."

"You're welcome." I pause, considering how to keep the conversation going, hoping to ease his nerves and mine. "So, um, where do you usually get food? And where do you go when we don't see you around the neighborhood?"

"I'm a volunteer test subject with the CDC. They're doing research on an AIDS vaccine, and since I don't have HIV and I'm not, you know, involved, I'm in their control group. They put me up a few days a month to monitor my health, take massive amounts of blood, feed me, and give me a little money. Ironic, isn't it, considering that's where my father worked and how he felt about me?"

"I don't know what to say except that I think your father was wrong to do what he did." I quickly change the subject, not only out of courtesy to Ron but also because I know Cameron is mentally recording every word spoken. She might not understand it all, but she is listening. "So, do you want me to just trim your beard, or do you want to shave the whole thing off?"

He thinks for a moment, then decides. "I think I'll keep the beard. Just less of it."

So I trim his scraggly beard until it is shorter and has shape. Then I use Kenneth's electric razor to shave his neck. The only sounds we hear are Cameron's coloring and the scissors and razor doing their thing. When I am finished, I encourage Ron to go look at the finished product in the full-length hall mirror. Before I put the tools away, I want to be sure he is satisfied with what he sees.

When he returns, he is smiling. "Thank you. It looks good. Real good. If you'll hand me a broom, I'll sweep up all this hair."

"The hair can wait. Let's get you across the street." And to my little picture-drawing daughter with big ears, I say, "Are you ready to help me take Magda her surprise?"

"Yes!" She takes Ron's hand in hers, and we walk across the street. First, we stop to get Magda's mail, and then we climb her steep driveway together. None of us says very much. I know Ron is nervous, and I believe Cameron has a sense of the importance of what we are about to do. She rings Magda's doorbell, and I hand Ron her mail.

When Magda opens the door, expecting only Cameron and me, her eyes cloud over for a moment as Ron hands her the mail. "Special delivery," I say, and then I take Cameron's hand as she and I head back to our house, leaving Ron and Magda for their special reunion. Before we are even down the front steps, we hear Magda say, "My Junior! Oh, my boy! You are alive; you are home." And then we hear her muffled cries as they embrace.

When we reach the bottom of Magda's driveway, we hear her front door close. I glance up, and her front stoop is empty. Cameron looks up at me and says, "That was a really good surprise, Mommy."

The lump in my throat is so big, I can barely respond. "Yes, my darling. It was."

- - - - -

Ron has moved in with Magda and has already begun putting on some much-needed weight. Would that I could personally donate to that cause! He is also now officially in charge of collecting Magda's mail. Cameron and I take walks, go to the library, and tend to the yard and household chores. And we visit grandparents, always bearing lovingly colored pictures and roses from our bush. The details my child includes in her art make me proud. Where did she learn that? Not from me, that is for sure.

She and I also schedule a visit with Kai at his grandparents' home. While Cameron and Kai play in the Butlers' backyard, Mrs. Butler and I sit under the shade of a patio umbrella and discuss the state's case against Kai's father and how Kai is adjusting to life without either of his parents. In the background, I hear his and Cameron's chatter and their laughter, unweighted by all that has occurred in his life, and that makes me happy. I am equally glad to hear that the case against Gabe appears to be so solid that he will likely plead guilty and spare the Butlers the agony of sitting through a trial. Whether or not we get Kai and Cameron together again, I will leave up to Mrs. Butler. Our presence might be a too-sad reminder of Willow. As we leave, I make some comment about her calling me if she'd like to schedule another play date. On our way home, I spot a new Joe loves Margaret art pop-up. It looks hastily constructed, and I imagine Joe created it mostly as an act of defiance rather than an homage to his wife and family. Since it is on city property, I am also reasonably certain it will be dismantled in a matter of days. Poor Joe. Poor Margaret. Poor Baby Makes Three. How dare the city of Atlanta continue to erase their testament of love for one another? What harm is Joe's art doing to a city that is experiencing such unrest? Aren't the wounds of Vietnam and racial tension enough? Rather than obsess over this travesty, though, I hurry us home. Cameron and I have an afternoon snack planned with Ron, and he is bringing Magda. This will be her first opportunity to see our azalea and rose bushes up close, and I am excited to show her how well they are faring. And then, just like that, summer is over all too quickly.

- - - - -

Another school year begins. I have five ESOL classes and one planning period. I have never before had the luxury of a planning period, and I have fantasies of getting far ahead of my students rather than my typical one step ahead. Cameron is in the third grade, and her teacher, Mrs. Samples, seems to understand that she is to keep our daughter challenged, maybe even a little off balance. If Cameron finishes a reading assignment or a worksheet before her peers, Mrs. Samples will give her more work to do. That, or ask Cameron to work one-on-one with another student. So far, we have heard no complaints from our daughter when we all do a daily debrief at the dinner table.

- - - - -

I am amazed at our capacity to use our ingenuity to make life better for our fellow humans. Not only is there a man in Salt Lake City celebrating Christmas with an artificial heart beating in his chest, but Kenneth has, once again, been asked to go to Africa, this time for the Carter Center. They need his infrastructure analysis of a few key projects in a few key countries. He is scheduled to fly out in early January. I am so proud of my engineer husband and his expertise. What an asset he is to Atlanta and to the worthwhile projects being undertaken by our former president! I am sure Mema Fields absolutely gloats when sharing the accomplishments of her son at her monthly Junior League meetings. I wonder what, if anything, she says about me.

Chapter Nine: 1983

KENNETH FLIES OUT first to Ghana, with his objective to be sure the infrastructure is in place for their access to healthcare and for fair elections to be conducted. He also has stops scheduled in Nigeria and Cameroon for other infrastructure assessments. How great it will be for him to check on the condition of some of his projects while we were in the Peace Corps! Part of his duties then were to train the locals in upkeep and making potential improvements. I have packed gifts for him to give to some of our former Cameroonian neighbors. Cameron has, once again, requested he bring home a baby elephant. I think this silliness has now become part of our family banter, and I enjoy listening to her exchange with Kenneth and his mock seriousness about the logistics of bringing an elephant back with him on the airplane. Her response is so witty: "But she's waiting for you and she's already packed her trunk." His response is to tickle her and soon we are all laughing.

- - - - -

Carlisle now has a permanent office at Bass, even though his responsibilities are to all schools in the Atlanta City Schools that house ESOL programs. Bass is, for him, home base, and this means I get to speak with him at least once a week. Occasionally we visit during my planning period, but more days than not, Tate joins me for tutoring. This is by arrangement with the guidance counselor, Ms. Hisley. Rather than make him sit through yet another class where he struggles to keep up, he brings his books and schoolwork to my classroom, eating his lunch while we talk through his assignments. I am struck by his native intelligence for "God's critters," accompanied by his inability to form a logical paragraph on his own. Reading, writing, and arithmetic are not just labors for him, they are torture. I am sure when he was deprived of oxygen at birth, some of the wiring in his brain got crossed. Or erased. The only way I know to help him, and this is with the school's consent, is to read out loud to him from his textbooks and then have him talk about what the reading means to him. This he can do. He does have ideas, however primitive they may sound to someone who doesn't know the depth of his soul. Then I have him write down those key ideas, one per line of notebook paper. After that, he cuts each idea from the paper and rearranges them in an order that seems logical to him. Then I ask questions, I push him for more details—usually "what else?" I challenge him to state what those ideas remind him of—anything to help him connect dots. I make suggestions, as well—"maybe you should write that down, too." And then he rearranges those ideas again and transfers the words, as connected as they can be, onto a clean sheet of paper to turn in for a grade. All the while, I know he will likely never earn high marks, he will probably fail most of his tests, and he'd much rather be outside. But I also have to believe the workout for his brain is ultimately doing some good. I must talk to Nell about what plans they have for Tate after high school, if he can, indeed, complete high school. Maybe Grant Park Zoo needs a critter sitter. Tate would excel at that.

On the days Carlisle and I do get to chat, we talk about many things, not just school and students and curriculum. I would go so far as to say we are becoming friends, and this sits well with me. Ever since Willow began distancing herself from me —which I now understand was to protect both of us—I have missed having a girlfriend. I would never say this to Carlisle, but he is the closest thing I have to a girlfriend. What an odd thing to think. Still, it's a comfort to me. **He** is a comfort to me.

- - - - -

Kenneth returns from his Africa trip, not with a baby elephant, but with flower garlands he bought off the Hare Krishnas at the Atlanta airport. So much for African souvenirs. Cameron is so thrilled with her gift, though, she wears it to school the next day, purposefully selecting clothes with colors that complement the flowers. And, although Kenneth is jet-lagged, he goes to work the next day and then resumes his chess club meetings. An old pattern re-emerges, including his avoidance of talking about us, his feelings, why he cannot just invite a friend over to the house to play chess once in awhile. After I work all day at Bass, I still need to devote time in the evenings to prepare for upcoming lessons. When I add in cooking dinner, making everyone's lunches for the next day, throwing a load of towels in the wash, and getting Cameron ready for bed, I resent his absence and he knows it. So he just doesn't discuss it. Instead, he announces his plan to go out after dinner. I fantasize about doing the same some evening and seeing his reaction, but if he calls my bluff, I'm sunk. I must be at home to get ready for the next day. If his precious chess club met only on Friday night or on a Sunday afternoon, I'd feel differently about his involvement, which looks more like an addiction to me. But they meet several nights a week. I don't care that they are preparing for a big tournament and I don't care that he is also teaching Cameron how to play. I care about a more equitable division of labor at home. But when I bring it up, he just listens to me rant, stone-faced, and he doesn't respond, doesn't react. And nothing changes. I am going to recommend to him that we go for marital counseling. I wonder if he will keep that poker face when I do, or if there will be any expression of emotion, of caring about the state of our marriage.

- - - - -

We have a nine-year-old. Cameron is a badge-earning, cookie-selling Junior Girl Scout. Kenneth teases her about being a Girl Sprout, which seems to get under her skin. She is quite serious about her accomplishments. When she takes offense at being called a Girl Sprout, or to selling Girl Sprout cookies, he tries to cajole her into laughing, but she holds her ground. Good for her! Maybe I should try his teasing techniques to get him to talk about this most recent episode of marital doldrums, our drifting apart again.

Magda and Ron have bought one box of each kind of cookie. I ask Magda if having them in the house is too much temptation for her, given her diabetes, and she says they are not. "I take blood sugar every morning and every night. No cookies for me." Is it foolish to wish I could have diabetes— just for a few months, so I can have a medical reason to avoid my favorite, Thin Mints? Or should I just admit that a sugar monster lives inside me? I have twinges of guilt when I see photographs and news reports of famine in Ethiopia. I have too much and they don't have enough, and it is not due to any merit on my part but, rather, my good fortune to be born here in Atlanta to two caring parents who had the means to keep me alive. My obsession with food is even more complicated by the recent death of Karen Carpenter. I have such a mix of emotions about anorexia. I eat too much; she ate too little—on purpose. Was she stronger than I? I look at my child and wonder what mixed messages she receives about her body and about food and about will power.

- - - - -

Kenneth has taken to reading the *Atlanta Journal* in the kitchen while I prepare dinner. Maybe this is his response to my request that we spend more time together. We are certainly in the same room, and he does occasionally talk about an article he is reading, and sometimes we discuss the current events in our city, our country, the world. Maybe this is how Kenneth really does define intimacy and maybe I should not complain. And maybe after that stupid chess tournament is over, he will stay home more evenings. I will hold off on broaching the idea of couples counseling until I see if my maybes are warranted.

Suddenly Kenneth gasps, and I see a look on his face that I rarely see. It is shock mingled with raw grief. "What is it?" I ask.

He is speechless for the longest time, and I wait, spatula in hand, watching him, waiting for him to compose himself. He points at the newspaper and whispers, "He's dead. Roger Isely is dead."

"Who is Roger Isely? A co-worker?" I know the names of most of his colleagues. This is a name I do not recognize.

"Roger is—was—in the chess club." Kenneth's Adam's apple bobs up and down as he tries to control his emotions. "I knew he'd been sick with a bad cough, but now he's dead. The **Journal** says he had cancer. He never told me he had cancer. I didn't know. He was only 40."

"I'm so sorry. Was he married? Did he have children?"

"No, he never married." Then, "I need to call someone in the club and find out what they know."

Kenneth steps out of the kitchen, making his phone call in our bedroom instead. When he returns, he stands in the doorway, ashen. I ask, "What did you learn? Will there be a funeral?"

"He had sarcoidosis."

It takes a moment for me to reach into my memory bank and pull that term up on a mental index card. The only time I have heard of sarcoidosis is in relation to patients with AIDS. "Kenneth, was Roger a homosexual? Did he have AIDS?"

Kenneth looks stricken, almost as if I've accused him. "I don't know if he had AIDS, and I don't typically ask someone if they're gay or not," he says, defensively.

"Don't get mad at me. I just never knew about sarcoidosis until we started hearing about AIDS."

"And what if he **was** gay? What if he did have AIDS? So what?"

If only he had this same passion in his voice when talking about us. Still, he has just lost a friend, so I decide to take the high road. "Look, I'm sorry you lost your friend. And I didn't mean anything with my questions. Come here." Kenneth steps over to where I am standing, and I wrap my arms around him. At first he is stiff, but in a few moments, I feel his body soften as he is wracked with sobbing. This tender moment uncoils so many conflicting emotions inside of me, I can barely catalog them as they arrive. I am touched; I am confused; I feel victorious that we are sharing something that feels genuine, that I have asked for, pleaded for; but I am also resentful that this moment was initiated by a friend in Kenneth's life that I didn't even know existed. I continue to hold Kenneth while he weeps, letting his tears soak the front of my shirt, while my feelings bounce off of one another.

Then Kenneth pulls away. His eyes are red and his nose is running. "I'm not hungry, Mer. I think I'm just going to go early to the chess club and buy a round of beers in Roger's memory. I'll go tell Cameron that I'm not eating dinner here tonight."

And before I can respond, he leaves the kitchen, and I, too, am suddenly not hungry.

- - - - -

Carlisle notices my vacant stare and calls me on it. "Where were you just now?" I wind up sharing with him my puzzlement over my husband's moods, his inability to be intimate with me but his weeping over Roger Isely's death. I try so hard not to cry, but the pent-up tears of confusion, frustration, and self-pity win and, before long, I am a mess. Mascara is streaming down my cheeks and my eyes are puffy and my nose is dripping. Carlisle takes me in his arms and pats my back, saying nothing except, "there, there, now." When I have finished crying, despite my resolve not to say so,

I tell him he is the closest thing I have to a girlfriend. He responds with a twinkle in his eye, laughing, "Good. I'm glad," he says. "I consider that one of the highest compliments I've ever been given." How wonderful is that? Out of this dam-burst, I discover that I have a confidant, a friend, a true intimate. And while it is not the person who I most in the world want it to be, my heart lifts. I will not look this gift horse in the mouth.

- - - - -

Another school year is, as they say, in the books. How apropos. My ESOL students have excelled. Nasim, Fatima, Gerardo, Hieu, and Felipe are graduating, and all five are going on to college. I could not be more proud of them if I had given birth to them. Tate has made great strides in his reading comprehension and his writing, but he still lags far behind his peers. The school, however, decides to promote him to the 11th grade. He repeated several grades in elementary school, so he is likely the only 19-year-old rising junior. I don't mind that he has been socially promoted, though. He is a hard worker and he is so earnest, and we have no illusion that we are preparing him for college. He and Nell stop by the week of post-planning to give me a little gift and to thank me for helping him. Nell has baked banana bread and Tate has drawn a picture of one of his pet bunnies. The drawing is very detailed, so much so, I will frame it and hang it in my classroom next school year. I never knew he could draw. Why did I not know that? Why have I not tried to find out more about him outside the world of academic achievement? I have been so intent on helping him catch up and learn, I have ignored the fact that he might have other talents, maybe even marketable ones. I will worry less about Tate's future now. He will make his way in the world with the gifts that he has. Thank you, Tate, for schooling this teacher.

- - - - -

Weekly picnics in our backyard or on our front lawn with Ron and Magda have become a regular event for Cameron and me. Ron plays checkers or chess with Cameron while Magda continues to coach me through plant care. Then Ron and I talk books while Cameron and Magda talk about the badges Cameron is working on. Magda offers to help Cameron with her flower badge and her new cuisines badge. They will make golabki, or cabbage rolls, together for the new cuisines badge, and Magda has a book of flowers she has loaned Cameron. She quizzes Cameron each week on her flower knowledge, and I listen with one ear to their conversation while Ron and I discuss what each of us is currently reading.

Kenneth travels more than usual for the Carter Center to follow up on some of their projects in Africa. The City of Atlanta is very understanding in letting him use his vacation time to make these worthwhile trips, but that also means he does not have enough leave accrued for us to take a family vacation. Instead, Cameron and I settle into a routine of visits to grandparents, trips to the library and to museums and the zoo, and our weekly picnics with Ron and Magda. I rather enjoy the pace of our summer, and I am reconciled to the demands on Kenneth's expertise, with the understanding that these commitments will not be long-term. We have even discussed some of the places where we might go next summer.

When Kenneth returns from one of his trips in late July, Cameron and I have a surprise waiting for him. We have scheduled a family movie night at the drive-in on Moreland Avenue. We pick up a pizza on our way to see **Lady and the Tramp**. Cameron sits between us, transfixed, as we enjoy a night out together as a family. Cameron falls asleep in the car on the way home. The love story between Lady and Tramp has put me in the mood, and the fact that our child is sleeping gives me hope that Kenneth and I can create a human reenactment of the restaurant scene, minus the mutual spaghetti noodle.

Kenneth carries Cameron to bed while I change into my pajamas and open a bottle of wine, pouring two glasses. As I walk into the living room to give him his glass, he is setting up his chess board. I hand him his glass and ask, coyly, "Hiya, Tramp, would you be interested in playing a different game just now?"

Kenneth looks up, distracted, his mind obviously already on his opening move. **Opening move!** I think, and, inspired, I place myself between him and the board, sitting on his lap.

"Uh, Mer," he tries to keep the irritation from his voice, "not tonight."

Rather than cajole him into foregoing a precious practice round of chess, I simply get up and take my glass to the bedroom. **Coyness is wasted on him**, I fume. **Maybe I need to dress like a queen chess piece instead.** Before I get to our bedroom, I pass by the hall mirror and get a good look at myself in my so-called pajamas, a floppy t-shirt and a pair of ragged panties. Shame engulfs me. **I don't blame him. I wouldn't make love to me, either.** And I immediately start plans for a new diet plus a trip to Rich's for a real nightgown.

- - - - -

I was right about the City of Atlanta removing the newest Joe loves Margaret art installation, but no sooner have they taken it down than, several blocks down, Joe has erected another testament to his devotion. Go, Joe! I do hope Margaret knows how incredibly fortunate she is to have Joe display his love so publicly. And I do hope Joe displays his love as emphatically, with such determination, in private. I would settle for some private devotion of my own, despite the fact that my most recent diet is not working. Although, if I'm to be honest, I have not been sticking with it too well. When Kenneth rebuffed my attempt to lure him into the bedroom, wearing my new nightgown, I think I decided that Girl Scout cookies love me more than he does. And just maybe, the sentiment is mutual.

- - - - -

Another school year begins, and I am excited to be returning to the classroom. Once again, Carlisle and Dr. Hendricks, the principal, have made certain that I have a planning period, which is a real gift this year. I have more new students than ever, and they are from nearly everywhere—Cuba, Poland, China, Ethiopia, Honduras, Czechoslovakia, Romania, Vietnam, Senegal, oh, everywhere! I have a feeling I will be mere seconds ahead of them this year as I plan learning activities for such a variety of locations, at all levels of learning the English language. I also have a feeling they are more nervous and excited than I am, and I would do well to remember this.

Cameron, once again, is in the thrall of her teacher, Mr. Edwards. That's right. She has a male teacher for fourth grade. Mr. Edwards is 32 years old, married, with one child, a three-year-old daughter, and he is a deacon at Ebenezer Baptist Church. I learn all of this in a letter he sends home the first day of class. My guess is this is his peremptory effort to allow any parents uncomfortable with their child's teacher assignment the opportunity to request a change. I wonder if Horrible Headlee's child, Collier, is in Mr. Edwards' class and, if so, if she has raised a ruckus about her precious child being taught by **that man**. I, for one, am thrilled that Cameron has a male teacher, and that he is black thrills me even more. She is being granted an opportunity that I was not in elementary school. Kudos to Euclid for expanding the educational horizons of their students and parents!

- - - - -

Tate continues to visit my classroom a few days each week for tutoring. I now look for opportunities to help him make connections between his school work and his love for animals and art. It is a stretch sometimes, but more often than not, if he can begin drawing what he understands about new concepts rather than speaking or writing about them, we can then talk through those concepts, adding in details as we go. I have even asked some of his teachers to allow Tate to sit through one or two of my ESOL classes each week so that he can help me by sketching out explanations to some of my students' most challenging concepts. His sketches become part of the instructional materials I have put on my back bulletin board. For example, he has drawn for my students the step-by-step process of getting on a MARTA bus, paying the fare, and then going through the turnstile of a MARTA train station, transferring to a MARTA train to get to their final destination. We often use Lenox Square as our example destination. The simple acts we Atlantans take for granted are extremely puzzling to so many others and, once Tate has intuited their confusion, he seems to naturally know how to demystify and simplify those things.

As we near the holidays, I have an idea of another way Tate can help me, and that I might also be able to help him. I ask him if he would like to custom-make Christmas cards for me to give to coworkers. I offer to pay him for his services. Secretly, I hope my colleagues will be so pleased with the cards that they will also consider asking Tate to design and create cards for them, and this will provide him with a small cottage industry after he graduates high school. Tate and I discuss a few design ideas and then he returns the next day with an elaborate drawing of a cardinal perched on an evergreen branch. It is exquisite, and I tell his so, having to explain to him what exquisite means. Tate adds this new word to his vocabulary and I ask him to put the definition in his own words. His definition is **more perty than ever-day perty**, and it takes my mind a split-second to translate—more pretty than everyday pretty. What an exquisite definition.

The following Monday, Tate shows me what he has done with his drawing. He has carved the reverse image of the cardinal, as well as SAMTSIRHC YRREM—no small feat for someone who can barely write words in forward order! —on to a wood block. He has then run a thin layer of red paint over the carving and stamped rectangles of high rag content paper with the image. Once the paint has dried, he has folded the rectangle into cards. They are, well, exquisite. They take my breath away. I ask Tate how much money he spent on the materials and how much time he spent on the project. As always, I try to weave in some sort of learning opportunity, today's being math. We sit down with a piece of scratch paper to determine how much he should charge for his work. Tate low-balls his hourly rate and so I send him, with a note from me, to the librarian, to help Tate research how much artists charge for work done on commission. Tate returns the next day, sheepishly quoting me a rate that seems more fair to me, but obviously seems outrageous to him. I write him a check for fifty dollars more than he asks for and encourage him to open a checking account for, what I hope, will soon be a fledgling business. In my card to Nell, which I hand-deliver to her in the cafeteria, I include a separate note with my encouragement for Tate to consider making his living from his art. I even encourage Nell and her husband to coach Tate through designing a flyer for us to post in the teachers' break room, advertising Tate's services. The flyer, I say, should mention such things as custom greeting cards, family pet portraits, and the like. And it is in this optimistic mood that I enter the holidays.

Chapter Ten: 1984

THIS YEAR IS flying by. I can barely keep up with my job and my family, not to mention current events. But I do try to be aware of what is happening so that I can help my child and my students better understand the world in which they live. They understand things like the L.A. Raiders winning the Super Bowl, and they are aware of the hoopla around the movie **Amadeus**, even if they are not particularly interested in classical music, but explaining to them the break-up of the Bell telephone monopoly is difficult. I commission Tate to help me with my students. I assume that if I can explain to him in a way that helps him grasp the essence and the implications of a monopoly, as well as the implications of that monopoly being dismantled, he can then translate that meaning into one of his drawings. What he draws is a playground bully in the form of a very outsized telephone, the handset being the bully's bulky torso. And, for perspective, there are a few small, cowering phones on the periphery of the playground. In the next two panels, Uncle Sam is spinning the behemoth phone around by the cord, shaking loose smaller phones within it, until the playground is populated with lots of equal-sized telephones, all grinning and no longer afraid. It's enough of a start, and I am appreciative of his rudimentary pictorial explanation.

- - - - -

Cameron is ten years old, and full of sass and smarts. I am grateful she still likes school and enjoys reading. What I am not grateful for is her attitude that she knows better than me about almost everything. She debates nearly everything I say. If I like a television show, she does not. If I want her to try a new food, like cauliflower, she already knows she will hate it. If I tell her to wear a sweater to school, she rolls her eyes and tells me it's not even chilly outside. I look to Kenneth to back me, which he does if he's around. And then the irritating part is, if he says so, Cameron relents without argument. If he has already left or is not in the same part of the house, words between my daughter and me quickly escalate. On the one hand, I'm glad my daughter is so strong-minded, but on the other hand, I want her to respect my authority. I wish Dr. Spock made house calls.

- - - - -

How is it already summer? The school year is over and Walter Mondale will run for President of the United States against Ronald Reagan. No sooner has he sewn up the nomination than my parents' world begins to fray. Dad is, once again, misplacing things but, this time, Mom says it's as if he is hiding specific items from some unknown intruder. So, not only his billfold but also his checkbook go temporarily missing. These episodes seem to come in spurts. Mom reports that Dad acts furtive and disoriented for awhile, then returns to his typical gregarious, organized self. Cameron and I step up our visits, especially on the days when Mom is working. At least on those days, Cameron remains charming and polite. And Papa Don is always kind and witty toward Cameron and me, engaging us in conversation, but Mom tells me on the sly that, occasionally, when she confronts him about his forgetfulness, he becomes defensive. This does not sound like my father, and I ache for Mom as she tries to determine what to do. She has mentioned retiring early so she can keep a closer eye on him; she has also mentioned his retiring, which he adamantly refuses to discuss. She feels stuck, and I do, too, in how to be the daughter they both need. Oh, Aging, you can sometimes be so cruel. You can turn sweet children into moody preteens and detail-oriented fathers into forgetful ones.

- - - - -

Another school year begins. Cameron, now in fifth grade, rides her bike to and from school, getting home before we do. There will be no more Grandparent-on-Duty rotation. She has a checklist of things she is to do after she gets home, including locking the door once inside and starting on homework. With Ron and Magda right across the street, available in case there's an emergency, Kenneth and I are glad to let Cameron spread her independence wings in this way.

My classroom is, once again, a study in United Nations diplomacy and cultural understanding. I swear, I learn more from my students than they do from me. And they are so supportive of each other, which makes my heart glad. Another thing that makes my heart glad is that Carlisle has taken a full-time teaching job at Bass. He will be teaching Spanish and French, and I will be tapping into his expertise more often on behalf of my Spanish- and French-speaking students. His lunch period is not the same as mine, but now that Cameron can get herself home from school, there are many days Carlisle and I linger over a cup of herbal tea after the last bell. I truly do not understand why that man is not already married. He is such a kind soul, with a clever sense of humor and boundless patience.

School has been in session for only a few weeks when Jorge begins coming to class late or not at all. My students are typically so diligent; this behavior distresses me. Is he in a restroom somewhere on campus smoking weed? Is he roaming around Little Five Points, getting into trouble? Is he so bored in class that he feels he can skip and still stay current on his assignments? It's such an affront to me that he seems not to value his ESOL lessons that I determine to call him on it the next time he attends. When I do confront him, I am distressed to learn his reason for so many tardies and absences. Jorge is the oldest of five children, the only one in high school, and the only one old enough to drive. Neither of his parents speak much English. His father, a custodian at Piedmont Hospital, has cancer and has had to cut back on his work hours because of his chemotherapy regimen. His mother cleans houses. They have one car. On chemo days, after they get the younger ones off to school, Jorge drops his mother off at whatever house she is cleaning, then takes his father to his treatment, translating for his father and the medical staff. When the chemo treatment is over, Jorge drives his father home, gets him settled, then goes to where his mother is, who then drives Jorge to school before driving herself back to work. When the school day is over, Jorge makes sure his siblings have all gotten off their buses and home safely, and he helps them with their studies until their mother gets home to start cooking supper. It just never occurred to Jorge to write an absence note and have one of his parents sign it for him to hand in at the front office. I tell him that he needs to start checking in at the front office when he's late to school or has to miss an entire day, and that I will meet with him outside of class as much as he needs to help him catch up. I also tell him what a good son he is and how proud his parents must be of him. I know I would be. I also know I need to stop complaining about anything in my life. Like I said, I learn far more from my students than they'll ever learn from me.

- - - - -

Joe still loves Margaret. The newest art installation is in the back of the Sevananda parking lot. I wonder if they have given him permission to profess his devotion; I wonder if Joe and Margaret and Baby Makes Three shop at Sevananda and, if so, if I've ever seen them there. I also wonder if Margaret realizes how special it is to have her husband go to such lengths to make his public declarations. I hope so. Joe seems like a spectacular guy to be so determined to tell the world about his beloved. And maybe, just maybe, this installation will get to stay so that Joe and Margaret and Baby Makes Three's followers can be kept up to date on the latest developments in their lives.

- - - - -

A week before Thanksgiving, Magda falls and breaks her hip. Every morning as I leave for Bass, I see Ron back Magda's purple Mercedes down their driveway, heading to Emory Hospital to spend the day with her. Ron promises to keep us posted on her recovery and to let us know when we may visit her. And even though Cameron can be so surly at times, her tender side is still evident in the many pictures she colors for Ron to take with him on his visits. It does my heart good to know that, beneath all that sass and argumentativeness, my sweet child is still there.

Meanwhile, on the heels of Reagan's re-election, I have the dubious honor of trying to help my students decode what "Reaganomics" means. I don't even try to get Tate's help with this because I am not sure I understand it myself. If anything is trickling down, I doubt many of my students and their families are getting even remotely damp.

- - - - -

Magda is now at Emory Rehabilitation Center. She has a new

hip but the same old plucky attitude. When Cameron and I visit, she gripes about the food and the fact that her therapist makes her miss her program and, instead, get in the pool to exercise. "I am not fish," she scowls. Ron winks at us over his mother's head; we take her crotchety behavior as a good sign, a sign that she feels well enough to express her opinions. We are all hopeful that she will be home in time for Christmas.

Chapter Eleven: 1985

MAGDA IS FINALLY home. Before she is discharged, Cameron and I scrub and dust her home from front to back while Ron installs grab bars in the bathrooms. Since she is not able to walk steadily without a walker, she is discharged only with the understanding that her home must be made ready for a diabetic woman with a hip replacement who gets around on a walker. All of her throw rugs are gone, and Ron has also seen to it that a ramp leads from the carport to her back door. To help celebrate her return, we have prepared many of her favorite dishes. Cameron's Girl Scout badge in cooking finally pays off. And Ron will have leftovers galore to reheat. Despite her spunkiness, she looks awfully frail and gaunt. They have both lost weight during her hospital stay. I cannot say the same.

Magda looks exhausted after our celebratory meal, so Cameron and I leave to allow her to rest and so that she and Ron can begin figuring out what their new normal will be. As we walk back home, Cameron turns to me and asks, "She'll be okay, won't she?" And my heart cracks a little, not only because my tender-hearted child is still evident but also because I, too, wonder how much longer we will have Magda with us.

- - - - -

My students and I spend most of January learning about sports and how American football is alike and different from what the rest of the world calls football, or what we call soccer. Why did I not think of this grand lesson in compare and contrast before now? We conclude our study with a Super Bowl party of our own on the Friday afternoon before the big event. My students have been given permission to spend the last period of the day with me. My classroom is decorated, there are typical Super Bowl snacks, and my students vote on which team they think will win. The student who predicts the outcome and comes closest to the final score wins a special prize on the Monday following the game. The boys are most distressed when Hosne, a girl new to the US this year from Bangladesh and rather indifferent to sports, wins by predicting the 49ers will defeat the Dolphins 35 to 17. The final score is 38 to 16, and none of the boys are even close. I hope they cannot read my expression as I hand her a box of colored pencils, an English dictionary, and a new spiral-bound notebook, for I am privately gloating.

- - - - -

We have an 11-year-old. Cameron has one toehold in the world of adolescence and one foot still planted in childhood.

I sometimes think the wars she wages with me over such insignificant things as what shoes she should wear are really evidence of the hormonal wars raging inside her and are evidence of her confusion over the tug to remain a guileless, wide-eyed child or become a world-weary young woman. If anyone can figure out how to do both and be both, it will be this one, for she remains one of the smartest kids I've ever known. I say that knowing it smacks of parental pride and bias, but I also know it to be true, and I would acknowledge that truth about anyone else's child if I knew it to be so.

- - - - -

Current events provide yet another opportunity for my students to learn about our language and culture. With the advent of New Coke, I hold a taste test in each of my classes and assign them a paragraph describing each drink: regular Coke, New Coke, and Pepsi. They are permitted to use a dictionary to search for adjectives, and they are allowed to work with a partner. I simply want them to express their opinions and to do so in grammatically correct form, exploring the myriad ways to say "delicious" or "nasty. I, for one, as a native Atlantan, think Pepsi tastes medicinal and any Coke product is divine.

- - - - -

Another school year is nearly over, and my beloved father is once again exhibiting curious behavior. Mom is concerned enough to take a leave of absence from her job and to let the

Dean at Emory know my dad will not be finishing out the quarter. This most recent set of behaviors has him again staring at squiggles of tar on one of the streets near their neighborhood, uttering, this time, such strange statements as, "What do they want?" or "They've got it all wrong," or "What are my instructions?"

Here is what Mom has been able to piece together so far. A road crew recently repaired some cracks on Harold Avenue, and a resident there was so alarmed at Dad's anguished and nonsensical statements that she called the police. Mom is not only shocked that Dad has taken to crossing Ponce de Leon on his daily walks, she cannot explain to the officer who brings Dad home what he might be referring to. So, while he is still in his agitated state, she and Dad get in her car, and she drives to Harold Avenue. They park on the side of the road and get out. Dad is immediately drawn to those tar squiggles again, stooping down to examine them as if they were a new piece he was putting on display at the Carlos Museum. He mutters; he frets; he walks around to the other side and squats down again, examining. Mom coaxes Dad into the car and, before she starts the engine, asks him what is going on in his mind. Dad's response sends chills up her spine and, as she later relates the story to me, mine as well. "If I told you, I would have to eliminate you."

That afternoon, while Dad is napping, Mom begins looking through all of his private papers in his home study. She finds scribbles that look to her like Arabic, which does not surprise her, as this is his academic area of expertise. And then it dawns on her that the pages with the scribbles look like the tar squiggles. Dad has been trying to "read" the road repairs! No wonder he is confused. This does not, however, explain his reaction to them or his answer to Mom's question earlier that day.

When Dad wakes from his nap, he's himself again and has very little recall of his walk earlier that morning. Sensing the time is right, Mom asks him for details about his travels to Egypt, his studies of the Ptolemaic Era, his specialty, and what he remembers about those days before they met. And for the next few hours, he relives his life, as he often refers to it, Before Jo. Once they started dating, all of his trips ended, and any acquisitions were handled by other antiquities dealers. Mom presses for more details, like who he associated with over there, where he stayed, who he stayed with, and what he did when he wasn't acquiring or viewing antiquities. At this point, Dad gets cagey, so Mom lets it rest.

Determined to make sense out of his bizarre behavior and his reaction to her probing questions, Mom gains access to his office at Emory under the guise of taking home some of his books and papers. And it is there that she makes her most shocking discovery. From what she can tell reading a journal he has marked In Case of Emergency, the State Department asked Dad to be a courier on his many trips abroad, his cover being that he was legitimately there to study and to purchase Egyptian artifacts. Apparently, once he fell in love with Mom, he stopped traveling abroad. He did not want to have to refuse the US's "request" to carry documents back and forth—documents that, while he may not have known what they contained, he knew were worth killing over. What an extraordinary secret he has carried all these years! On top of this, Mom must now decide what sort of medical treatment to seek on Dad's behalf, especially since this secret is so old and nobody should have to die for uncovering it. What else don't we know about the people we love?

- - - - -

Kenneth's consulting money allows us to take a family vacation. I am somewhat reluctant to leave Mom and Dad, but she assures me all is under control. There have been no more bizarre episodes recently, and Dad is his old self. Once again, I do not know if Mom is being completely honest with me, protecting me from her deeper worries, or if she genuinely believes all is okay for now. I can only assume she wonders, as I do, not if another episode will occur, but when. Still, she practically begs us not to stick around Atlanta on their behalf. And so, we spend a glorious week at Jekyll Island, swimming, beach-combing, reading, relaxing, eating seafood, and playing board games and card games after sunset. I enter the new school year more relaxed than I have been in a long time.

- - - - -

Cameron is in the sixth grade at Inman Middle School. I tell her that when her dad and I were in sixth grade, it was a part of the elementary school, and that our high school started in eighth grade. I immediately become ancient in her sight, and she looks at me as if I have suddenly sprouted a dowager's hump. She is also no longer permitted to ride her bike to and from school, as it is too far away. We are making her ride the dreaded "cheese wagon" instead. Most days, Kenneth can drop her off at school in the morning, so she only has to ride it once a day. Still, she resents this loss of freedom, even though she still has unsupervised time at home in the afternoons. I will share with her my own school bus stories another time, lest she believe her parents are actually aliens.

As for me, I still have many of the same students from last year, plus a crop of new ones. My heart aches to hear the stories of deprivation and war that have driven many families to migrate to the US. And then, when I hear Atlantans, including Kenneth's parents, speak disparagingly of these brave travelers, I have to restrain myself to keep my temper and control my tongue. I vow to use my energy to help my students find their way in a strange culture, to help them prove to the naysayers that they have a genuine right to the same things we take for granted: food, shelter, work, health, peace, and safety.

- - - - -

Am I the only person in the world who did not know one of the most famous actors was probably a homosexual? Now that this dashing actor has died, his private life has become public fodder. I am by turns fascinated and offended by reporters' assumptions that they may now reveal to an eager public the details of his life beyond the camera lens. And yet, what does it say about me that I read them, as if I personally knew him and he kept secrets from me? He wasn't married, and he didn't have children, so I honestly don't care that he preferred men. I'm not sure I would have said that before getting to know dear Ron. That said, he was a good actor. I completely believed every leading man's performance opposite his lady love.

– – – – –

Oh, my hormonal daughter, how you torment me. One moment you are open and sweet, giggling with me about something we both find amusing, and the next moment you treat me as if I am the only thing between you and the pot of gold at the end of your rainbow. Your sharp words and your disdain for all things maternal cut me deeply. We are looking at the latest addition to the Joe loves Margaret art installation behind Sevananda, depicting their adoption of a kitten, and we are enjoying Joe's delightful depiction of the kitten—its ball of yarn head and pine-straw-stuffed onesie body—when suddenly, your lip curls into a sneer and the laughter abruptly stops. Did you see a school pal out of the corner of your eye and fear that being seen enjoying your mother's company would be deemed uncool? Did I say something? Do something? Where did you go, my little girl, who used to hang on every word I said? And why won't you answer my questions about what's bothering you? I think I would rather hear your angry words than be completely shut out by your icy silence.

- - - - -

When Kenneth goes out this morning to get our Sunday edition of the *Atlanta Journal*, he informs me there is an ambulance in Magda's driveway. I quickly pull on a pair of jeans, put a sweatshirt over my nightgown, and run across the street, still in my slippers. There are no emergency lights running on the ambulance, but Magda's front door is wide open. I poke my head in and call, "Ron? It's Meredith. Is everything okay?"

I step into Magda's living room as the paramedics are wheeling a gurney out her back door, down the ramp Ron installed earlier this year. He is sitting at the kitchen table, his head in his hands. I pull up a chair and sit beside him, somehow knowing what he'll tell me.

"She's gone," he states simply. "I went in to get her up for breakfast, and she was ice cold. They're taking her to the hospital to be pronounced, but I know she's been dead for hours."

The lump in my throat makes it difficult for me to speak. "I'm so sorry." I put my hand on his shoulder. "I am so, so sorry."

Ron nods. "I just wish she hadn't died alone. I wish I'd been with her."

As he says this, Cameron, still in her pajamas and barefooted, runs into the kitchen, her eyes wild. "What's happening?"

I look up at her, and she instantly knows. Cameron covers her face with her hands and slumps into the chair beside me. I keep one hand on Ron's shoulder and put my other hand on Cameron's head, but she pulls away, making it clear to me that she will have nothing to do with my comfort at the moment. The only sound in the kitchen is our sniffling. After a few minutes, Cameron stands, bends over to kiss Ron on the cheek, and leaves. She doesn't acknowledge me on her way out.

- - - - -

Ron has decided to have a graveside service. Magda will be buried next to her husband, Ron, Sr. Her funeral is held on a beautiful late November afternoon. The sky is clear, and the temperature is mild enough that we are comfortable in long sleeves and sweaters. We can hear birds chirping in the trees, and the smell of fallen oak leaves reminds me of my mother's White Shoulders cologne.

Kenneth, Cameron, and I sit beside Ron. A few of Ron Sr.'s old CDC colleagues are there, as well as the woman who faithfully cuts Magda's hair every eight weeks. A few of the Emory Rehabilitation Center staff are there, too, along with the minister the funeral home contacted about conducting the ceremony. Ron has asked that the ceremony be kept brief and informal and that anyone who wishes to say a few words be allowed the opportunity before Magda's casket is lowered into the ground.

The minister, the kindly young Rev. Howell, who recently graduated from Candler School of Theology, begins by thanking us all for being there. He very honestly admits he did not know the deceased, but that he and Ron have spent some time together talking about Magda, her life as a girl, as a young bride, as a transplant to the US, as a caterer, and as a mother. He good-naturedly describes Magda's initial struggle to understand Southern English. She often made mental notes about words she could not decode so that, later, in the privacy of their own home, she could ask her husband to translate. When Ron, Jr. was just a baby, a neighbor tried to teach Magda that standard bedtime prayer, "Now I lay me down to sleep..." Magda asked her husband afterwards, "Vat is this 'fyshudye?' When Ron, Sr. could not understand the question, she parroted the neighbor's recitation: "fyshudye before I vake, I pray to Lord my soul to take."

This anecdote gets a warm chuckle from all of us. Whether we've known her for a few weeks or much longer, we know this is our Magda. The laughter lubricates the memories of others, and several more take turns telling a Magda story, not sugar-coating her tendency to be unapologetically honest but also highlighting her generosity and pluckiness. I share my oak leaf weed story, glancing out of the corner of my eye at Kenneth, as this is the first time he's heard the full version. Soon, the tears of comic relief and the tears of grief have mingled, and we are feeling grateful for having known this remarkable woman.

When it becomes obvious that nobody else wants to say anything, Ron Jr. stands up and says a few words. I am touched by his love for his mother. At the same time, I wonder if he was ever a testy teenager and gave his mother the silent treatment. If so, I wonder what prompted him to once again let her into his heart and to treat her with dignity. I then chastise myself for thinking of my relationship with Cameron while we are here to celebrate Magda. When Ron says, with emotion clotting his voice, "I only wish I'd been with her when she died," my daughter pipes up, saying, "Magda liked her privacy. She was just stubborn enough to wait until you went to bed to die. If you'd stayed up, she would've sent you on some ridiculous errand to Plaza Drugs in the middle of the night just to get you out of her room." And in that moment, the bubbles of levity provide just the emotional release we all need to say our final goodbyes.

- - - - -

Ron joins us for Christmas brunch. He contributes a bowl of cut-up fruit to go with our scrambled eggs, grits, bacon, and biscuits. The mood at the table is at times lighthearted and at times somber. We continue our reminiscences about Magda, and Ron tells us about his boyhood Christmases. Cameron no longer believes in Santa Claus, and this prompts her to ask him how he, also an only child, discovered the truth. Ron then regales us with a tale of seeing his father unload a bicycle from the trunk of his car one night. We anticipate hilarity to ensue, but instead, Ron, Sr. spanks his son when he catches him investigating what is underneath a blanket in the back of the garage. I am certain I would not have liked Ron, Sr.

Next, we exchange gifts. Cameron has drawn a portrait of Magda that is quite good. Ron is clearly touched. Kenneth and I give Ron a set of VCR tapes on ancient history, which also seems to please him. With the tapes is a Christmas card, custom-made by Tate, whose cottage industry is thriving. Ron gives Kenneth a very handsome tie, and I'm sure it set him back a good amount. To Cameron, he gives a set of books on drawing, everything from portraits to nature, a new sketch pad, and quality colored markers. My gift is a notebook Magda compiled for me on plant care. She lists every type of house plant and ornamental bush native to the area and what to do for them and when, everything I need to know to keep them alive. Did she know she was dying, and did she also know how much I would need to nurture plant life to literally keep me grounded? I picture her cheering me on from beyond, celebrating with me when Mema Fields realizes I actually do have a green thumb. Oh, Magda, what a genius you are, and how I miss you!

Chapter Twelve: 1986

OUR NEXT HOME project is foisted upon us when our heat dies in mid-January. Our entire heating and air conditioning system needs to be replaced. If we can scrounge up a 20% deposit, we can finance the remainder without interest. While Kenneth tries to line up some outside consulting work with the Carter Center and the City of Atlanta, I make sure we have enough firewood to last the rest of the winter. I also go around all our windows and seal them with plastic sheeting. Meanwhile, we wear multiple layers at home and sleep under several blankets. My pity party was short-lived after news of the space shuttle Challenger explosion. Still, I hope we have an early spring.

- - - - -

Cameron is 12 years old. We ask her if she wants a birthday party and, if so, where. She asks for a skating party. I had no idea she was interested in roller skating. Maybe this is just her way of earning another Girl Scout badge. Whatever her motivation, the prospect of someone else setting up and

243

cleaning up appeals to me, so we schedule the party for a Saturday afternoon in mid-February. We purchase invitations for Cameron to hand-deliver at school, limiting the party to 12 children, Cameron included. I am interested in who shows up and how many of her friends will be males and how many females. She is definitely at that age when they begin showing an awkward interest in each other.

The day of the party, we arrive early at the Medlock Roll-a-Rama with balloons, a sheet cake, 11 gift bags, and presents from us for Cameron to open. Kenneth courageously rents a pair of skates for himself. I choose not to skate, telling them both that at least one person in the family needs to remain uninjured. Cameron's friends arrive in ones and twos, and, as I introduce myself to their parents, Kenneth helps them into their roller skates. I will stand guard over the presents while they whirl around the floor. I am stunned—and pleased—to see Kai come in with Mrs. Butler. I have no idea how Cameron got the invitation to him, but I'm so happy to see him. I spend a few minutes chatting with Mrs. Butler before she excuses herself to get some shopping done during the party. Kai is growing into a handsome young man, and he seems poised and respectful in his interactions with his grandmother, Kenneth, and me. It makes me glad, too, to see hints of Willow's features and sweetness in him.

The party seems to be a great success, and Cameron is her chatty, cheerful self in the car ride home. If I knew the precise formula for keeping this version of my daughter around, I would act on it. Is it balloons? Cake? Being with friends? Skating? A part of me knows that the formula includes time when she is not the center of her mother's attention, and part of me regrets not pushing for a second baby years ago. If we had another child now, though, Cameron would be mortified, I'm sure.

- - - - -

The school year is over, and the installation of our new heating and cooling system has begun. We survived the cold temperatures of winter, and, hopefully, the new system will be in place before the hottest part of summer descends on Atlanta. I have borrowed box fans from both sets of parents to keep the air moving in the house until we can turn on our new, and very expensive, unit.

- - - - -

We take a few day trips during the summer, but we are really pinching our pennies to pay for the new heat and AC in under three years, so we spend most of the summer in Atlanta. Cameron's favorite day trip this summer is to Callaway Gardens. She remains intrigued by the FSU Flying High Circus, less so by the hordes of people swarming the beach area of Robin Lake. This keenly observant child of ours can spot a redneck or an ignoramus from a mile away, and she does not attempt to hide her disdain. After we watch the circus perform, we go on a bike ride, both to get her away from the people who irritate her just for being born and also because I have no desire to be seen in a bathing suit. I will start another diet when school begins again in a few weeks. I must.

- - - - -

A new school year begins. Cameron, now in the 7th grade, announces at dinner after the first day that her bus driver is "disgusting." "She has this beehive hairdo that, I'm not kidding, almost touches the top of the bus. And, get this," she says, dramatically, "there are rumors that there was actually a spider's nest in it a few years ago. Gross! She must smoke a pack of cigarettes a day, too. You can smell it on her, and it makes her voice all scratchy and husky. Oh, and the worst part is that she wears sleeveless shirts, and when she turns the steering wheel, all that flab on her arms wobbles back and forth. Disgusting."

I don't know whether to smile at or scold my story-telling daughter. Has she paid attention to my physique lately? Just in case she has and is secretly hoping my arms won't one day resemble Bus Driver Lady's arms, I vow to start that diet tomorrow. And I question my choice of starting my ESOL classes this month with lessons on different cuisines of the world.

- - - - -

Joe has added some embellishments to his Sevananda sculpture. Apparently, they have now added a hamster to their menagerie. I wonder if having a fluffy pet would help

Cameron stay in touch with her softer side and help her learn more responsibility, or if I would wind up being the caretaker. I quickly talk myself out of the idea, especially because Cameron has never expressed any sort of interest in having a hamster, a dog, or a cat. Only a baby elephant. Also, we need every spare cent to help pay for coaxing our old house into the modern age. Maybe a hermit crab, though? Would caring for a crab make her less crabby?

- - - - -

Out of the blue one day, Cameron asks how she got her name. It turns out her classmates are calling her "Cannon," and she is embarrassed by our choice for her first name. She is considering going by her middle name, Laine. I break it to her gently that if someone wants to make fun of your name, they will find a way, even if you start using your middle name. "Your buddies would probably start calling you Lame,"" I tell her.

"That's just great, Mom. First of all, they aren't my buddies. And you just called me lame."

"I was just saying that changing your middle name might not stop the name-calling, Cameron. Can you not make me out to be the enemy here, please?"

"So how did you and Dad decide on Cameron? I'm the only one in school with that name."

I proceeded to tell her about our time in Cameroon and how

we thought it was a cute play on words to name her Cameron. If preteen looks could injure me, I would be mortally wounded. This child of mine can cut me down with her words and her contemptuous glares. I suggest to her that, when those classmates call her Cannon, she respond by simply saying, "Boom. "Otherwise," I explain, "their mission to irritate you has been accomplished."

I expect her to roll her eyes again at this suggestion, but a smile creeps up on her face, and she nods. "I like it. Thanks, Mom." Well, circle this date on the calendar as a minor victory in the ongoing skirmishes between mother and child!

- - - - -

I am late getting home from a faculty meeting in early November, and when I walk in the back door, Kai is sitting at the kitchen table with Cameron. They are talking and laughing like old times. I cannot disguise my initial confusion at seeing him in our home, though, and they stop mid-sentence to explain.

It seems that, on the route home from school, the bus driver lady hit a mother cat crossing the street, carrying a kitten in her mouth. "Mom, she kept driving. She didn't even stop to see if she'd killed them. She didn't care. She's always trying to get through her route as fast as she can. Yesterday, she ran a red light and said," and here she imitates perfectly a backwoods drawl, "I guess I squeezed the last droppa yaller outta that light."

248

"That's awful. I should probably report her, then. I'll call first thing tomorrow."

"Whatever. I'm just telling you that I'm not riding her bus anymore. Ever. I made her let me out at the next intersection."

"You what? Cameron, you cannot just get off the bus anywhere you like. How would I know how to find you if anything happened?"

"Calm down, Mom. Nothing happened. It was at Springdale Park. There were lots of people around."

Kai interrupts, "And that's where I saw her when I was riding my bike home from Paideia. We walked together from there."

"Thank you, Kai. But, Cameron, you can't do that anymore. We need to know where you are at all times."

"Well, you wouldn't have to worry if you'd let me ride my bike to school, like any normal parent."

There she goes again, turning the tables and making me out to be the bad guy. I take a deep breath so that my response will be calm and measured. I am, after all, the adult in the room, and I do not want things to escalate, especially in front of witnesses. "Your father and I will talk about this later. For now, you will just have to hope that the school can quickly find a different driver. That, or wait at school until I can get there after I get off work. Before she can protest, I shift my attention and say, "Kai, it's always great to see you. Thank you again for walking Cameron home. You should probably head home now. It's getting dark outside. I'm going to go change out of my work clothes and start dinner." And I do just that.

Chapter Thirteen: 1987

THE NEW YEAR starts off with a bang, literally. Someone down the street begins shooting off fireworks at dusk and continues to launch those illegal missiles long into the night. If they are foolish enough to engage in an illegal activity, there's no guarantee they are smart enough to avoid setting something on fire or sending a bottle rocket through someone's front window. Kenneth calls the police at about 11 p.m., and the noise ceases. For a short time. Apparently the police didn't confiscate what those revelers had, and they didn't issue a strong enough warning because, shortly after midnight, the noise starts up again. Every dog in the neighborhood is howling about it, too. When I see Ron the next day, he seems especially haggard. I ask if the fireworks kept him awake, too, and he sheepishly tells me he hid under the bed, mumbling something about mortar rounds in Vietnam. I'd like to strangle those revelers.

- - - - -

My daughter is officially a teenager. God help me; she is every inch a teenager. As our big birthday gift to her, she gets her own phone in her room, and we hope we won't live to regret it. She is already so furtive and no longer shares very many details with us. Still, we want to respect her privacy and her need to have conversations that we cannot overhear. We establish rules like no calls after bedtime, which is 10 p.m., and no taking calls during dinner. Is this the middle way? Time will tell.

- - - - -

My daughter is not speaking to me. My already-sullen 13-year-old woman-child is punishing me. She glares at me over her bowl of Cheerios and refuses to acknowledge me in any way, ignoring all of my questions or attempts at conversation, more interested, it seems, in reading the ingredient panel on the cereal box. I am no match for the oaty goodness of the Cheerios.

Yesterday, I took Cameron and ten of my ESOL students to the Lakewood Fairgrounds. I thought it would be a great Saturday treat for some of my younger students. So few of them even had a concept of what a fair or carnival is, and none of them had ever been to one. The weather was perfect, and so was, I thought, all my planning. I had secured permission from administration and parents as well as funds from the PTO, and I had lined up a male chaperone—none other than the popular Mr. Carlisle.

We leave the Bass High School parking lot at 1 p.m.,

promising the parents we'll have them back at 9 p.m. The thinking is that if we leave the school after lunchtime, we will only need to feed them one meal, and we'll be back in time for them to get a decent night's sleep. I thought I had all my bases covered by bringing along Cameron and Carlisle to help. That and two pockets stuffed full of dollar bills. Carlisle drives one school van and I drive the other. And since he speaks both French and Spanish, I figure he can help explain things to some of our newer students—the ones from Cote d'Ivoire, Guatemala, and Senegal. I've known the other students for at least a year, and we communicate well enough, even though they are still learning English and the ways of Americans. Ah, but Robbie Burns, how right you were about best-laid plans!

Everything goes pretty well at first. We walk together through most of the fairgrounds, pointing out exhibits, games, rides, and restrooms and answering their questions. Many of their questions are about the food. A few of them seem more intrigued by the variety and smells of food than they are by the rides. I guess corn dogs, funnel cakes, candy apples, and hot pretzels **could** seem exotic. I enjoy seeing their wide-eyed expressions and their sense of enthusiasm and adventure as they watch people get off the rides. I catch Cameron rolling her eyes a few times at the types of questions they ask, and I give her the stink-eye to let her know I'd seen her. Obviously, the stink-eye is no longer an attitude deterrent since she continues to be exasperated by their naiveté. When did she become so jaded? Anyway, we set a few rules and a location for checking in every hour. I station myself at our established check-in location, near one of the restrooms.

The students divide themselves up into groups of three or four, according to which ride they want to try first. I put Suki in charge of her group, which includes Meridia and Rolph, and Dmitri in charge of his, which includes Nikolai, Pham, and Sebastien. And I only give them enough money to last about an hour—for just a few rides or a few rounds of ring-toss. The three new students—Marine, from Cote d'Ivoire, Arturo, from Guatemala, and Muhammad, from Senegal—seem to know they are to stay together with Carlisle. I tell Cameron to go with them. Arturo is naturally outgoing; Muhammad seems pretty self-sufficient; but Marine is shy and speaks such broken English that I worry about her. I asked Cameron to take her under her wing. I expect another eye roll, but she seems to take this assignment to heart. So, there is compassion and maturity under that glib and sulky demeanor.

Each group checks in with me at about 4:30 and again at 5:30, reporting on how thrilling or boring certain rides are or how much trouble they have understanding some of the other fair-goers. Meridia, from Spain, who is nicknamed Didi, says she keeps hearing her name called all around her. "Didi, look!" "Didi, can we go on that ride?" "Didi, I'm hungry." "Who are these people, and why are they calling my name?" she asks. Which leads to an impromptu lesson in Southern diction from my daughter.

"They're hicks, and they're saying, 'Daddy.'" She then proceeds to imitate them so perfectly that I have to hide how proud I am of her performance and linguistic prowess, scolding her instead for name-calling.

At 6:30, the students check in again. This time, some of them bring small stuffed animals, miniature Atlanta Braves baseball bats, or fake snakes and vampire teeth that they've won at ring toss, skee-ball, or one of the other arcade games. Some of them are now talking about eating dinner. I check my supply of dollar bills, evenly dividing up the rest—enough to cover dinner and several more rides. Rolph, from Poland, a linebackerish 6'2" and probably 200 pounds, says he's never had a corn dog before. He thinks about six of them would make a good snack. I tell him that six is not only not a snack, it is too many to even call a meal. I hold up four fingers and say, "No more than four, Rolph."

"Yes, Miss," his always-polite reply to my instructions.

Cameron's group had split a bag of popcorn earlier and they want to keep riding the rides for now. They say they'll buy their dinner just before we leave and eat on the van ride home. Muhammad points at the Ferris wheel, telling us that's where they're going next. I catch my fearless daughter rolling her eyes. She wants to go to the haunted house, stating the Ferris wheel is for "amateurs." Arturo, the peacemaker, in broken English and gestures, indicates they will first ride the Ferris wheel, then go to the "casa medrosa," the scary house.

Dmitri's group is eager to try the bumper cars. We need to leave the fairgrounds at about 8:00, so I hand out the remaining cash. Carlisle and I agree that they are free to explore for the next hour and a half. "After I get some dinner, I will be right back here, waiting for you all," I tell them. "Have fun!" Cameron shrugs, and off they go.

I am just finishing a bag of peanuts and a Coke when Suki runs up to tell me that Rolph has gotten sick. "Sick? Where? What do you mean?" She mimes puking, and just the power of suggestion makes me queasy. She leads me to a picnic table where Rolph is lying on one of the benches, looking very green around the gills, his elbow hooked over his eyes. Didi, looking concerned but grossed out, stands just near enough to keep an eye on him. Evidence that the corn dogs—so many corn dogs! —didn't agree with him is in several putrid piles on the ground. A family at another table stares at us, snickering and elbowing each other. What a sideshow my students and I are providing for those, well, hicks! All my protective instincts kick in. "Rolph, can you sit up?" He responds by rolling to his side and retching again, splattering my tennis shoes. I look at Suki and Didi, who are holding their noses and covering their mouths. "How many corn dogs did Rolph eat?" With her free hand, Suki holds up five fingers, Didi four. "Well? Did he eat five, or did he eat four?" They put their hands together. "Nine?! He ate nine? Rolph, you ate nine corn dogs?!" Just the thought makes me bilious as I relive the effects of my failed hot dog, banana, and boiled egg diet, and I'm afraid my peanuts will soon be on the ground with Rolph's corn dogs. The Hick Family Robinson is now openly staring, not even pretending not to. I lower my voice. "I gave you each the same amount of money for dinner. How did you pay for nine corn dogs?" Turning back to Suki and Meridia, "What did you two eat?" Turns out, the girls had each bought French fries and two corn dogs, but decided there wasn't enough catsup at Lakewood Fairgrounds to choke down the corn dogs. So Rolph had eaten them.

"Those are **not** Oscar Meyer wieners," Didi states, emphatic and serious. I have to make myself not smile.

"No, you're right. They are not." I look at my watch. I have about 30 minutes to get Rolph in good enough condition to walk back to meet the others, then to the parking lot. And to make sure he is not going to baptize the floor of the school van on the way home. I hand Suki and Didi enough money to buy all three of them a Coke, hoping the carbonation will settle Rolph's stomach and prevent the two girls from puking. "Come right back, okay?" They nod, obviously relieved to have a mission to help their classmate—one that, at least temporarily, takes them away from Rolph and his sour stomach.

When Suki and Didi come back with the Cokes, Cameron and Muhammad are with them. Cameron's eyes are flashing. I know something has gotten her dander up. "Where's the rest of your group?" I ask.

"With Carlisle. He sent us to find you since you weren't waiting where you said you would."

I nod toward Rolph. "He got sick. Can you go ask Carlisle to wait there for the last group?"

"Gee, Mom, I don't know. Can you tell me why you saddled me with the girl who has a heart condition?"

"What are you talking about, Cameron? Can't you see I've got my hands kind of full here?"

"Marine. She has a heart condition. How could you not tell me?"

"I didn't know. Is she okay? Do I need to go see her?"

"Carlisle is with her. I think she'll be okay, but when she fainted, I thought she'd died."

"She fainted? Oh, Christ." At the mention of our Savior's name, my students and the Hick family all look at me. Then it's Cameron's turn to give me the stink-eye. "You're sure she's okay?"

"I said so, didn't I? Holy crap, Mom. Keep your voice down. Carlisle is with her. Let's just get everyone together and go."

Well, circle another date on the calendar; we'd arrived at something we could both agree on. Turns out the curative powers of Coca-Cola helped both Rolph and Marine, and we were able to get everyone to the vans and then deliver them back to their parents at the school parking lot without any more vomiting or fainting.

After we get home, Cameron starts to head for her room, but I stop her. "What makes you think Marine has a heart problem? How do you know she didn't just faint from hunger or fright?"

"I'll tell you how I know." My indignant daughter proceeds to tell me how they were all five walking together through the haunted house, which she, by the way, found lame. Of course she did. Whenever a ghoul jumped out to scare them, Marine screamed and clutched her chest. Cameron thought she was being dramatic and was losing patience until a blood-dripping corpse sat up from a coffin, looked straight at them, and let loose with a mournful moan. Marine grabbed her chest and then slumped over, nearly knocking Cameron down as she landed on the ground. I guess this happens occasionally because the haunted house staff jumped right into action. They stopped everyone in whatever room they happened to be in, turned on the lights, and came over to where Marine was lying, out cold. They unbuttoned the top two buttons of her shirt and applied cold compresses to her neck and forehead. While they were speaking to her and trying to rouse her, Cameron noticed the edge of a jagged scar that starts near Marine's collarbone. Marine came around in a few moments and a staff member checked her pupils, asking her questions—was she hurt anywhere, did she have any bumps on her head from landing on the floor, was she dizzy, when was the last time she ate? When it was determined that she was okay, Cameron and Carlisle helped

Marine sit up and then stand. While Marine was buttoning her shirt back up, Cameron pointed to the scar. "What's that?" And that's when, in gestures and broken English, Marine told my daughter about the open heart surgery she'd had as a baby and how she'd almost died, and that was one reason her parents were so anxious to get to the US—because she will likely need more surgery after she reaches maturity.

"I had no idea. I can't believe her parents let her come today. The permission form clearly states the same rules that the fairgrounds post on their rides. I'm sor . . . ."

Cameron cuts me off, shaking her head. As she heads to her room, she says, "Don't you ever saddle me with one of your students again." From the warble in her voice, I know just how scared she was. And rightfully so. And when Kenneth comes in from his chess match later, he finds me sitting on the sofa, crying, shocked, angry, and afraid, all of the what-ifs flying at me faster than I can duck, explain, or rationalize. The FearGuiltShame Triplets are back in full force. I tell him I am a failure as an ESOL teacher and a mother. What made me think I could be responsible for other people's children off school grounds? What will Carlisle think of me? I will now lose my job, and my daughter will shut me out even more than she already does. Way to go, Mer. Way to go. And Kenneth does not try to divest me of my self-loathing.

- - - - -

Something's happened to Joe and Margaret. Or, at least, that's what my imagination conjures up when I notice there is no new installment and the current one has fallen into disrepair. It's late fall, and even though I'm knee-deep in lesson plans for my new ESOL students, each time I shop at Sevananda, I've continued my habit of checking out Joe's devotion to his beloved Margaret. Have they argued? Split up? Have the demands of child-rearing and pet care driven a wedge between them? Or left Joe too tired to make new art?

I check myself. Maybe they've simply moved, or Margaret has asked Joe to cease memorializing their love affair to all of Little Five Points. Maybe that's all it is.

I don't know why I take their relationship so personally, why I fear the worst, or why I even care. It's not as if I know them. It's not as if they know me. So why does Joe's art have such a barbed hook in my heart? In proud Scarlett O'Hara fashion, I vow to think about all of this tomorrow. For now, I have lessons to prepare, papers to grade, dinner to cook, and Christmas lists to make.

Chapter Fourteen: 1988

WE BEGIN THE new year by paying off the new heat and air system with money Kenneth received for one of his consulting jobs and with an ambitious plan to refurbish the dining room. Our goal is to strip the paint that covers ancient wallpaper, remove the wallpaper, install crown molding and a chair rail, replace the ugly light fixture with a nice, but modest, chandelier, and repaint. The plastic sheeting between the living and dining rooms should keep most of the dust contained. Kenneth has the name of a contractor who can do the electrical work as well as the carpentry—Lyle Something-or-Other. We think we can complete this project in about four months, and we go ahead and pick out the new light fixture and the paint color to keep us motivated. I am eager to see Mema Fields' expression when we host our first family get-together in our restored dining room. That, too, serves as motivation for me to keep stripping layers of paint when my arms are screaming for rest.

- - - - -

We have a 14-year-old. Cameron Laine Gardner has definitely left her childhood behind. There is not a trace left of her inquisitive, occasionally compliant, playful nature. None that I can see, anyway. Instead, she is increasingly moody and has even started back-talking her father, which is a new development. Kenneth and I very much hope that this change is mostly hormonal and that she will level out after she adjusts to being at the mercy of her cycle. We even discuss taking her to the doctor if she continues to be snippy and sarcastic with us. That, or removing the phone from her room. We decide not to use that threat as any sort of leverage for the time being because we want her to want to be nicer for the sake of being nicer. The only adult I see her being kind to is Ron, so we know she is still capable of doing so. If we can tolerate another year of her moods, we can at least use getting her learner's permit as bribery. She may have a driving lesson if she agrees to say nothing when she cannot think of anything thoughtful to say. I'd add no eye-rolling and no exasperated sighing, too. I will say that one benefit of Cameron's moodiness is that it often fuels my energy to strip layer upon layer of old paint in the dining room after she has angrily cloistered herself in her room because we "make" her eat dinner with us. Should I thank her for that?

- - - - -

He said he knew of a contractor. He said we shouldn't punish Cameron too harshly for being who she is. He said he had to go to his chess club meetings more evenings in March to prepare for an important competition. And I didn't question him. I did not suspect anything. What is wrong with me? How can I be so stupid?

I get all the way to Bass, park my car, and enter the building before I realize I have not only left my classroom key at home, I have also left my purse. I blame my absent-mindedness on the argument Cameron and I had at breakfast. The front office staff is collecting money for a gift for one of our janitors, Dennis, who is having back surgery. Today is the last day they are collecting. I stop in the front office and let them know that, since first period is my planning period, I am running home to get my keys and my purse, and I will be back shortly to give them money. I drive home as carefully as possible since my driver's license is not with me. As I pull in the driveway, I see a familiar pickup truck parked in the back, and a wave of nausea hits me.

I hear laughter when I open the back door, and I follow the sound. Kenneth and Aleksander are in the master bathroom wearing only their underwear, shooting at each other with water pistols. It is evident that they have been shooting each other in the crotch just as much as other places and that they are both aroused. And my first thought is, "Why don't you laugh like that when you're with me? Why are you not that playful with me?"

Their laughter stops when they become aware of me standing there, gasping. Aleksander makes a motion to leave, but I stand in the doorway, trapping them both inside. We all stare at each other for awhile, the only sounds being each of us trying to catch our breath. I continue to stand in the doorway, mute, and eventually Kenneth sits on the toilet seat and Aleksander on the ledge of the tub. Nobody speaks, but they very much understand that I am not moving.

"You never stopped seeing each other, did you?" I ask them both, accusing They look at each other and then at me, like two kids who have been caught stealing candy from Kroger. "And Lyle," I turn to Kenneth, "he's another one of your homo friends, isn't he?"

Aleksander answers. "He works for me."

"Well, you can tell him he no longer works here. Do you understand?"

Aleksander nods.

"I want you to leave now," I say to Aleksander, and he scoops up his shoes and his wet clothes and slips behind me as I maintain my sentry duty at the bathroom door. After I hear the back door close, I unleash a depth of fury I didn't realize I was capable of, barraging Kenneth with question after question, louder and louder, leaving him no time to respond. "How could you do this to me? How could you not tell me? How could you expose me to AIDS? How could you let me believe for years that you thought there was something wrong with me and that I repulsed you because I had gained so much weight after Cameron was born? What is wrong with you? What kind of man are you?"

That last one is the one that seems to stick the deepest and results in Kenneth's confession. He sighs, resigned, and replies in an even, calm voice, "I am the kind of man who is attracted to other men. I didn't let myself believe it for years. And I avoided you because I was trying to protect you. For what it's worth, I am HIV-negative, and I do love you and our daughter. Very much."

"Protect me?!" My voice is now so loud that I'm sure if someone were passing by on the sidewalk, they could hear me. But I do not care. I am livid. And I am scared. "How long have you known? How long have you been seeing other men? And how do you know for certain that you're HIV-negative? God, Kenneth, you disgust me! I feel like I don't even know you! I do not understand you."

"Yes, you do. How can you say I disgust you when you are such good friends with Ron? And Carlisle?"

"Wha-? Wait. First of all, I am not married to Ron. I married you. Besides, Ron has never lied to me about who or what he is. Second, what are you saying about Carlisle? How do you know he's queer? You've only met him once. Don't you dare try to insert anyone else into this situation. This is about you and me. This is about us."

"Okay. You're right. I'm sorry. And I was recently tested, okay?"

My mind is whirling, but I am already deciding what must be

done. Kenneth cannot live here any longer, and I must divorce him. In the span of a second, I wonder how I will tell Cameron, what her reaction will be, what my parents will say, and how Kenneth's parents will respond.

I look Kenneth fully in the face so he will know how serious I am when I say, "I am going now, but when I get home, I want you gone. You no longer live here. Leave me a phone number where my attorney can contact you." And I turn around and walk out, grabbing my purse and work keys on the way.

Once I am in my car, I am shaking so badly that I cannot turn the key in the ignition. I take in gulps of air, commanding my hand to cooperate. Once I get the car started, I realize I don't know where I am going. Should I go see Kenneth's parents and drop this bomb about their precious son? My parents for moral support? For the first time in a long while, I miss Willow in a fierce and palpable way. Should I talk to Ron? Not yet. Later, but not now. I decide I need Carlisle, my mentor, my colleague, and my rock-solid friend, and I head back to Bass. I skip the front office and head directly for Carlisle's classroom, hoping to catch him when the bell rings at the end of first period. My students will just have to wait outside my locked classroom until I get there.

Carlisle can tell with one look that I am in distress. He furrows his eyebrows, and all I can manage to say is, "I need to talk to you after school, okay? Will you come see me?"

He nods, and I make it back to my room with five seconds to spare before the late bell rings. I have no idea how I make it through the rest of the school day, but I do, fueled in part by indignation and in part by the eager faces of my students, willing to accept anything I say. **They appreciate me more than my husband and my daughter do.** I realize I would rather be here right now than anywhere else.

When the last bell rings, I let out a sigh, and that is when the tears come. Carlisle appears in the doorway, and I beckon him in, motioning for him to shut the door behind him. "I kicked Kenneth out this morning. I think I'm going to divorce him." I then proceed to tell Carlisle about Aleksander, episodes one and two, about the disastrous date night years ago, about Kenneth's and my problems in the bedroom, and about his stupid chess club. Carlisle listens patiently while I talk and weep, occasionally stopping to blow my nose.

When I am finally silent, Carlisle reaches over and pats my arm. "I suspected Kenneth might be queer or bisexual. I assumed you two had some sort of agreement or understanding."

"What?! You knew? How? And you didn't say anything?!" My sense of betrayal is so agonizing that I wonder if I can ever trust another human being again, including myself.

"No, I didn't say I knew, just that I suspected. Meredith, I know you are hurt by this revelation, but please try to understand that it was not my place to say anything. Imagine if I had and it wasn't so. How bad would that have been?"

My head hurts, and I am now having trouble processing his words. In the ensuing silence, Carlisle keeps his hand on my arm, and I do not brush it away. We just sit there, both stewing in our own awkward truths. Finally, I look up, and the compassion in Carlisle's eyes provides just the strength I need to leave my chair, this room, this building, and do the next thing. I know that if I do not go over to my parents' house right now for a referral to an attorney, I might chicken out. And that just cannot happen.

- - - - -

I knock on the back door before stepping into Mom and Dad's kitchen, expecting to find Mom preparing dinner and Dad puttering elsewhere in the house. Instead, I hear his anguished voice: "I told you, I don't know!" I have never heard my father raise his voice before. Ever.

I call out, "Hello!" and then I hear Mom walking rapidly down the hallway toward the kitchen, where there isn't so much as a pan on the stove or a morsel of food on the counter awaiting preparation.

"Meredith!" I can't tell if she is glad to see me or not.

"What's going on, Mom?"

"Your father is having another one of his episodes, and this time he has misplaced his wallet and mine, his car keys and mine. She points at the empty organizer by the backdoor, where those items are usually kept. "We've looked everywhere, and I'm beside myself."

Another? Her admitting this is telling. Things must be much worse than I knew.

"What can I do to help?"

"Go sit with him while I look. He's too agitated right now to remember much of anything."

I walk down the hall to his study and find him standing at one of the bookshelves, running his finger over the titles of some of his prized possessions, books on antiquities. I stand in the doorway for a moment, watching him engage in this self-soothing behavior. "Dad?" I interrupt. He looks in my direction. "Hey." I smile. "I just popped in for a quick visit. Do you have a moment to sit with me?"

He looks at me and smiles back, but he is clearly confused. He has a **Where do I know you from?** look on his face. I thought my heart couldn't break anymore in one day, but I was wrong. I walk over to the settee and sit down, patting the empty place beside me. This he understands and, like an obedient little boy, he sits down with me, his breathing ragged. I take his fluttering hand in mine and pat it, searching my brain for something to say or something to ask that can help alleviate this suffering and confusion. I point at

271

the bookshelf. "Those books. They mean a lot to you, don't they?" He nods. "Tell me about one of them, one of your favorites."

He is quiet for a moment. Then, "The Ptole-, the Ptole-." He is stuck. He cannot finish saying Ptolemy. And all I can think to do is continue patting his hand. I came over needing my mom and dad, and suddenly I am the parent, soothing my restless, confused father and my distressed mother.

Shortly, Mom calls out, "Found them!" This does not seem to register with Dad. He is lost somewhere in thought or in some rumination of the past, but he has, at least, calmed down. I stand up and walk to the kitchen. Mom is standing by the sideboard in the breakfast room, and the drawer where she keeps extra silverware is open. "I don't know what he's thinking when he does this, and why he cannot remember where he puts things or why he stashed them somewhere else in the first place. I'm at my wit's end, Meredith."

I don't know how to respond. I do know that I will not say anything about my decision earlier in the day. The news that I am divorcing Kenneth can wait. "What will you do?"

"I should take him back to the doctor. And start keeping my wallet and keys in my purse," she says wryly.

"Want me to go with you? To the doctor?"

"Thank you, but no. That will only make him confused or agitated. I'll just tell him that the doctor wants to see him back in a few months for a follow-up. He won't remember that's not exactly what the doctor said, but he'll remember I'm a nurse and won't question it. I'll let you know what Doc Melton says."

"Meanwhile?"

"I'll let Eggleston know not to schedule me for any more shifts. Not until we know something. I should probably hide his car keys, too. I can't have him misplacing himself too, can I?"

I know she is trying to be upbeat, but it hurts my heart for both of them.

"Do you want me to stay? Fix you both some dinner?"

"I think I'll just heat up some tomato soup and fix us a few girl-cheese sandwiches. You go on home and fix dinner for your own family."

My own family. What a strange concept that is to me now. It will be just Cameron and me. I can feel the tears start to sting my eyes, so before I start to cry in earnest, I give Mom a hug and leave, saying, "Call me, please."

When I get home, Cameron is sitting at the kitchen table, seething. She is holding a slip of paper and waving it at me. "What's this?"

Now it is my turn to act like the kid who got caught stealing candy from Kroger. On the slip of paper is a note, "I'm sorry. Here's where your attorney can call me." And there's a phone number written on it.

"Attorney? Mom, what the hell?"

I have never heard my daughter utter a four-letter word before, and I know it will be a very long night.

- - - - -

I don't know how we finish out the school year, but we manage. It is not pretty, but there are glimmers of better days to come. While Dad has been diagnosed with stage five Alzheimer's, Mom has found an organization that offers adult day care, allowing her the opportunity to resume working part time and to take a break from near-constant watchfulness. She has convinced Dad that he is going to take a new teaching job. She hands him one of his artifacts and one of his books each morning and wishes him well in teaching that day's continuing education course. These objects seem to tether him to some semblance of normalcy. Most days. There are days, the staff reports, when Dad has an audience of a few willing listeners, and there are days when he has trouble stringing together a sentence. On those days, he seems content to watch television or listen to LP records with his "students."

My attorney and Kenneth's attorney help us work out as amicable a divorce as possible. They cannot, however, help me pull Cameron out of her increased moodiness and sour disposition. She still does not know all of the details about why her father and I are no longer together; only that I told him to leave. His parents, too, do not know everything. I don't know if it's the FearGuiltShame Triplets making me reticent or if I'm just too tired to exact the revenge of seeing the people who idolize Kenneth Fields suddenly see him differently. At any rate, Cameron is only allowed to visit with her father at neutral locations, not at the house he now shares with Aleksander. I know this arrangement cannot continue indefinitely, but that is what our attorneys have specified, at my insistence. For now, I am too tired and too worried about my mother and father to care that The Fields and my daughter believe that I am not woman enough to keep my man. Apparently I wasn't man enough.

In the final week of classes, I have my students look through dozens of old magazines and create a collage of what they hope their futures will be—careers, family, travels, hobbies. On the last day of class, they will stand in front of their peers and talk about the images they have chosen and what they will do this summer to help them begin to realize some of their goals. This assignment will help them put English names to things as well as practice different verb tenses. They are enthusiastic about this project, and I enjoy walking around the classroom and listening to their conversations as they swap magazines, share glue sticks, look up words in translation dictionaries, and dream out loud. Maneet, a shy girl of 14, innocently asks, "Are you going to make one, too,

Miss?" I start to laugh off the idea, but something sparks in me, and I am soon at my desk between class periods, flipping through magazines and cutting and gluing images onto my own 11x15" piece of poster board. Maybe it is because the first magazine I look through is an **Architectural Digest,** or maybe it is because I readily admit that the plastic sheeting still hanging up between the living and dining rooms mocks me and has become a sort of symbol of my failed marriage, of destruction, and of unfinished business. Whatever it is, I now know what I want most in the near future is to finish the dining room and renovate the carriage house so I can rent it out for extra income. And I want to learn to do as many of these big projects myself. No more do I want to defer to a man about home renovations. Or much of anything, honestly. Just because I took home economics in high school and most guys took shop does not mean they are any more ideally suited to make home renovation decisions. If I can learn how to sew a dress, I can learn how to measure and cut wood for a chair rail.

- - - - -

As soon as I put Cameron on the bus for two weeks of 4-H Camp at Rock Eagle, I head to the library to check out books on home improvement. Cameron is as desperate to get away from me as I am for her to stop sulking around or to do it somewhere else. For a change, let her punish her camp counselor for her miserable life. Every time I write a letter to Cameron, I will also write to the counselor and offer my condolences and encouragement.

From early morning until late at night, I scrape, strip, measure, saw, hammer, and paint. Every time I mess up, like when the beveled edges of the chair rail don't meet the way they're supposed to, I learn a new, more reliable technique. I also decide I didn't want crown molding to begin with and that I was only agreeing to that because I thought I would win points with Mema Fields. The only points I want to score right now are with my home improvement skills.

When Cameron returns home, I don't say anything about my project. These two weeks at camp have done wonders. She is chatty; she is lively; she is interested in world events again, and I want her to keep talking for as long as she will let me in. I must send another letter to her counselor, thanking her. One to the camp director, too. I have my daughter back. The only question I ask her is what she would like for dinner her first night back home. And the only reference I make to the dining room is that dinner will be served there. She looks at me quizzically and then walks through the house to look for herself.

"Wow, Mom. Wow. Did you do this?"

I nod. "What do you think? Do you like it?"

"You did this all by yourself?"

"Mostly. Ron came over a few times to hold up one end of the railing while I installed it. And he helped me put on the last coat of paint. Other than that, yes, I did this all by myself." I cannot keep from smiling. I'm proud of myself, and I may have even given the FearGuiltShame Triplets the boot.

"And, do you know what else?" I tell Cameron. "Ron convinced me that I should let you spend time with your dad at his new home, so tomorrow night, that's where you'll be going for dinner and a sleepover. He wants to hear all about camp, too."

Well, circle yet another date on the calendar. My usually smart-alecky, jaded, argumentative daughter is strangely silent and awe-struck as she takes in so much newness. I bask in her sunny smile.

- - - - -

During the completion of the dining room, I'd hired a general contractor to talk me through the multiple stages of renovating the carriage house. I took lots of notes and asked a lot of questions. I have now prioritized the renovations, from the ones that are the most straightforward and easiest to learn to the ones that are the most complicated and will require outside help. I know I will need to call on experts from time to time, but I am determined to do as much of it myself as possible. And, of course, I intend to enlist Ron's help when I need an extra pair of hands. Mom and Dad have loaned me money for building supplies, and I will begin repaying them interest-free once I have a tenant.

One of my first tasks is to install a window air conditioner unit. I cannot work in the carriage house in this summer heat without it. Before I am able to do that, though, I need to seal the window frames to keep as much of that precious cold air in as possible. My Helpful Hardware Man at Ace shows me how to load a caulk gun and keep the stream of caulk thick enough to do the job but thin enough not to make a mess. I begin on the outside of the window in the back, the one with a large wax myrtle growing by it. (Thank you, Magda, for making sure I know that shrub's name.) After washing the exterior, I am ready to caulk, and if I make a mess, Myrtle will forgivingly cover my tracks. In almost no time, I am wielding the caulk gun like one of Charlie's Angels. My confidence soars, and within a couple of days, all of the window frames are clean and airtight, inside and out, and I have installed the window a.c. unit. How gratifying it is to turn it on and listen to it hum as I begin crossing renovation to-dos off the massive list. Windows caulked—check. A.C. unit installed—check. Since Cameron is doing light clerical work at Kenneth's office during the rest of the summer, I will need Ron to help me with the drywall. I am appreciative of his help, and to show him my appreciation, he eats dinner with Cameron and me most evenings. His easy presence is comforting to both of us, and our conversations are always pleasant and engaging. My goal is to get most of the renovation roughed in during the summer so that, once the school year resumes, I can work on completing weekend projects or contracting them out. I know this is an almost unrealistic expectation, but one can hope. I also plan for Cameron and me to spend as much time with my parents as possible. We all need that time together, so we set aside

Sunday afternoons for brunch and whatever else Mama Jo and Papa Don are up for that day. I feel tugged in so many directions. Am I able to be a good mother, a dutiful daughter, a kind neighbor, a decent home renovator, and a professional educator?

While the pace of the weekdays this summer is ambitious, the more tasks I complete, the harder I work. That is not to say I have not, on multiple occasions, questioned my sanity and my decisions. I have wanted to admit defeat so many times— when I underestimate the time or the expense of a project, when I fall off a ladder, when I spill an entire bucket of paint on the floor, the many times I hammer my hand instead of a nail, and when I get part-way through a project I think I can manage, like installing a ceiling fan, and realize I don't know what I'm doing at all and that I could have electrocuted myself. Just who do I think I am? Oh, and my hands and my hair! I have callouses on every finger of both hands, despite wearing gloves, and specks of paint in my hair that will not wash out.

I decide fairly early on to allow myself Saturdays to catch up on grocery shopping and laundry as well as leisurely reading. I cannot, though, give my brain a rest. Included in leisurely reading are the many books on home improvement I have checked out of the library. Perhaps one day I will write my own for the newly single gal who foolishly believes she can do almost anything, despite all odds.

- - - - -

On the Saturday before pre-planning week, I wake up earlier than usual. Cameron is still sleeping. I decide to surprise her with breakfast from Sevananda, so I slip on some shorts, the only clean t-shirt I have left, and my sneakers, and head out. It has been weeks since I really paid attention to the goings-on in my neighborhood, so engrossed have I been in my renovation projects. I notice new flower beds in some yards and evidence, like Little Tykes swings hanging from tree branches, that more and more young families are moving in to fix up older houses. Ordinarily, as I'm walking to Sevananda, I would be fantasizing about what I would buy to eat, scolding myself for wanting fattening foods, which I will still most certainly buy. Yes, I would still buy them, and then I would hide the evidence from my family—in the cupboard or in the back of the freezer—sneaking in to treat myself when nobody was looking. As I pass by houses today, though I notice the smells of their weekend breakfast preparation—the bacon, the hash browns, the pancakes—I am surprised to discover that I am not all that hungry and that I am, in fact, craving cantaloupe and eggs and not much more. I think back on how few times this summer I have bought ice cream sandwiches and potato chips and how little of them I have eaten. This is such an unusual realization for me that I am compelled to weigh myself when I get back home. I knew my clothes were looser, but I am surprised to see that I have lost 25 pounds without really trying. Who knew divorce and home renovation could be such a great diet plan? The next week, during pre-planning meetings, a few of my colleagues comment on my weight loss, asking me what diet I'm on and how much I have lost. I tell them I have lost 185. When they look shocked, I qualify that. "160 was Kenneth, and 25 was me."

- - - - -

It was too good to last, this post 4-H Camp version of Cameron. She is once again moody and snippy with me, although never in Ron's presence. It seems everything I do exasperates her and annoys her. I secretly hoped she would be offended that her father had moved in with and was "in love with" another man, but she is enamored with Aleksander— Alex to her. And her dad, to hear her tell it, can do no wrong. I don't notice her attitude so much after coming home from working in Kenneth's office; it's more noticeable after her overnight visits with Kenneth and Aleksander. According to her, I have too many rules. Alex and Dad treat her like an adult and let her stay up as late as she wants. Alex and Dad let her talk on the phone as long as she wants, with whomever she wants. Alex and Dad let her listen to whatever music she wants, whenever she wants, at whatever volume she wants. And Alex and Dad let her read whatever she wanted. I sure hope they don't have any scandalous magazines in their house! I keep trying to tell her this is a phase the two men are going through, trying to win her affection while she adjusts to the divorce. I have even tried speaking with Kenneth about this on the phone. He doesn't see any problem with their lack of rules. I swear, if Aleksander didn't live so far away from Bass, I'd let Cameron stay over on school nights. Then those two would have to deal with having to get a grumpy girl up and to school on time. So, this, then, is the slag of Kenneth's and my relationship—living with a daughter who thinks she hates me and who wants to live with her father and his lover. I know I need to bide my time until this post-divorce adjustment period is over, but in the meantime, I admit, but only to myself, that, while I love my daughter dearly, there are days when I simply do not like her. I know she feels the same way about me.

- - - - -

As Christmas approaches, the carriage house is close enough to being finished that I have posted ads in the *Atlanta Constitution* and the *Atlanta Journal* for a boarder. With the help of my many books, my Helpful Hardware Man, and Ron, and contracting out the plumbing and electrical jobs, the carriage house now has a large living/dining/sleeping area, a small bathroom, a kitchenette, and freshly painted walls. The final cleaning and preparations, like window dressings, should be no problem. In an effort to show Cameron that I, too, can treat her like an adult, I ask her to sit in on the interviews with the two people who have responded to the ads so far. Whoever we choose may move in soon after January 1, giving us all the Christmas break to complete the renovation.

The first person we interview is a young man in his early 30s, Jared. Jared works downtown for an investment firm. I get the distinct impression he was born with a silver spoon in his mouth and the keys to the BMW he drives in his hand. He is pleasant enough, but he does not seem to appreciate the work that has gone into refurbishing his potential digs or that a woman did much of the work. I'm not even sure why he wants to live here. He is not very forthcoming about much. What he is, though, is entirely too flirtatious with my daughter. At first, she seems flattered by the attention, but as the interview progresses, I can tell she is becoming increasingly uncomfortable.

After we escort him to his car, letting him know we'll be in touch soon, Cameron turns to me and says, "I sure hope the next one is okay, 'cause that one's a no." I am relieved that she still shows evidence of common sense and can see through Jared's smug charm. I wonder what he acts like around his clients and if he sucks up the most to the ones who have the most money.

The other applicant is a young, quiet, mild-mannered viola player with the Atlanta Symphony Orchestra. Camela, originally from Cairo, Georgia—and I can tell because she pronounces it "Kayro," goes by Cammie. In addition to playing viola, she also works part-time for the ASO's marketing department to supplement her income. We all seem to click, and so, after we agree on a reasonable viola practice schedule for when Cammie is at home—nothing past 10 p.m.—she signs the lease and puts down her first month's rent.

After she leaves, Cameron turns to me. "Thank you for letting me be a part of that, Mom. I think I'm going to like having Cammie live here. She might even end up being kind of like a big sister." **And, if so, I think maybe you won't be so determined to go live with your dad.**

Chapter Fifteen: 1989

I HAVE A 15-year-old. Cameron insists on getting her learner's permit the day she turns 15, and insists on a driving lesson in the empty parking lot of Druid Hills Methodist on the way home. I indulge her because I have decided her ability to drive is just the leverage I need to gain her cooperation when she digs in her heels. And she digs in frequently, as if it were a matter of teenaged principle. I will have to be selective, though, about when to dangle the driving privilege carrot. So, while I will occasionally let some things go without an argument, like her choice of certain outfits, there will be other times when, I, too, will dig in. She cannot leave the house half-naked, looking like she forgot to finish dressing.

- - - - -

Since I am turning 40 next year, and since Dad is continuing to decline, I decide I need to schedule my first comprehensive physical exam since Kenneth and I divorced. I also want to make double sure I am not carrying the AIDS virus. I had a blood test shortly after walking in on Kenneth and Aleksander the second time, and it was negative. Call it paranoia, even though we were so rarely intimate, I just need that reassurance of a clean bill of health.

After I get my lab results back, with the blood work and Pap smear all clear, I decide I am also long overdue having a conversation with Kenneth. I still have so many questions. Besides, I owe it to our daughter to be as cordial to her father as possible. I'm done wanting her to be mad at him for my sake. And, to her credit, she never has been.

Kenneth and I meet at The Majestic for lunch on a Saturday afternoon. Until now, he has usually only seen me seated in the car as I drop Cameron off for a weekend at his and Aleksander's house. I purposefully don't meet Cameron at the door when he's bringing her back home. When I walk into The Majestic, he's already sitting in a booth. He stands to greet me, clearly unsure of the new protocol—to hug, shake hands, hold my elbow while I slide into my side of the booth? He eases the situation by saying, "You look great, Mer. Living without me obviously agrees with you."

"Yeah, well, um, thanks . . . ." His touch of humor allows us both to relax a little and take a seat without having to negotiate this bit of post-marital awkwardness. That detail can wait. We place our order and, while we wait for our food to arrive, before things get more awkward, I start the conversation.

"Like I said on the phone, I want things between us to be as cordial as possible, for Cameron's sake." Kenneth nods, listening. "But in order to get there, I need to ask you some questions, and I need you to answer honestly." He again nods. "So, for starters, how long have you known you're a homo?"

"Gay, Mer. We prefer to refer to ourselves as gay."

I almost spurt the water I've been sipping out of my nose. "Gay? For Pete's sake, you have been anything **but** in all the years I've known you."

"Duly noted. I know I can be somewhat of a stoic."

I don't know whether to be angry with him for being so conciliatory, or pleased that I've landed a zinger. I continue. "Did you know when we were dating?"

"I didn't have words for my conflicted feelings, Meredith. I knew that I loved you, but I also couldn't escape the fact that I was attracted to men. An attraction, by the way, that I didn't act on for years."

I am filled with such a wild chorus of emotions and thoughts, I barely know what to ask next. I mean, if we hadn't married, there would be no Cameron, but if he hadn't lied to me, to himself, I wouldn't be a divorced, single parent. I try to shush the chorus by taking a deep breath. **What would Dad ask?** I take another deep breath and continue. "Tell me what that was like, being conflicted. What were you thinking? What were you feeling? When did you decide you were, um, gay?"

It's Kenneth's turn to take a deep breath. I think he was anticipating another zinger. "I knew I wanted to be married and to have a family one day. That much I was sure of. As a teenager and a young adult, I didn't know anyone I could talk to about my attraction to men, though. I struggled, Mer, I really did. And I thought once I settled down with you, the confusion would go away. And it did—for awhile. Or, at least, it wasn't a daily thing. I also thought my parents would be so disappointed in me if they thought I wasn't straight, that I would embarrass them."

"Do they know now? I mean, they were pretty disappointed in your choice of a wife. At least, your mom was. Surely they want what's best for you, your happiness, and surely Mema believes that means someone, anyone, not like me."

"One thing you need to understand about my parents' relationship is that they don't talk about their feelings. Ever. And just so you know, Mom has never said a negative word to me about you."

"Oh, she didn't have to. She said them to me, with words **and** her facial expressions . . . ."

The waitress brings our food and leaves as quickly as possible, sensing the seriousness of our conversation.

"Let's not bring them into this just yet, okay? In answer to your question, they know I am living with Alex and that I was unfaithful to you. They do not hold you responsible for our marriage breaking up."

"Wow. Okay. Fair enough. So, you said you didn't act on your feelings for years. What changed? When?"

Kenneth lets out a long, audible sigh, almost like air suddenly leaving a bicycle tire. "In Africa, when we lived there, after Cameron was born."

My face must register that same wild chorus of thoughts and emotions because he quickly continues. "It had nothing to do with my dissatisfaction —with you or with fatherhood. And it was never in Cameroon. Only when I traveled in the region." He pauses.

"Tell me."

"The first time, I was drunk. We'd just finished that infrastructure job in Kenya and I was celebrating with the crew. I drank way too much beer and the next thing I knew, I was in bed with one of the guys. Thing is, it wasn't as sordid as all the stories one hears in high school. But, still, the next day I vowed it would never happen again. And it didn't happen again for many months. It's just that there was something about that first time that seemed to confirm a truth about myself that I hadn't been willing to acknowledge." He pauses again, thinking. "I felt like all the right numbers of the Master's lock suddenly lined up, and -click! —I was free. Sort of. Honestly, Mer, I'm glad you caught Alex and me. I've been living in hell for so long," his voice cracks, and he reaches across and lays his hand on top of mine, then quickly removes it. "And I now know . . . admit, I have put you through hell, too. I wanted to be a good husband and father, but I wanted to be with Alex. I wanted to be able to say, 'This is me. This is who I am.'" He shrugs his shoulders.

And just like that, with his quick gesture of reaching out to touch my hand and his acknowledgment of how he hurt me, a few cylinders in my own lock line up, freeing me, at least for now, from resentment and anger. And my first concern is this: "Kenneth, have you and Alex been tested for HIV?" I try to lighten the mood. "I mean, I still need the alimony and child support to get by. Plus, that'd be an awful way for your folks to find out."

Kenneth smiles and assures me that both he and Alex are clear. They are apparently clear and committed, so I need not worry about either of them developing AIDS.

"And your chess club. Are all of you guys gay? Do you really play chess?"

"Yes, and yes, and we don't have orgies, if that's what you're wondering. We're serious about the game, and just as serious about having a few hours a week where we do not feel like we need to hide. One of the rules of the club is that we don't out each other and we don't just randomly have sex with each other. We are an organization of gay men devoted to playing chess. Period."

"Well that certainly explains your devotion." I pause, considering. "I think my ESOL kids must feel the same way about class with me. It's the one time each school day when nobody makes fun of them for their accent or for not being American enough. So, yeah. I think I get it."

Relief spills from Kenneth's face, and we spend the rest of our meal picking at our food and talking about how, together, we can better parent our strong-willed daughter.

- - - - -

The school year progresses, at times too quickly for me to keep up, and at other times at a workable pace. Our tenant, Cammie, seems respectful, concluding her practice sessions long before 10 pm, and exchanging niceties with us when we pass each other getting into and out of our cars. She mostly keeps to herself, though. Cameron and I plan to attend at least one ASO concert to hear her play.

My students continue to challenge me, delight me, keep me on my toes, and make me proud, sometimes all in the span of one class period. As for Cameron, she continues to excel in the 9th grade, but she is not very forthcoming about everything. I wonder sometimes if she is trying to keep her life as a Bass student separate from my life as a Bass teacher so that her classmates won't associate her with me. I can't say I blame her, but what I do know is my furtive daughter often closes her bedroom door when talking for hours on her phone. And she thinks she is hiding from me archived copies of **The Great Speckled Bird** she has checked out of the public library. Little does she realize that both Kenneth and I read **The Bird** when we were high school journalists. I wonder if she would be shocked to know we, too, had counter-culture tendencies. Probably all teens do. Since I occasionally use **Creative Loafing** in my classroom, I decide to coax Cameron out of her room by asking her what articles in each issue she thinks they would find interesting, worth discussing and writing about. She seems to enjoy being my instructional consultant, and I am grateful that she takes that role to heart. Still, I know she is keeping something, or some things, from me, and I wonder what.

My answer comes in the week leading up to our spring break. Ron, almost apologetically, informs me that he has seen Cameron hanging out after school with the hippies and the Hare Krishnas in Springdale Park, across from Druid Hills Methodist. I tell him maybe she is meeting Kai there, on his way home from Paideia, but Ron says he does not see Kai when he sees Cameron. I ask him if Cameron knows that he has seen her, and he doesn't think so. I ask him if she seems more interested in the Hares or the hippies, uncertain which answer would concern me most. Of course, I am concerned that she might be dabbling with drugs, but I'm also concerned that she could just as easily be dabbling with weird religion. I wish Dad were of sound mind. He could help her sort through her fascination with both groups. Ron swears he isn't spying on Cameron when he happens to see her, and he is not sure if she prefers one group over another. Maybe she **is** just waiting there for Kai. I do think Ron is being protective, and intentionally schedules his errands to coincide with her getting out of school. So, do I confront her? Take her bicycle away and make her ride to and from school with me? Remove her phone privileges? Threaten to suspend driving lessons?

Last year, I would have fretted about it and made a decision on my own. This time, though, I call Kenneth at work and ask for his thoughts. His response is "Why don't I see if she will take MARTA to my office after school and earn a little money doing our filing, like she did last summer? The bus has a rack for bicycles, and I can fit her bike in my trunk when I bring her home." That solution sounds ideal to me. No confrontations, no accusations, our daughter is safe and earning money, and Ron can stop worrying about her, as well.

- - - - -

As the school year concludes, Cameron brings home a flyer about the Close-Up program. Each fall and each spring, groups of high school students may go to Washington, DC, for a week of meeting with their legislators, observing the Supreme Court, touring the Smithsonian, and meeting with interns and lobbyists to learn about their roles in government. Cameron seems eager to go with the October group, and Kenneth and I agree the experience would be invaluable. We tell her, though, that she will need to earn the money to go, including airfare, hotel, snacks, and souvenirs. She is all too happy to work at Kenneth's office again, and I am glad my daughter has worthwhile goals and is willing to work toward them. She seems willing to forego summer camp for this DC experience. If my argumentative, opinionated daughter can witness first-hand how to channel all of that conviction toward a greater societal good, I'm all for it.

- - - - -

After a fairly ho-hum summer of Cameron working and my doing household maintenance, catching up on long-neglected yard work, visiting with my parents, and reading a few books for pleasure, a new school year begins. My daughter is in the 10th grade, and we occasionally talk about her college plans. For now, she continues to work after school, make preparations for the Close-Up trip, and help me decide what articles in **Creative Loafing** to highlight with my students.

My students continue to inspire me with their courage and their earnest efforts to assimilate while also maintaining their cultural identity. They are aware of the fact that not everyone in Atlanta welcomes them, and helping them navigate those turbulent waters challenges me. Would I be so understanding if I had not been the stranger in Cameroon?

- - - - -

One Saturday, Collier Headlee—yes, the daughter of that

very Headlee, comes over to work on a school project with Cameron. I hadn't realized they were classmates until she rode up on her bicycle and knocked on the front door. For what it's worth, Collier is nothing like her mother. Cameron and Collier camp out at the dining room table, spreading out their notebooks along with poster board, markers, glue, scissors, and old **National Geographic** magazines Collier has brought in her Jansport backpack. I interrupt only to bring them sandwiches, chips, and drinks for lunch, leaving them to their project. I cannot, however, avoid overhearing their conversations, and I enjoy their deep thoughts and playful banter. I wonder where Collier gets that from. Certainly not from her gin-soaked mother. Or is it whiskey?

Around 4 pm, Collier's mother calls. Her words are slurred, and she does not bother to introduce herself, opening with "Is Collier Headlee there?" To my ears, it sounds like a 45 record slowed down to 33. "Is Callya Headlee they-ya?"

"Yes, she is. Would you like to speak with her?"

"No. Just tell her to get her tail home."

"Okay. I sure have enjoyed having her over today."

"Uh-huh. You tell her, now. Bye-bye." And with that, she hangs up.

I walk into the dining room and say, "Collier, that was your mom on the phone. She needs you to come home now." It's my first real opportunity to see what they've been working on. The heading on their poster is Atlanta: A City of Immigrants, and the poster board has a map of the world overlaid with images of people, many of them children, from quite a few nations. Each image has a string connected to Atlanta, depicting the melting pot that our city is becoming. At the bottom of the poster, Collier and Cameron have attached a pocket made from a large manila envelope, and filled it with a stack of index cards with key facts about each nation and its people that they have gleaned, apparently from sources in the school library as well as the magazines they've been cutting apart. I'm honestly a little stunned that the Headlees have a subscription to **National Geographic**.

As Collier packs up, Cameron asks, "You sure your neighbor won't mind that we cut up all her magazines?" Aha. Collier shakes her head, then thanks me and Cameron for letting her come over. I can only assume she gets her manners from their housekeeper. Or from her generous neighbor.

"You're welcome any time, Collier. Be safe riding home."

After she leaves, I decide not to say anything to Cameron about Horrible Headlee or ask her if Collier talks about her mom. Maybe she isn't so horrible to have such a delightful daughter. Maybe, but I doubt it. Instead, I point to the poster board and ask, "It's for the Geography Poster Fair on Wednesday, right? Do you want to ride to school with me that day, or do you want me to take it and you still ride your bike?" Then, "I like it, Cameron. Very much. I'm proud of you and Collier."

Cameron shrugs as if it's no big deal. "I'll ride with you." And, without my asking, she starts cleaning up, even grabbing Pledge to polish the table. I hope Cameron and Collier will become good friends, for both their sakes.

The day of the Geography Poster Fair, I am walking through the bank of posters lined up in the school library, looking at the contributions of the 10th grade Geography students, some of whom I teach or have taught. I stop to study the poster contributed by Cameron and Collier when Mrs. Headlee walks up, accusing.

"How dare you indoctrinate my child with your filth!" She points at the poster. "Don't you know God tells us not to mix the races? How else are we going to remain pure?"

I am so stunned by her strident tirade and misguided assumptions that I am temporarily mute. I am aware that her religious ideology is merely fear in disguise, but I am also aware that I must not overreact or be defensive, as tempting as it is to set her straight. I need to be careful not to place Collier in any more of an awkward position than she's undoubtedly already in.

"I'm sorry you feel that way, Mrs. Headlee. I think Collier and Cameron did a fine job on their project. And if you're ever interested in getting to know people from other races or cultures, you are more than welcome to visit my class some time."

"I wouldn't be caught dead," she hisses. "Now, you leave my child alone, y'hear?"

At this fortuitous moment, Dr. Hendricks, Bass Principal and Knight in Shining Armor, shows up by my side and effuses, "What an excellent poster, Mrs. Headlee, Ms. Fields. I know you are so proud of your daughters." I give him a grateful look and then move on to the next poster, glad for the reprieve. But still, I wonder what it is about me that acts as the match to the fuse of Horrible Headlee's unexploded ordnance, and I wonder about the reasons behind such hatred toward everyone who is not just like her. If she had her way, the Bass PTA would stand for Parent-Teacher Artillery and would be pointed at students just like mine. Poor Collier.

- - - - -

When Cameron returns from her Close-Up trip, she is fired up. The experience was everything she'd heard it would be. Her group was fortunate to be in the Supreme Court for opening arguments in Hallstrom v. Tillamook County, and now she is interested in EPA regulations. So interested, Kenneth reports, that she peppers him with questions about his projects for the City of Atlanta and whether or not the city is conscientiously adhering to regulations or attempting to circumvent them. I love her intensity when it is aimed at something worthwhile; I also love that she picked up the word "circumvent" and can use it correctly in a sentence. I almost want to dare her to ask her Mema and PopPop Fields about regulations in their work, but I decide to keep my nose out of it, especially since Kenneth apparently recently told his parents about the nature of his relationship with Alex. That can't have gone well, and I am almost positive the Fieldses were more concerned about their reputation than they were with Kenneth's happiness. Their precious boy is human after all. How disappointing.

- - - - -

In early December, I arrived home late after a PTA meeting, having stayed behind to speak with several parents of my students. As soon as I step out of my car, I smell marijuana. It is a unique odor that is not unfamiliar; I occasionally smell it wafting out of the restrooms at Bass. Lights are on in the carriage house, and I can hear giggling and Cammie saying, "... and when he said 'capisce?', I said 'no thank you,' because I thought he was offering me an hors d'oeuvre! Talk about a girl from the backwoods!" More peals of silly laughter "Well, he **was** holding a tray..." More giggling.

I walk up to the carriage house door, indignant, ready to lay into my tenant and possibly terminate her lease for bringing that stuff on my property, where I am trying to responsibly raise my daughter. Before I can knock and enter, I very clearly hear my daughter's voice. "We should get Ron over here. Then it would be Cam, Ron, and Cameron. Get it? Cam, Ron, Cameron?!" And she dissolves into silly laughter, clearly amused at her drug-induced sense of humor.

I knock on the door and attempt to turn the knob. The door is locked, and there is scurrying. "Just a minute," I hear Cammie say. More scurrying. More giggling.

Cammie opens the door, and I now smell marijuana and Lysol. They both look like small children with their hands in the off-limits cookie jar. Small children with very red eyes.

I point to Cameron, glaring. "Go wait for me in the kitchen." She scuttles out. I turn my glare on my tenant, a young woman I had assumed was quite innocent. "You're the adult here. Explain. Why did you bring illegal drugs onto my property? Why did you give them to my daughter?"

Cammie is suddenly very sober and remorseful. Tears slide down her cheeks. "Ms. Fields, I promise you tonight is the first night I've ever smoked a joint. Smoked anything. And Cameron brought it to me, not the other way around."

And I believe her. "Right now, I need to go talk to Cameron, but I am warning you. If anything like this ever happens again, your lease is terminated. On the spot. Am I clear?" She nods. "And just to be safe, it's probably best if Cameron does not visit you in here anymore unless I'm with her. Understood?" Again, she nods.

I am trembling as I walk the footpath between the carriage house and the back door. Cameron is sitting at the kitchen table, still as a statue. She, too, seems to have sobered up, but instead of tears in her eyes, there is defiance.

"Cammie says you brought the marijuana to her, not the other way around. Is that true?"

"Yeah. So what? Lots of kids are doing it. What's the big deal?"

"The big deal is it is illegal, it is a drug, and you are not an adult, so you don't get to decide what laws you will break and what laws you will obey."

"It's a harmless drug, and it relaxes me. Haven't you noticed we haven't been arguing as much lately?"

"We can learn not to get on each other's nerves without resorting to drugs, Cameron. I will not tolerate this." Then, "Do you have any more marijuana anywhere in or around this house? If so, I want you to go get it now."

Cameron stands silently and goes to her room, returning moments later with a used Folgers Coffee can. She opens the lid and shows me that it contains several joints in a sandwich baggie. Wordlessly, she hands the tin to me.

I stand and walk over to the phone.

"Mom. Wait. Are you calling the cops?"

"No. I am calling your dad. I need him to help me sort this out. You stay right there."

I dial Kenneth's number, and Alex answers. "Alex, it's me,

Meredith. I need to speak with Kenneth, please. It's urgent."

Kenneth comes on the line and asks, with concern in his voice, "Is everything okay? What's going on?"

"It's Cameron, Kenneth. I caught her and our tenant smoking weed. Weed that our daughter supplied. We're sitting in the kitchen with the rest of her stash. What do we do? How do I dispose of it?"

"Put her on," he says.

I hand the phone to Cameron, and all I can hear is "no, sir," and "uh-huh." She then hands the phone back to me.

"I'm coming over. I think it's best that Cameron spend the night here tonight. I'll take the stash and dispose of it. Be there in about 20 minutes."

"Are you sure? How will you get rid of it?"

"Don't worry. I'll get rid of it. It's probably best if you don't know where or how. See you in a few." And he hangs up.

I am suddenly so tired. Ancient tired. In the marrow of my bones, tired. And as difficult as things are for my parents right now, I need my mother. As soon as Kenneth leaves with Cameron, I call and tell her I'm coming over to spend the night and that I'll explain when I get there.

- - - - -

By mutual consent, Cameron goes to stay with Kenneth and Alex until the Christmas holidays. They will upend their routines to get her to school, and they will decide whether or not to dangle driving lessons in front of her to buy her cooperation. I will get a rest from my worries, and Cameron will get a break from me. We'll still occasionally see each other in the hallway at school, and that seems like just the right amount of contact for both of us right now. I love my daughter dearly, but, right now, I don't care for her company. I'm sure the feelings are mutual. At least, I hope she believes that she loves me.

Chapter Sixteen: 1990

AS THE 1990'S begin, instead of making a New Year's resolution, which I gave up years ago, I am going to try choosing one phrase that I want to define my life in the coming year, even though I know doing so risks the FearGuiltShame Triplets trying to take up residence in my head when I fall short. The older I get, though, the more I realize I need to be as kind and gentle with myself as I am with my most struggling students. If that means falling down again and again before I get something right, so be it. I just need to continue getting up and trying. So, my phrase, my mantra for 1990, is Get Back Up. I explain this to Cameron one Saturday afternoon before school resumes, and she responds, "Far out, Mom." I guess that ringing endorsement just about sums it up. I think our break from each other has helped, and we settle into a fairly easy routine around school, work, and grandparent visits. Both Kenneth and I have made it quite clear to her that we are not able to buy her a car for her 16th birthday next month, and, as far as Cameron is concerned, that is "fly." Who is this kid, and where is my teen-speak dictionary?

- - - - -

My now-16-year-old daughter is still, in some ways, a little girl. She still sleeps with Mr. Whiskers, as battered as he is, and she still takes the occasional bubble bath with Mr. Bubble instead of some perfumed bath oil beads. She also has one foot solidly planted in the grown-up world. She devours the newspaper and the evening news. And she has opinions about nearly everything happening in the world today. Maybe she will become a lawyer, arguing and advocating for the downtrodden. Or, following through on Kenneth's and my experience working for our high school newspapers, a journalist exposing grave wrongdoings like Watergate. From time to time, we discuss colleges and majors, but I know not to push too much. Most things with her must be her own idea, or seem like her own idea, for her to embrace them. I remember, as a teenager, thinking my parents didn't know as much as I did about the world and then realizing, as a young adult, how wrong I had been. That day cannot come soon enough for my willful, bright, and opinionated daughter.

- - - - -

Kenneth calls for me at the front office of Bass one early March afternoon, about 45 minutes after school has let out. Cameron was not on the MARTA bus and has not shown up for work. I had not realized he was in the habit of meeting her as she got off the bus and helping her take her bicycle off the rack.

"Could she be on a different bus, one that gets there later?"

"I've waited for her usual bus and the one that comes after it. I don't think she's coming."

A prick of panic runs up my spine, and I steady myself on the office counter. "I think I know where she might be. Ron has seen her before at Springdale Park, hanging out with the hippies and the Hare Krishnas. I'll leave now and go look for her. Should I call you at the office or at home once I know something?"

"Don't you want me to help you look?"

"Let me look. It'll take too long for you to get through traffic to the park, and I want to start looking now."

"Okay. I'll head home. And I'll leave word with the receptionist to call me if she shows up here." He pauses a moment, then says, "Mer, when you find her, please don't yell at her before you make sure she's okay. After you get her and her bike home, call me so I can yell at her."

I hang on his choice of word—"when,," not "if." I also appreciate his attempt to lighten our parental anxiety as well as his offer to be the disciplinarian. "It's a deal. I'll call you when I know something."

I drive faster than I should toward the corner of Moreland and Ponce de Leon, then slowly down South Ponce, looking for my daughter. There are so many people milling around that it's difficult to tell if Cameron is among them, so I pull over and park. I take her school photo out of my wallet, stow my purse in the trunk of the car, and then walk into the park. I move from group to group, showing Cameron's photo and asking if anyone has seen her today. All the while, I'm bargaining in my head, pleading with the cosmos that, if she is here, it is with the Hares and not the hippies. I know not all hippies are into drugs, but, given Cameron's recent experimentation and some of the stories Willow told me about her life before Kai, I'll take the prospect of dealing with cult religion over illicit drugs any day.

I walk up to a group of glassy-eyed youth milling around a swing set and interrupt their conversation to ask, "Has anyone seen this girl here today?" They stop bantering with each other to look at the photo, but their response is non-committal. They are clearly humoring me. Then a young girl who looks about Cameron's age flashes her eyes up toward one of the old houses behind South Ponce. It's obvious which one because there are other young people milling around it, hanging off the banister of the front landing, sitting on the lawn, and leaning out the upstairs windows.

I walk up to the house and nobody stops me from entering. Inside, there are more young people with seemingly nothing better to do except hang out there with each other. **Don't you**

all have homework to do? My teacher's mind wants to scream, **or jobs to go to? Or families to be with?** Then I hear Cameron's distinctive laugh from the back of the house, and as I walk down the hallway, I can smell it. Marijuana. Without knocking, I open the door where the smell is coming from, and I see my child sitting on the lap of a bearded, bedraggled man who appears to be twice her age, passing him a joint. He, too, is laughing.

"Hey, Mom," she casually remarks. At which point The Bearded One pushes her off of his lap and attempts to stamp out the joint.

"Where's your bike?" I ask, trying to keep my voice level. She starts to answer me, but I interrupt. "Never mind. Take me to it."

Cameron giggles, says to The Bearded One, "See ya, dude," then hooks her elbow with mine and leads me out the back door. Her bike is in the backyard with several dozen others, her backpack dangling off the handlebars.

We wrestle the bike into the trunk of my car, and as soon as Cameron has climbed into the passenger seat, I announce, "You're grounded."

Rather than argue with me, her response is, "Chill out, Mom." And in that moment, I dispense with taking her home, heading straight to Kenneth's instead.

When we pull up in his driveway, I lay on the horn. Kenneth

and Alex both walk out with puzzlement on their faces. I roll down my window and explain, "I came straight here. Alex, will you please take my very stoned daughter into your house? I'd like to speak with Kenneth."

Alex walks over to the passenger door, hefts Cameron's backpack onto his shoulder, and then guides her out of the car and into the house. Instead of remaining at the driver's side window, Kenneth walks around and sits in the passenger seat.

"She was at a flop house, Kenneth. I've never seen so many aimless, strung-out kids in one place. She was smoking pot and," my voice raises with anger and worry, "she was sitting on the lap of some hippie guy who looks to be in his early 30's. Oh my God. What if she's sleeping with him?"

Kenneth gently touches my arm. "I'll talk to her. You did the right thing bringing her here."

"I didn't yell at her, but I did tell her she was grounded. Do you know what she said? 'Chill out, Mom.' That's what. Kenneth, what is happening to our daughter? What do we do?"

"I'll talk to her. You go home and try to relax. I'll call you later. Okay?"

Once again, the anger and worry have made me so suddenly weary that I do not argue with him. Maybe it would be better for both of us to talk with her together, but Kenneth knows and I know that if I talk to her right now, I will say things to my daughter that I will later regret. But, like a puppy who has just chewed your favorite shoe, she must be disciplined now, not later. Or maybe now **and** later.

Kenneth gets out of the car and turns to wave at me as I back out of his driveway. After I get home and wrangle Cameron's bike out of the trunk, I head straight for her bathroom and prepare a Mr. Bubble bubble bath, and while the water is running, I pour myself a glass of wine. I, too, can be a kid and an adult at the same time, and this is what Get Back Up looks like today.

- - - - -

Cameron seems to be getting back on track after spending a week with Kenneth and Alex. She remains on a short leash with me until she can prove she is once again trustworthy. For the time being, she does not have the privilege of riding her bike to school but, instead, she gets to drive us both to Bass, and then she rides MARTA to work at Kenneth's office afterwards. She understands in very clear terms that she is to go straight to work from school and straight to the dining room table for homework once home. No more hiding herself away in her bedroom for hours with the door closed. I have also unplugged her phone and hidden it in my closet. I will return it to her when I decide to. While I know we cannot live like this indefinitely, I want desperately to impress upon my daughter that her actions matter, that bad choices have consequences, and that trust is easily broken but sometimes difficult to repair. When she gets mouthy with me, saying things like, "You forgave Dad for much worse," I respond by saying, "There's a difference between forgiveness and trust."

- - - - -

I am reading aloud to my youngest ESOL students an article in **Creative Loafing** while they follow along. The article, on the dismantling of the Berlin Wall, is one Cameron and I selected the night before. We agree that classroom discussions can go in many different directions, from the literal wall in Germany to the barriers they face as immigrants, from living under communism to living in a democracy that sometimes sees them as "other." So many possibilities. I lose my focus when I see the assistant principal, Mavis Brown, hovering outside my classroom door, peering in. I say to my students, "Please finish reading the article silently while I step into the hall. We will discuss it in a few minutes."

I step out into the hallway, expecting bad news about my father. My voice shakes. "Is anything wrong?"

"I wanted to let you know that two of Cameron's teachers have reported her absent today. Since you didn't let the front office know she was out sick, I thought you should know sooner rather than later."

Mavis is aware of some of my most recent parenting challenges, so I appreciate her informing me this early in the school day. "Oh, dear. Thank you for telling me. Would you mind watching my class while I call her father? I need to let him know. I'll be back in a couple of minutes." I nod toward the classroom door. "They're reading silently."

"Not at all." She looks back at me as she opens the door. "Take all the time you need. Good luck."

I call the house first, leaving a message for Cameron on the answering machine, asking her to call the school if she gets this message before I get home. I then called Kenneth at work. We decide that if she shows up for work, he will immediately take her home to pack her things for a more permanent move to their house. We want to nip this errant behavior in the bud, and he has a more calming influence on our daughter than I do. We also agree, finally, that the three of us should see a counselor together. Cameron has tapped out any parental expertise we imagined having.

There is not much more I can do until the school day is over. Except worry. If Cameron doesn't show up for work, I'll go back to Springdale Park and look there for her first. If she does show up for work, she has quite a surprise in store.

The rest of the school day goes by in a fog. I am distracted, so after reading the Berlin Wall article to all of my classes, I have them draw or write about walls in their own lives. Right now, I could fill a notebook with information about parental competency walls.

- - - - -

Apparently, work is important to Cameron, but so is getting stoned. Her rationalization is to skip school and get stoned early in the day so that she shows up for work clear-headed and sober. Cameron is now living for the remainder of the school year through the summer with Kenneth and Alex. She is, essentially, under house arrest, and Kenneth and Alex are her wardens.

Kenneth has not spoken with her yet about counseling, saying he first wants her to get used to her new routine at their house before adding a new element to our lives. I suspect he also does not want to talk to a counselor about being gay. I am okay with waiting until the new school year to see if Cameron can straighten herself out. I will spend the summer reading, catching up on household chores, meeting Ron for coffee and book discussions, and occasionally taking Cameron out to lunch during her work day. That's how I plan to straighten myself out and Get Back Up.

- - - - -

Things are going so well with Cameron living at her father's house that, when the new school year begins, we decide to leave our arrangement as it is. Kenneth has made it very plain to her that she is to stay at school for the entire school day, attend all of her classes, ride MARTA to work, and sit in their kitchen or dining room to do her homework after work.

I broach counseling again with Kenneth, but he hedges. I'm beginning to think that he believes I am part of Cameron's problem, and the longer she lives with him, the less likely she is to return to her drug buddies. Maybe that is true. Maybe not. Which would I prefer to be true? I wonder if Kenneth's neighborhood has the equivalent of a Springdale Park and, if so, has Cameron found it? What I do know is that I miss my little girl, and I miss the woman-child who is eager to engage in conversation about things happening in the world. I do not, however, miss the daily skirmishes, the questioning of my authority, the yelling, the eye-rolling, and the exasperated sighs—hers and mine. For the first time since I've returned to teaching, I begin the school year with only myself to get out the door in the morning. Since I do not have to nag, plead, and cajole, I am able to apply my makeup at home, not in the car. And I am able to savor a second cup of coffee before leaving. Cammie seems to be less guarded around me as well. If I let them, the FearGuiltShame Triplets will convince me that my daughter is better off without me, but I have read enough literature about adolescence that I hold on to the notion that this is just a phase. The older Cameron gets, the more she will realize I am not the enemy, and I was not put on this earth to squelch her identity and her rights. I have told her that my job as her mother is to help her navigate her way to adulthood and help her develop a set of coping strategies that do not involve illegal activities. That elicits a sigh, but at least she does not roll her eyes while sighing. I am fairly certain that there is intrinsic comfort in knowing exactly where her boundaries are, but that she also feels obligated to test them.

- - - - -

The new school year cruises along fairly uneventfully for all of us until right before the Christmas break. As Alex is changing the sheets on Cameron's bed, he finds her stash of drugs. Maybe Kenneth's part of town does have its own version of Springdale Park. She's getting those drugs somewhere, from someone. I suspect The Bearded One. We schedule a showdown that evening in their living room. We will skip the counseling and, instead, admit Cameron to a drug treatment facility after Christmas. Kenneth understands this will necessarily include counseling for all of us, but we agree she needs to be away from her bad influences as soon as possible. So, after our family meeting—Kenneth, Alex, Cameron, and me—which involves a great deal of tears and shouting, Cameron moves back home with me since I am not working over the Christmas break and Kenneth is. I am now her warden, and my child will have zero personal freedom until we deliver her to Breakthrough on December 26. I have even removed the door from her bedroom. Merry Christmas, indeed.

- - - - - -

She's gone. The Friday before Christmas, Cameron is still sleeping, so I make a quick grocery run to Sevananda. I take the car to make sure I am home before she wakes up. When I return a mere 30 minutes later, she is not in her room, and her backpack along with some of her clothes and personal items are gone. Her bike is still parked in the backyard. I believe she has run away.

Frantic, I call Kenneth just to make sure she is not with him. She is not. Alex stays there, in case, and Kenneth heads over to Springdale Park, while I start calling everyone I can think of. I start by calling Ron to ask if he's seen her today. I know he still drives by Springdale Park in Magda's old Mercedes when he's running errands or taking meals to friends who have AIDS, but he's also been keeping an eye out for Cameron since she returned home, and I love him for that. It turns out that Ron has not seen Cameron for some time.

I call Mrs. Butler and ask to speak to Kai. He has not seen Cameron in a long while, either, but promises to let me know if he does. I sense he's been worried about her, too. I hang up the phone and head over to the carriage house to knock on Cammie's door. She is packing a suitcase to go home for Christmas, and she, too, has not seen Cameron nor had any contact with her, adhering to our agreement. I wish her a Merry Christmas and walk back into the house, wracking my brain for whom to call next. I wish I knew more about those aimless kids she'd been hanging around with and which ones she considered friends. And I wish I'd pushed her for more details about The Bearded One, like his name. I suspect if Kenneth speaks with him, though, he'll get the full story, and that it might involve wearing his old steel-toed work boots from our days in Africa.

I decide to call my parents on the off chance that Cameron is there. Of course, she is not, and I speak to Mom only long enough to hear that things are currently fairly calm there and that there have been no recent episodes to cause concern. I call Kenneth's parents and leave a voicemail. I don't hold much hope that Cameron is there, though. The only other person I can think of to call is Collier. I dial Headlee's number and hold my breath, hoping Collier will be the one to pick up. No such luck. Horrible answers with irritation in her voice, slurring even her one-word "Hello."

"Mrs. Headlee, this is Meredith Fields, Cameron's mom. I was wondering if she was there."

"Uh, no," she says, her distaste and disdain obvious.

"May I speak with Collier, please? I'd just like to know when the last time she saw Cameron was. I'm afraid she's run away." Why I share this tidbit with her, I do not know, but I am a mom, she is a mom, and I am desperate.

"Oh. Hold on." She covers the phone and hollers, "Call-ya! It's Mrs. Fields. She wants to talk to you."

I'm honestly a little surprised she's so accommodating, but I'm grateful. Collier picks up an extension in another part of the house. I can hear two sets of breath on their end of the line. I apologize for bothering her and ask if she's seen Cameron recently. She has only seen her in passing at school, as they did not have any classes together this quarter. I ask her if she knows of any friends Cameron has at Bass that I could call. She does not. I thank them both and hang up.

I have hit a dead end. How is it that I do not know my own daughter well enough to know who her accomplice might be in helping her run away? I wish now I'd asked Cameron to take me back to Springdale Park and introduce me to the kids she hung out with and got stoned with. Unless Kenneth can find her or get information from the ragamuffins at the park, we don't know where else to search for our daughter. I sit at the kitchen table and wait to hear from Kenneth, aware that my breathing is ragged and shallow. I hear a tap at the back door, and Ron walks in, bearing a pot of freshly brewed coffee. He insists on waiting with me.

- - - - -

We have exhausted all leads, filed a police report, and are living in the peculiar hell of waiting for news of some sort. Kenneth's folks have put their usual Christmas trip on hold and are being quite supportive. We are in a time warp, and the Christmas season passes with absolutely no merriment on our part. There is no way to recover from this.

Chapter Seventeen: 1991

THE DEKALB COUNTY have police have assured us that Cameron's is an open and active missing person case. They try to be reassuring when we call for updates—that kids typically come home when they get hungry enough, that they're rarely very far from home, and that their officers know all of the teen and drug hangouts and check them regularly. They also assure us they have located and interviewed The Bearded One and have him locked up on charges of contributing to the delinquency of minors as well as drug trafficking. Good! His name, as it turns out, is Bruce Calloway, and he is 32 years old. Exactly twice Cameron's age. So, points for knowing he was a bad character and for guessing his age correctly, but demerits, the FearGuiltShame Triplets scold, for not even thinking of reporting him to the police after finding Cameron with him, And they are right to scold.

I go from wanting my child home and safe to wanting to know where she is and who she's with to wanting to just know she is okay. I would now settle for just knowing she is alive and well and that she is not pregnant with The Bearded One's, with Bruce Calloway's, child. Cameron is smart and resourceful, so as long as she is able to fend for herself, she will survive. I occasionally think about Willow, who was also smart and resourceful, but then I make myself stop. The FearGuiltShame Triplets torture me enough; I do not need to torture myself more with mental images of Willow's broken body, lying partially hidden for days before being discovered. Under these conditions, I have no business declaring a yearly affirmation, unless it's Find Cameron.

- - - - -

Arthur Ashe died yesterday. Today is Cameron's 17th birthday, and there seems to be no good news anywhere about anything. If a good man like Arthur Ashe can be infected with AIDS-tainted blood during a transfusion, what hope do any of us have of outrunning disaster in this world? I am already in such a funk when the alarm clock goes off that I call into work and request a substitute teacher for the day. Now I regret doing so, sitting at the living room window, looking out at the bare trees and the brown grass, alone with my thoughts and my anguish. If I were in the classroom, I would at least feel like I was contributing to making the world a tiny bit better. I am feeling so adrift.

Kenneth and I speak on the phone in the early afternoon. He, too, is thinking of our girl on her birthday. Only he seems to be bearing up fairly well. I am not. That evening, Ron knocks on the back door, bearing a birthday cake. I am so touched by his thoughtfulness and generosity of spirit that I let him cut me a slice, and we eat our cake together in companionable silence. I am dangerously close to asking him to lie down with me and hold me, but I chicken out, and he leaves soon after we finish our cake. Mom calls, and that's when I completely let my guard down, weeping until snot runs down my face.

- - - - -

I turn 40 on March 1, and for my birthday, Kenneth and Alex offer to hire a private detective to search for Cameron. They bring over takeout, and Ron, Kenneth, Alex, and I sit around the kitchen table to strategize. How much are they willing to pay? What leads can we provide that we haven't already provided to the police? How long will we retain the detective's services? I feel like I've been plopped into the middle of a Grade B mystery movie—only this is Cameron we're talking about and this is real life. How surreal. Still, I am grateful for this most unusual birthday gift.

- - - - -

The school year is over. I'm relieved for many reasons. I know my co-workers mean well, but I am tired of the look of pity on their faces and their averted gaze when they see me coming down the hall or into the faculty break room. Carlisle is the only one who acts the same around me. He asks me every week if we have any news or if the private detective has turned up any leads. He also remembers to ask me about my parents, asking how my father is doing and how well my mother is coping. I love him for his caring and for helping me feel somewhat normal under such abnormal circumstances. I have for five months neglected all but the most basic housekeeping tasks. I need to direct any energy I have toward household maintenance. My summer to-do list is long.

The detective is nearly certain Cameron is no longer in the Atlanta area, possibly not even in Georgia. He has contacts with law enforcement throughout the state, and no young girl matching Cameron's description has come to their attention. I don't know if this is necessarily good or bad news. I almost wish someone in a neighboring city would catch my daughter shoplifting at the local Piggly Wiggly. The detective assures us he is pursuing all viable leads, so we continue to retain his services.

- - - - -

I have just finished cutting the grass and am about to put the mower away when the mail truck comes earlier than usual. Before I stash the mower and get the edger out, I go to the mailbox. Ron is walking down his steep driveway at the same time. We chat a bit, remarking about the weather and how the mail delivery is surprisingly early, and he has already started to climb back up his driveway when he hears me gasp. I have received a postcard from Cameron with a Little Rock postmark. Ron quickly crosses the street and helps me to the steps on the front stoop, seeing that I am suddenly weak.

Dear Mom, It reads, **Please do not worry about me. I am safe and well. I will call soon. Give Dad and Alex my love. Cameron.**

So, not **Love, Cameron,** but at least **Dear Mom.** My child is alive. She is okay. "Ron, I need to call Kenneth and the detective. You're welcome to come in, if you'd like."

"I'll leave you to it if you're sure **you're** okay." I nod. "I'll check on you later." He gets halfway across the front yard and turns around to shout. "I'm so glad our Cameron is okay! I love that kid, you know?"

"I know. I know. Thank you. You're the best." I close the front door and head straight for the phone.

- - - - -

By the time the private detective and the local police department's contact in Arkansas get to Little Rock, there are only traces of Cameron having been there. It appears she worked an odd job or two, getting paid under the table, before moving on. Moving on to where, though? I am a tidal wave of emotions: relief that she is okay; worry about where she is and where she's going; anger at her for putting us through this; curious if she is continuing to do drugs, even recreationally; wondering who she is with. The detectives are not able to shed light on my worries and curiosities. Once again, we are forced to wait, forced to operate on Cameron's timetable.

The mix of emotions has me both weary and keyed up. Too keyed up to rest well and too weary to focus on much of anything. I go to the bookshelf and pull out the gardening book Magda created for me and thumb through it, looking for a plant project to occupy my mind and my hands. I decided to be bold and plant rose bushes right in the middle of the front yard. I plant three double knockout rose bushes—a yellow, a red, and a pink one—thinking if just one of them survives, I'll be pleased. Magda left detailed instructions for how to care for roses throughout the year, and I've had good practice with the one in the backyard she gave me. Plus, I am a dutiful student. So much so that all three are still alive when the new school year begins.

- - - - -

In the last week of September, Kenneth receives a postcard. The postmark is from Albuquerque. Once again, the message is short, with the same news—that Cameron is okay and well and will call soon. It is clear from her definition of "soon" that we are not using the same dictionary. Still, we are elated that she is alive. We assume she is inching her way west. Kenneth, Alex, Ron, and I have dinner together to celebrate and strategize, once more, about using the services of the detective or not.

This meal is more upbeat than our first strategy session, and I drink far too much wine. At some point during the meal, I point my fork at Alex and confess, "I used to have a bit of a crush on you, you know?"

To which Ron adds, "Me, too."

Followed by Kenneth's, "Me, three. Obviously."

To laugh again from the bottom of my belly is a true gift, and I look at these three men in my life with gratitude. Kenneth loves Cameron, of course, but so do Alex and Ron. How I long to say that to Cameron when she calls. If she calls. She is loved. She is dearly loved.

- - - - -

As Thanksgiving approaches, I decide to invite Ron, Kenneth, Alex, Kenneth's parents, and mine over for a meal. Perhaps Cameron's running away has left me deranged, but I no longer care if I can pull off the perfect meal and please everyone at the table. I just want all of us who love Cameron here at the same time. Then it occurs to me to invite Carlisle as well, if he is not seeing his elderly mother that day. He promises to stop by after eating lunch with her, even if it's just to say hello and have an extra slice of pie.

Kenneth and Alex bring a smoked turkey, and everyone else contributes a dish or two toward the meal. We have butternut squash, sweet potatoes, mashed potatoes, green bean casserole, macaroni and cheese, cranberry salad, rolls, cornbread dressing, and pecan pie. The first few minutes are awkward, but very quickly the meal becomes a joyful event, with lots of story-telling and reminiscing about the old Atlanta. Mema and PopPop really do know their Atlanta history. My dad did, too, at one time, but he lives increasingly in a world of silence, smiling sweetly when addressed but mostly trapped in the haze of dementia.

After the meal, while Mema and I wash dishes, Mom serves coffee to the menfolk, who are gathered around the television watching football. For the first time in my life, Mema Fields does not frighten me or intimidate me. In fact, she surprises me by saying, "Those rose bushes out front are glorious! Who's your yard man?"

"Me," I say, with no pretense or bitterness.

"Well," she stammers, "I thought Kenneth took care of your other rose bush." She points to the one in the backyard, "and that beautiful azalea in the front. I might have to have you come over and look at **my** roses."

Was that a compliment? I think so, and I'll take it. I do not expect an apology for previous slights, but I'll certainly take a compliment.

"Just name the day and time, and I'll be there," I respond. Then we hang up our dish towels and join the others in front of the television for a carbohydrate-induced afternoon of football and dozing.

Chapter Eighteen: 1992

ANOTHER NEW YEAR begins. The Christmas card Cameron mailed to me still sits on the mantle. Kenneth and Alex received one, too. The postmark was from Phoenix. She is apparently very good at getting short-term work to support herself before moving on. She was vague on the details except that she is okay and working on getting her "head on straight." I cling to that phrase, hoping it means she is not doing drugs and not hanging out with those who do. I so badly want to hear her voice, convinced I'll know if she's genuinely okay if I can just hear her speak.

- - - - -

On the evening of Cameron's 18th birthday, the phone rings. Right after she went missing, I started paying extra for caller ID. The number that pops up just indicates a San Francisco number without a name. I pick up immediately, expecting the private detective to be the caller with news of my daughter.

"Hello."

"Mom? Mom, it's me, Cameron."

"Oh, my gosh! Cameron! Honey, how are you? Happy birthday! Wher-" I start to ask where she's calling from but realize if I ask too many questions, she might hang up. "I'm so happy to hear your voice. Are you having a good birthday so far?"

"Slow down, Mom. Yeah. Today's been a good day. Thanks."

"Do you want anything for your birthday? Do you need anything?"

"No, I'm good. How are Mama Jo and Papa Don? And how are your students? What sorts of fun learning activities have you created for them?"

"Your grandparents are managing pretty well. Things seem to have stabilized for now. And my students are good. I have kids from Africa, Central America, South America, Cambodia, and Europe. They're so sweet and eager to learn. They are currently learning about the Grammy Awards and different styles of American music. Why? Do you have any suggestions for me?"

"No. That sounds good. I'm sure they're enjoying your lessons."

"I hope so. If they aren't, they're good at pretending. We've been listening to different radio stations during class, studying lyrics, and discussing popular music." I so badly want to ask her a bunch of questions, but I know if I pry too much, she'll shut me out. And she's far too smart for me to trick her into disclosing her location. I tried one more tactic, though. "This call must be costing you a fortune. How about I send you some money to reimburse you?"

"It's okay, Mom. Really."

"Alright. Are you planning to call your dad, or do you want me to tell him anything for you?"

"I'm going to call him after we hang up. How's Ron? Is he doing okay?"

"He's doing great. He'll be pleased that you asked about him." Should I tell her he misses her, or would she think I'm being manipulative? "He brought cake over on your birthday last year. Wasn't that sweet?"

"He's a sweetheart, that's for sure. Well, I should probably call Dad before my break is up. I'll call you later, okay?"

"Okay. I'd like that." What does "later" mean? In a week? A month? Next birthday? "I'm so glad you called. I love you dearly."

"Thanks, Mom. I'm going to call Dad now." After she hangs up, I stand there, lost in a sea of thought, holding the handset until the incessant beeping of the phone brings me back to the present. I hang up, waiting to hear from Kenneth, share notes, and strategize again.

Kenneth calls after he and Cameron talk, excitement in his voice. "Our girl's okay. She's really okay."

"I know. Isn't that great? She sounds good, too, don't you think? Were you able to get any details about her life? I was afraid to ask too many questions. All I know is that the call came from San Francisco and that she mentioned being on break."

"That's about all I know, too. And I agree. She sounds good. Alex and I have just talked about it, and we're inclined to dismiss the private detective. We think that if he goes out there and drags her back here against her will, she'll just disappear again, maybe forever. Besides, she's technically an adult now. We're just not sure what to tell the police department."

I feel like a hole has swallowed me up. The months of anguish, of not knowing, of getting little tidbits and then having the leads not pan out, of not seeing my daughter for so long, of wanting to know why she left in the first place, all rush toward me at once. And now Kenneth and Alex have decided, without asking me, to stop looking for her. I can barely comprehend what this will mean. I definitely cannot afford to hire a detective myself. I wouldn't be able to afford Barney Fife searching the town of Mayberry, much less a private detective searching all of San Francisco. "I've got to go. I need to think." That's all I can think to say; my heart and head hurt so much.

After I hang up with Kenneth, I walk across the street and ring Ron's doorbell. He answers with a dishcloth slung over his shoulder.

"Am I interrupting? It's just that Cameron has just called me, then Kenneth, and I need to talk to someone."

Ron takes my hand and leads me to the sofa. "Sit," he says. "Tell me."

And I spill out the contents of my heart and soul to him, holding nothing back, while he patiently listens. And then he folds me into a hug while I sob on his bony shoulder. It's only after I finish drying my eyes on the dishcloth that I see Ron has a guest in his home, a handsome man who looks to be about Ron's age. His guest is patiently waiting, leaning in the doorway between the kitchen and the living room. His eyes sparkled with devotion to Ron.

"Oh, Ron. You have company. I'm so sorry I bothered you."

"You didn't. Bother me, that is. This is Guy. Guy, Meredith. She's my friend from across the street. I've told you about her."

"Nice to meet you," Guy says, walking over to shake my hand.

I stand up to leave, but not before Ron says, "For what it's worth, from what I know of Cameron, I have to agree with Kenneth. If she's okay, as you both think she is, then going after her is only going to backfire. Her calling you on her own and paying for it herself is big. You've raised a sensible, smart girl, and she's strong. Rely on that, okay?"

I nod, then walk back across the street into my quiet home, my heart partly at peace and partly numb. Maybe I have done a somewhat decent job of raising my daughter, despite what those Triplets occasionally hiss in my ear.

- - - - -

The school year rolls along fairly smoothly, with its typical bumps and turns. Most days, I think I have the greatest job in the school system. I get to work with a wide variety of students from all over the world; I have a supportive administration, including Carlisle, Mavis, and Dr. Hendricks; and I get the summers off to putter around home.

Both Kenneth and I get the occasional postcard from Cameron, but no more phone calls. That is, if Cameron calls her father, I am not privy to that information. The sharp ache of not knowing has become a bit duller over the past many months. I decide that no news is probably good news. Plus, there really isn't anything I can do to resolve my own questions except remain open to having any sort of relationship with Cameron that she's willing to have with me. If anyone had told me when they laid that baby girl in my arms for the first time how many ways my mother's heart could break, I would've accused them of lying. Now I know it is true that sorrow is the price of admission for being allowed to love someone deeply. I suspect it's true of all parents, not just the parents of runaways or addicts.

- - - - -

On the first full day of my summer break, I spend the morning with my parents. One hears horror stories of dementia patients becoming angry and lashing out at their caregivers. Fortunately, that is not the case with my dad. He does sometimes get agitated, but he has never said cruel things to anyone, and he is generally agreeable. I shudder to think what might happen if **my** editing faculties were stripped away. What wretched things might I say?

Back home, I am just emerging from an unintentional afternoon nap when the phone rings. I am still in that bleary in-between state of consciousness and do not check caller ID first.

"Hello."

"Mom, it's me. You sound sleepy. Or sick. Are you okay?"

"Cameron! Hi! I'm okay. I just woke up from a nap. I was visiting with Mama Jo and Papa Don this morning, and after I got home, I laid down for just a minute—about an hour ago." I hope she can hear the amusement in my voice. "Tell me about you. I'm eager to hear."

The pause is so long, I fear she has hung up. Then she starts, slowly at first but in increasing and rapid fire detail, to tell me what she has been doing, where she has been, and why she left. "I want you to know that I've been going to Narcotics Anonymous every day since I left. Even while I was still using, I went. I've been working the 12 steps, and I knew I couldn't do them if I was there. I need you to know that." I so badly want to ask questions—**Why would being with us not help? Narcotics? Steps? Every day in how many cities? How does that work?** but I resolve to just listen.

"Go on. I'm listening."

"I had to leave. I was surrounded by bad influences, and no matter how hard I tried to get away or stay away, I got deeper into the drugs. I thought I was just having fun, but now I know I was just avoiding dealing with stuff." Again, my mind whirls—**What stuff? Stuff you cannot ask your mom or your dad about? What kind of drugs? How often? Where did you get them? How could you afford them?**

"The final straw was when I caught my boyfriend shagging one of my so-called friends. I should've known long before, but I chose not to notice. I believed him when he said he saw us having a future together. I just knew I had to get as far away as possible before I did anything really stupid." I think she has just confirmed that she was, indeed, sleeping with The Bearded One, Bruce. **Yuck. Have you been tested for STDs? Oh, my little girl, how I want to hold you!** "Anyway, I went to the Greyhound station when I left him and asked where the next bus was going, and that's how I ended up in Memphis. I found an NA meeting, and then I got high afterwards with another newcomer. But I kept going back. And I kept getting stronger. And I was able to pick up odd jobs here and there, enough to buy food and the next bus ticket." **Where'd you sleep? Shower? Wash clothes? What kinds of odd jobs are out there for a kid?** "I kept heading west. I felt like I could not put enough distance between me and Atlanta." **Do I tell her Bruce is in jail and it's safe to come back?** "Anyway, I'm in San Francisco now, and I'm going to keep working for a year until I have residency status and can start at Cal State. I want to study psychology and help other kids."

"That's great, Honey. I think you'll be so good at that." **Again, how many questions am I allowed to ask? What kinds of questions will the rapprochement tolerate? I must be very careful and tread lightly on this new path.** "May I ask you something?"

"Yeah, sure."

"Where are you working, and where do you live? I've heard that San Francisco is expensive."

"I'm working in a coffee bar, and I live in an apartment with a bunch of other girls I met at NA. Some of them are already in school. All of us want a college degree."

"Oh, I'm so glad. I'm glad you have a job, and I'm glad you

have roommates who all have the same kind of dreams. Do you need anything? Can I send you anything for your apartment?" **When can I see you? How about I send you money for a plane ticket?**

"No, Mom. That's okay. But thanks. How's Ron?"

"He's doing well. He has a boyfriend; his name is Guy. He seems nice, and I think he's good for Ron."

"Oh, good. Give him my love. I'm glad he has someone to share his life with. How about you? Been on any dates?"

I almost snort, her question catches me so off-guard. "I should be asking **you** that question. But, no, I have not been on any dates."

"Tell me about Papa Don. How is he doing? And Mama Jo."

"They're hanging in there. I think he's finally reached the point where he doesn't remember that he used to know stuff, so he isn't as frustrated, you know? He's just very sweet and quiet. He enjoys listening to music and looking at photographs in some of the books he has accumulated over the years. If he recognizes some of the places or artifacts, he doesn't show it. And Mama Jo is a trooper. Very resilient."

"Please give them my love." **Okay, I'll give Ron your love and your grandparents, too. I'd rather you give it to them in person. Is there some in there for me, too?**

"Will do. Hey, remember the Turrets house? It's for sale again."

Pause. Long pause.

"Are you still there, Cameron?"

"Yeah, but I've got to go." Her voice is clipped. "Tell Dad I'll call him on my break Saturday about this time. I'll talk to you later, Mom. Bye."

I don't know what I've done, but the change in Cameron's tone of voice tells me I messed up somehow. I call Kenneth at work to report on this latest phone call, then take two aspirin to soothe the sudden pounding in my head. It has no effect on the ache in my heart.

- - - - -

Cameron does not call Kenneth on Saturday. He chalks it up to her either not remembering, not getting a break, or not having the spare change to place the call. We both should have told her she could call us at any time. Another week goes by without a call, though, and I detect concern in his voice. We don't even know the name of the coffee shop where she works or the apartment building where she lives. We don't know any of her roommates' names. In fact, in our attempt to keep the lines of communication open and cordial and not push her, we know so very little about our daughter and, while she probably prefers it this way, we should have found a way to get more information from her, about her. We should have sent the private investigator out there to get information. She need never have known. I go over our last conversation with Kenneth, hoping he has insight into this new freeze after such an encouraging thaw. He's as clueless as I am about the sudden cessation of contact. I ask Kenneth if we should call the San Francisco police or send the investigator out there, and he promises he'll call Officer Riley, the Dekalb County officer who was in charge of Cameron's case when she first went missing. He'll let me know what Riley suggests.

Before I hear back from Kenneth, though, I receive another call from Cameron. As soon as I see the San Francisco exchange on caller ID, I pick up the phone, my heart beating so wildly that it's roaring in my ears.

"Hello?"

"Ish me," a slurred voice informs me.

"Cameron? Are you okay? Are you sick?"

"Not sick. Drunk. 'Sall your fault."

"What do you mean? Tell me. What did I do? Or not do? Cameron, talk to me."

"D'you know," her words slide together, "I think you cared more for the Turrets and for Joe and Margaret than your own flesh and blood? Why do you think Dad played so much chess?" Her tone is increasingly accusatory and biting. "You couldn't even see what was happening to your family—to me, Dad, Papa Don—you were so wrapped up in your fantasy people. Is there anything about yourself that you actually like enough to just be okay with your life? Is that why you feel like you have to stick your nose in other people's, into fake," she hurls the word **fake** like an insult, "people's business? What was so wrong with the real people in your life? Even Kai thinks you could've kept his dad from murdering Willow. What do you think of that, huh?"

"Wait. What? Cameron, I don't understand. Surely you knew that the make-believe was just that, make-believe, a way to entertain you with stories and spark your imagination." As unfair as her accusations are, I think I finally understand. The very bait I'd tried to use to finish reeling her in during our last phone call, to get her to reveal more of her life in San Francisco, was precisely the wrong kind of bait and had opened up a wound that apparently had barely scabbed over. How could I not know this about her? Why had I not seen that my stories about these fictitious people, while entertaining at first, ended up irritating and hurting her? And why is she just now telling me that Kai thinks I'm partially responsible for his mother's death? Or maybe it's the booze talking. Then I remember how truly connected I felt to Joe, to Margaret, and to the Turrets, and how every time I got curious about my emotional attachment to them, I ate my way out of that curiosity and distracted myself from acknowledging I was using those make-believe people and food to try and patch over the holes in my existence. The rushing sound in my head intensifies, but I understand I may have just one shot at starting to make things right again. "You're right. There you were, right in front of me, and I created imaginary people to fill a void in my life. A void that I should never have asked **anyone** to fill for me—not you, not your dad, not Ron, not Carlisle, not Magda, not Willow, and certainly not people who lived solely in my imagination. I'm sorry." A dam bursts in me, and I am then sobbing. "I'm so sorry. Can you ever forgive me?"

Cameron is now crying and sobbing. Her words become nearly incomprehensible; she is sobbing, heaving, and hiccupping. "Friends... take... rehab... dry out... clean... once and for all... call... later... out...." Click. It's like the final piece of thread on the seam of my sanity has come undone, lost in the gale-force winds of Cameron's anger, hurt, and inebriation. I have nothing left to hold on to in that moment. Not even the promise—I think it was a promise—that she is entering rehab and will call when she gets out. Even that feels like too much to hope for. All I am left with is, finally, an understanding that my smart, sassy, sensitive daughter mistook my sense of being so adrift in my world that she believed that I believed there was something wrong with **her**. And that pain grew inside of her, so large that she tried to shadow-box it with rebellion, medicate it with drugs, drown it with alcohol, and run to the other side of the country from it. And I failed to notice. Chose not to notice. Just as I chose not to tell Willow's parents my suspicions about Gabe.

- - - - -

Officer Riley thinks contacting the San Francisco police or sending the private investigator out to California right now would be a waste of time and money. Cameron is an adult, she's not technically missing, and trying to determine what rehab center she's in, what coffee shop she works in, and where her apartment is would be considered a low priority and a nearly impossible task, given the number of young people who migrate to that area. He thinks the fact that she called before checking into rehab is a positive sign, even if it was to unload her fury on me. She apparently wants us to know just enough about her to allay our worst fears. So, there is that. He counsels us to wait at least six weeks to hear from her and then call him back if we have not received any news. Does he not know that six weeks is five weeks, six days, 23 hours, and 45 minutes too long to know that your child is going to be okay? But what choice do we have?

In hopes that Cameron does contact us after rehab, I commit to looking in every nook and cranny of my life for ways I can be a better person, a better mother, and a better friend. I take to heart what my fifth-grade teacher, Mrs. Norton, said to our class when there were kids cruelly teasing other classmates: **I behave as I behave because I believe what I believe**. "What do you children believe about yourselves when you say mean things to someone else? What do you believe about that other person? Is there another way?" Of course, this erudite approach to classroom management was a little over our heads, but for some reason, it stuck with me. And that is what I'm mulling while aimlessly pushing my shopping cart up and down the aisles of Kroger when I nearly bump into Horrible, that is, Mrs. Headlee. **What DO I believe about her? Could there be another explanation for why she says and does such hateful things? Could she, in fact, be a badly hurting human being, offloading her hurt onto others?**

"Oh, hi. How are you, Mrs. Headlee? And how is that **wonderful daughter of yours? What's Collier doing these days?"**

She seems so shocked by my overture, my interest, that it seems to momentarily take all the spite out of her sails. Instead, she looks lost and wounded. Her voice is grave, but in a tired way, not her typical whiskey-soaked way. Or is it gin? I can never remember. At any rate, she tells me Collier is getting ready to go to Agnes Scott in the fall, where she'll live on campus, and that she doesn't quite know what she'll do with an empty nest.

Talk to your husband, maybe? Scratch that. C'mon, Meredith, show some kindness. "I know what you mean. Cameron lives out in California, and I rarely hear from her. The house just isn't the same without her, even when she was yelling at me." I smile a little at this admission. "I was thinking of taking a stained-glass course at Callanwolde. Would you like to go with me?"

She sputters, as taken off-guard by my offer as I am at having made it. "I'll have to think about it. When is it?"

"It starts next week, and it's a four-week course. It should be fun. Maybe you can make something for Collier to decorate her dorm room, a reminder of how much you love her."

"Yeah? Yeah. That sounds good. I'll call you and let you know."

There is a lightness in my heart as I finish my grocery shopping. I realize a lightness that has been missing for a very, very long time.

- - - - -

When the new school year begins, I hang my stained-glass creation in the window closest to my desk. In keeping with my ongoing personal inventory, I chose to make a tree to remind me to take in the bad air and put out only the good air. To remind me to offer shelter, shade, and nutrients when I can and to trust that, even when my leaves are brown, things are happening inside me that will eventually bring forth new life. To remind me that my root system is not my child, my friendships, or my relationships with my parents, and definitely not imaginary characters, but my relationship with myself. When that system is intact, then the people that I care about, the people I love, like good ground cover, can help strengthen those roots, can help provide protection from erosion. I hope Collier is as pleased with the stained-glass sunflower her mother made for her as I am with my tree.

- - - - -

Six weeks and two days after the last phone call from Cameron, she calls.

"Hello?"

"Mom, hi. It's me." Her voice sounds airy and upbeat. Sober. "Are you free to talk for a bit?"

"Yes. Oh, it's so good to hear your voice. And before I forget, I want you to know that you can call me and your dad collect at any time. Okay?"

"Yeah. Okay. Anyway, I called to say I'm sorry. The last time I called you, I said some really mean things—things I shouldn't've said."

"You're sweet to say that, Cameron, but you said things I needed to hear."

"That's just the thing. I should never have let things build up like that. I accused you of not being honest with yourself, but I hadn't been honest with you either. I have spent the last six weeks doing that—being honest about myself. Being honest **with** myself. It's so much easier to blame someone else for my misery, but when all is said and done, I am responsible for my own happiness or my own misery."

What ensues is a tender, emotional, truthful, at times difficult, and heart-wrenching conversation about our mutual endeavors to reorder our lives and to accept responsibility for ourselves. We are a mother and a daughter, we are two adults, we are two women, finally walking side-by-side through this thing we call life, and that feels so right, although it still feels a bit shaky—to both of us, I suspect. Before she hangs up, Cameron provides me with a mailing address, the name of the coffee shop where she works, the names of her roommates, and the names of their apartment building and their landlord, "just in case." Who would ever have thought that these tidbits of information could constitute a mother's wildest dreams? To shore up this tenuous start, we also set aside a regular time to talk every other week, which is the icing on the cake.

Chapter Nineteen: 1993

IT'S SUCH A pretty spring-like day this early March weekend that I spend most of my time outside. Cammie has a U-Haul truck backed up to the carriage house, having taken a job with the Savannah Symphony. While I help her load the truck, I also take the opportunity to survey the yard, especially the area just around the exterior of the rental property. I'm thinking of ways to spruce things up both inside and outside the carriage house. My many years of ineptitude at growing plants used to make me hesitant to put in new ones, but if I've learned anything in the years since Kenneth and I split up, it's that I'm far more capable than I gave myself credit for. I've also learned that even when I screw up, I learn something. Boy, is that an understatement, especially when you consider the magnitude of some of my screw-ups, like pushing Cameron away.

Cameron. She turned 19 a month ago. She's been in San Francisco long enough now to earn residency status. She completed her GED while working two jobs, one in the coffee shop and one at a thrift store, then applied to community college. For her birthday gift, I send her a card with a check to buy textbooks. I'd forgotten how expensive they are! She replies to the birthday card and gift by sending back a short letter, providing a new address, the name of her new roommate, Ivy, and details about her new job doing intakes at a methadone clinic, which allows her to quit her job at the coffee shop. This new job excites her and makes me both nervous and proud. Probably sensing that that would be my reaction, she states that she is continuing to go to her weekly NA meetings. She is now in her second quarter at City College and has chosen behavioral psychology as her major. I get that. Who wouldn't want to figure out what makes people tick, especially after some of the things she's seen or heard about: Ron's abandonment by his father; Willow staying in an abusive relationship until it kills her; Kai plucking the feathers off pigeons at Springdale Park to express his pain; her father lying to himself and his family for years; and her mother living in a fugue state through most of her daughter's childhood?

As I am getting a shovel and a rake out of the small utility shed to tend to my rose bushes, exactly like Magda instructed, the phone rings. I don't recognize the number on the handset caller ID, but I recognize the area code, so I answer. "Hello?"

"Hi, Mom."

"Hi, Cameron. I was just thinking about you. This isn't our usual day to talk. Is everything okay? You could've called collect, you know."

"Yeah. Everything's great, as a matter of fact. Thank you again for the birthday money. I was able to buy a new copy of my Abnormal Psych text. I want to keep it, not sell it back, and I want to be the only person who's ever written in it."

"You're welcome. How is school? And do you still like your new job?"

"Yeah, but I have one on campus now, too. I was able to quit my job at the thrift store, and I'm keeping my job at the methadone clinic. I can make more at the clinic than I did folding t-shirts and ringing up sales. And the on-campus job is in the bookstore. They let me do homework when we're not busy with customers."

"That sounds great." Despite these free exchanges of information, I still feel a bit of trepidation. Fear that I will say or do the wrong thing, and we'll be back to mostly silence with occasional postcards and short, perfunctory phone calls. Or that I'll send her over the edge, back to the drugs.

"Anyway, Ivy is going to be gone for a couple of weeks in April, and I wondered if you'd like to fly out for a visit."

Did I hear correctly? Am I dreaming? "I'd love to. What are the dates?"

353

"She'll be gone April 5–25." As much as I'd like to know more about why Ivy will be gone for so long, I dare not pry.

"That actually might work," I say as I walk into the house to check my calendar. "Yep, our Spring Break is the week of April 13–17."

"That's our break, too, 'cause it's Easter. So you'll come?"

"Of course I will. Do you want me to call once I get the details sorted out?"

"Yes. This is my new number. Ivy and I each have our own line now."

"Cool. What's the best time for me to call you?"

"How about our regular time, Sunday afternoon, 4:00 your time? Would that work for you?"

My daughter is asking me if something is okay. She's not telling me what's not okay. Some tectonic plates in the Universe continue to re-center, and I wasn't even aware of them shifting. "Sounds good. I'll call you next Sunday."

"Good. I gotta go now so I won't be late for work. I love you, Mom."

I am so startled by these words and the ease with which she says them that I can barely breathe. I half-sob, half-choke, "I love you, too," before we hang up. And then I sit on the floor of the kitchen and weep one of those gut-heaving, soul-cleansing weeps before I call Kenneth to tell him the good news about our daughter.

- - - - -

I take the red-eye out to California so I can spend as much time with Cameron as possible on my two-day, three-night visit. I do not want to be presumptuous and overstay my welcome, so I keep my visit short, hoping she will think I didn't stay long enough instead of too long. She tells me how to get BART to her neighborhood and is waiting for me when I get off the train. We walk together up the steep hill to her charming little apartment. She lives within walking distance of the college and the clinic.

We chat about superficial things at first, just getting used to being in each other's company again. Then she asks me what my ESOL students are up to.

"They're fascinated by space travel, especially with the recent Discovery launch. So we're exploring, well, space exploration. I even took a big group of them to Fernbank, to the planetarium. That was a great field trip."

"And Mr. Carlisle? Did he go, too?"

"You know, I wouldn't dare take a field trip without him. But guess what?"

"What?"

"As soon as the guide turned off the lights so we could see the simulated star show, he nodded off. The whole bus ride back to school, the students imitated his snoring. It was priceless. He won't live that down any time soon."

"That's hilarious." As we walk the eight blocks to her apartment, she points to landmarks and historic buildings and pitches ideas for touristy things we might enjoy doing together later. This young woman I am walking beside is confident, self-possessed, and mature, and while I would have taken credit for it a few years ago, I know she has scratched and clawed against several odds to be this put-together. And I am proud of her for that.

She shows me around her tiny apartment, which is obviously furnished from her job at the thrift store. She offers to get me a cup of coffee or tea, asking me if I'd like a nap instead. I decline the nap, and while she makes me a cup of tea, I splash cold water on my face. I sit in one of two very used but elegant chairs in their small living room area, running my finger down the spines of the various textbooks on the table beside it.

"So, tell me about your classes. What all are you taking besides Abnormal Psych?"

"English Comp 2, Stats, US History, and Marriage and Family. My professors are great. I think my psych professor is going to let me work on research with her next quarter when I take her for Adolescent Psych."

356

"That sounds promising. Do you know what you'll be researching?"

"I've asked her to let me look into the effects of divorce on children." She looks at me without any guile whatsoever, and so I know this is not a dig at her parents.

"Well, who better than you to research that? I'd love to hear more about it when you get started. So, tell me about this Marriage and Family course."

"Hmmm. One of the things we're learning is that there are many ways to define a family. Your generation might not have thought so, but, for example, Dad and Alex could be considered a family. And in some contexts, Ivy and I might be considered a family, or you and Ron, or Ron and Guy. I went into this course believing we," she points back and forth to me and herself, "were never really a family, but I'm rethinking that. We were and are a family, but a dysfunctional one."

"True. We are a family, and we are dysfunctional. Your dad and I thought, for the most part, we were doing okay. It's like we were two airplanes taking off from the same airport at the same time, heading in the same general direction. We flew in each other's airspace once in awhile, just often enough. I think that's one reason it took me so long to realize he was struggling with his sexual identity. I was not conditioned to even think of such things."

"I can see how that could happen. You know, I blamed you for such a long time for driving him away. But when I saw how he was with Alex and that there was genuine love and attraction between them, I decided your divorce from Dad was actually a good thing. A hard thing, but a good thing."

"You're not kidding; it was hard. I don't think I really grew up until I had to learn how to be on my own. I kind of think you and I grew up together." I smile at my beautiful, wise daughter, hoping this admission isn't too uncomfortable for her. Instead, she smiles back warmly, seeming to appreciate my honesty. I continue, "I feel like I'm just now coming into my own. As a woman. As a human being. As a mom."

Her eyes light up as she engages in the conversation. "One of the things we learned early in our Marriage and Family course is that we're all products of our era and our upbringing. I love Mama Jo and Papa Don with all my heart, but I also know they raised you according to the standards of their generation. There are just certain things you wouldn't question..."

Oh, my precious daughter, how grateful I am for you! "I'm just sorry I had to be practically forced to question those things and that I put you through that. I'm sorry; I am just now learning to trust my intuition, to listen to myself, and to take notice. I'm sorry I didn't do my 'work' earlier, and that my reluctance made you feel abandoned."

"I don't know that I felt abandoned. Sometimes I felt over-loved, if that makes sense, but other times I didn't know where I fit, and it made me sad that I couldn't make you happy. And then, as I got older, I got mad that I **had** to make you happy. It was just easier to be around Dad, you know? He didn't come with so many expectations. I don't know if that's a mother-daughter thing, an engineer thing, or a personality thing. Maybe I'll find out later this quarter." She smiles, a twinkle in her eye that I have not seen in far too long.

I get up from my chair and go to Cameron and hug her, and she lets me. This moment, this trip, is golden.

- - - - -

Cameron waits by the front door to walk with me back to BART so I can catch my flight home. She has been sleeping in Ivy's bed, giving me hers. Before I leave her room, I put a gift on her pillow, one that she will find when she gets back—Mr. Whiskers, sitting sentry duty over his beloved girl. My beloved girl

I sleep most of the flight home, then retrieve my car from the airport parking lot. As I pull into the driveway, the roses are in full bloom. It is a glorious sight, and the bubble of gratitude rising up within me is nearly intoxicating. I am home. I am **at** home. Finally within myself.

Deidre Ann deLaughter

Acknowledgements

Thank you to the VMH Publishing Team for the handholding, guidance, encouragement, and patience. Thank you to my UNG colleagues for standing behind me, believing in me, and for 21 years of student-focused, learning-centered collaborations. For my dear friend and mentor, Terry Kay, may you rest in eternal peace—ok, maybe with the clack of a typewriter in the background. I know this book would not exist were it not for your advice and your consistent nudging. How you found the energy to check in with me even while undergoing chemotherapy is simply astonishing.